Seashells, Gator Bones, and the Church of Everlasting Liability

Stories from a Small Florida Town in the 1930s

by

Susan Adger

Text © 2013 by Susan Adger
Illustrations © 2013 by Grey Gecko Press

Published by Grey Gecko Press, Katy, Texas.

www.greygeckopress.com

Printed in the United States of America

Design by Grey Gecko Press

Library of Congress Cataloging-in-Publication Data
Adger, Susan
Seashells, gator bones, and the church of everlasting liability / Susan Adger
Library of Congress Control Number: 2013935821
ISBN 978-1-9388213-4-9
10 9 8 7 6 5 4 3 2 1
First Edition

For my mother,

Isobel Keathley Harwell,

our southern matriarch, whose family stories entertained and educated us through the years.

She took great pride in helping to edit this book but, sadly, died before its publication

CHAPTERS

Preface
by DeLoyd Stroudamore

It was 1971, the one-hundredth anniversary of Toad Springs, Florida, when I got the phone call from Sully Cook about the old cedar chest. Sully's the new feller in town thinks he's gonna turn Toad Springs into some kind of fancy resort, but ask me, he'll just end up circling the drain.

Sully had bought up sixteen acres out on Grasshopper Lake Road, and the old house we used for the Church of Everlasting Liability years ago was smack-dab in the middle of it. He said when they was fixing to tear the place down, somebody climbed up in the attic just to make sure we hadn't hid a pot of gold up there or something, and found an old cedar chest full of papers. They looked to be some stories that folks had wrote about living here back in the 1930s and since he knew my family's been here forever, he called me.

Me and my wife, Peanut, went through the papers and some of 'em really took me back, they did, like Granddaddy's three-legged gator with a picture of Jesus on his side that started up his famous reptile ranch, and when we found out our new pastor had learned to preach while he was serving time up in Raiford Prison, and how Grandma Only and all the church ladies was always raising sand and trying to outdo each other. I even learned a family secret my sister, Jolinda, had wrote about but nobody'd ever told me. Anyway, we took them stories to the preacher, and him and the church deacons decided we ought'a put 'em in a book to sell. So here it is.

If it turns out you want to read more than we got in here, just let us know 'cause we got lots more stories.

DeLoyd Stroudamore
Toad Springs, Florida
1974

I Should of Stuck with the Kewpie Doll
by Elsie Lou Only Swigfellow

Mama always said you don't never forget your first love, and for once she was right. My first boyfriend taught me a lot, most of which I wish I hadn't ever learned. He was a feller name of Galen Dodge that I met at the Hillsborough County Fair in downtown Tampa when I was sixteen. Our whole family, that's Mama and Daddy and us four girls, we'd gone down to the fairgrounds early of a Saturday morning, like we did every year, so we'd get to the cattle judging where Daddy could watch. When he was a teenager, his steer, Maurice, got second place and Daddy thought he should of won the blue ribbon. So like always, he put Maurice up against the new winner, in his own mind you know, to see who would of won.

Soon as it's over, like he done every single year, Daddy says the exact same words to Mama: "Sorrey May, Maurice would of beat that steer by a mile. Ain't no better steer ever been born than Maurice." And then Mama'd always pat him on the shoulder and say, "All right, Lucas. We know."

That year the rest of the family went to see the Snake Lady while I run off to the Ferris wheel by myself. I'd seen that snake lady the year before and like to of fainted. But mostly, I just loved the Ferris wheel back then.

It was fun, walking down the Midway through the sawdust by myself, listening to all the men hollering out from the booths for you to come and win a prize. Little kids were yelling to their mamas about what they wanted to do next and could they have some cotton candy, pleeeease. At one booth I smelled barbequed ribs already cooking, the next one had strawberry muffins covered with powdered sugar, and another one had coffee and hot chocolate.

When I get to the Ferris wheel, this fella, all tall, dark, and handsome like they say, he helps me into the seat and locks the safety bar down in front of me. When I go up high I can see the boats out in Tampa Bay, and then when I round over the top and start coming down and the seat kinda swings back . . . I get butterflies in my stomach. It always gives my heart a thrill.

When my turn is up, that good-lookin' feller unhooks the bar and puts out his hand to help me off. I give him my best smile, hoping he'll say something, then step out of the chair. Another man walks up and starts talking to him real serious, so I go on my way and buy myself a little Kewpie doll on a stick, like I do every year.

Her skirt's made of fluffy little colored feathers and she's got sparkles all over her. I know I'm too old for dolls, but I just love 'em. So, after I get my new Kewpie, I go back over to the Ferris wheel; just want to look at that fella again. He's helping three little boys into their seats and laughing with 'em. Once he pulls the crank and has 'em going, he sees me standing there.

"Come on over and take a free ride," he calls out. "What's your name?"

At first I can't believe he's talking to me, but I walk his way. "Elsie Lou Only," I say.

"Why, Elsie Lou Only," he says, taking my hand and kissing it. Then he looks me up and down. "Onlyest girl in town with a smile like the sunshine peeping through the clouds on a rainy day. I'm Galen Dodge."

I know my face is turning beet red. I'm blonde and I'm real bad to blush. I look down at the ground like I always do when somebody says something nice about me, and I say, "Why, thank you, kindly."

"Got yourself a Kewpie doll, I see."

"Well," I say, looking down at it. "It's . . . It's . . . for my little sister."

"It's right pretty," he says, reaching out to touch her.

I stand there smiling like a real dumbbell.

"I'll give you another ride if you want. For free."

My heart's beating faster. "You will? That's real nice of you."

He lets me stay on for a long time, and when he finally stops it, I thank him. Then I don't know what to do.

I'm turning to walk away when he says, "You ever go to the beach? I've been in town two weeks and still ain't been over there."

"Oh sure," I say, turning back. "We go to Indian Rocks all the time."

He gives me a big grin. "Well, maybe you could go there with me one of these days." When he says something with an *s* in it, he makes a little hissing sound—so cute.

"I . . . I don't know," I say. "I ain't allowed to go off with people I don't know . . ."

"Oh," he says. "Well, I didn't mean you no harm. Just wanted to collect me some pretty shells. But I wouldn't never find one as pretty as you."

I don't have no idea what to say so I just smile and look at the ground.

"Elsie Lou," he says. "How's about I'll buy you lunch?"

I'm so surprised I can hardly talk. "Oh, okay."

"Good! Meet me at the barbeque booth at noon."

"All right," I say. "Um . . . that'd be real nice." He gives me a wink that nearly about melts my heart and I run off.

Before long I run into Mama and Daddy and my sisters. The girls tell me all about how slithery and scary the Snake Lady is, doing it just to make my skin crawl. Then Mama says, "Elsie Lou, don't forget to meet us at the hot dog stand at noon."

"Well, yes, ma'am," I say. "But I met this fella who wants me to have some barbeque with him."

"Feller? What feller?" she says, looking around.

"He runs the Ferris wheel, Mama, and he's so dreamy."

"He what? Elsie Lou Only! You ain't gonna have nothin' to do with no carnie!"

"But, Mama." I look over at Daddy for some help, but he's staring off at the cotton candy machine. He always acts like he's interested in something else when Mama's on her high horse.

"You got no business hanging around with some lowlife. Them kind ain't nothing but trouble."

"But, Mama! He's not . . ."

"*No!* You meet us at the hot dog stand. You ain't getting mixed up with no damned carnie."

I feel the tears start up, but there ain't nothing I can do. I walk away, looking down at the straw and little pieces of trash all over the ground and start wondering what my big sister Dancy would do in my place. Dancy never cared a fig for the rules. After thinking for a minute, I go right over to Galen and tell him I'll meet him for lunch at one o'clock. He smiles and gives me one of them winks and my knees get weak.

Galen buys me a barbequed pork sandwich, which I can't hardly eat since I'd already had a hot dog, and he talks about how he's from Georgia and is working at the fair, just doing them a favor 'cause the guy who was supposed to do it was in jail for getting drunk and beating up a bartender. Galen's real job is lots more important. He goes door-to-door selling Encyclopedia Britannicas all over the state of Florida. Says he ain't making a whole lot of money yet, but business gets better every day and he has a great future ahead. Says he's been in five different states and seen all kinds of sights everywhere. He's so smart and so funny, he makes me want to start selling encyclopedias, too.

When Galen finishes eating he gives me that beautiful smile and says I'm the prettiest gal he's ever seen. He had the nicest, softest way of talking, and I especially like that little hissing noise he made.

Anyhow, he asked if he could call on me, and much as I wanted to say yes, I was sure there wasn't no way Mama'd let me so I told him no. Then he has to go back to work. After that, I'm so mad at Mama that all the fun of the fair's long gone. I dragged around the fairgrounds 'til we finally went home.

I moon over him for days, knowing I'll never get to see him again 'til even Dancy's feeling sorry for me, and that's saying something. About a week later, I hear a knock on the front door late in the afternoon and there stands Galen, wearing a suit.

"Well, hello there, pretty lady," he says, taking off his hat. "Don't I know you from somewhere?"

I'm so flustered all I can do is smile.

"How you been? Let's see, what was your name again? I can't quite call it up."

"Elsie Lou. Elsie Lou Only."

"That's right! Elsie Lou Only. I been hoping I'd run into you, Elsie Lou Only."

I just keep smiling.

"I'm selling these Encyclopedia Britannicas," he says, "like I told you at the fair. Think your folks might be interested?"

When he says "encyclopedia" and "interested" he does that cute little thing with his tongue and my heart just leaps. "Just a minute," I say. "I'll call Mama and Daddy."

I come back out and sit on the swing while Daddy's shaking Galen's hand. Then Daddy sits in the rocker and Galen sits down beside me. Mama just stands at the door, and when she sees he's selling something, she says, "Young man, we ain't gonna be buying no books. The young'uns get their fill of reading at school."

"Yes, ma'am," Galen says. "Now schools have good books. But they don't have the whole history of the world like these do."

"I don't care about the world," Mama says. "All's I care about is how long it takes them collards out back to get big enough to eat. That soil ain't fit to grow sandspurs. Your books gonna tell me something about that?"

"Well, you know, that's an interesting comment you made, ma'am. I got a book here, shows you how the whole state of Florida used to be on the bottom of the ocean. No wonder the land ain't too friendly, after being buried underneath all that saltwater. And there's another book that shows you all about different fertilizers."

For some reason that gets Mama's attention, and she sits in the other rocker and hushes up long enough to let him talk a little. I watch her, hoping she'll like him. He tells her that everything that's ever happened since Adam and Eve is in them books and the first one was printed way back in the 1700s. Even Jesus and the Seminole Indians was in it, he said. Once Galen got her listening, she warmed up and asked him to stay to supper. But on her way back to the kitchen, she called over her shoulder that she wasn't buying no damned books 'cause didn't nobody in our house have time to read 'em.

Daddy takes right to Galen 'cause Galen listens to his stories and even acts like he believes 'em. Daddy tells him about Maurice winning second place at the fair, the tarpon he caught that was so big he couldn't fit him in the boat and had to cut the line, and the day he jumped out of a boat in the middle of Bass Lake to save somebody that turned out to be a big old gator and if it hadn't of been dead, Daddy would of been. Galen stays 'til nine o'clock, and when Daddy invites him back to eat with us the next night he says, "Much obliged, sir. See you tomorrow, then."

Every evening after supper, him and Daddy sit in the old green rocking chairs on the porch, smoke cigarettes, and talk. After us girls finish the dishes, me and Mama would go sit in the swing, that is, 'til the night Mama found out that Galen was the feller invited me to lunch at the fair. Then that same night she started in on him about his church back home, and when she found out that his mama was a Catholic and his daddy was a Jew and he didn't go to church at all, she near about had a conniption fit and set right out to save him.

Mama always thought if you didn't go to the Church of Everlasting Liability you was going to hell and it was her job to make sure that didn't happen. After three hours of working on him real hard, Mama could see that likely Galen wasn't gonna change, and from then on she didn't sit with us after supper. Said she had too much to do inside. I was kind of surprised she didn't raise sand about him eating with us every night, but she just said one more mouth wouldn't make no difference.

A couple of times Galen sat on the swing with me and held my hand; 'course he did it where Daddy couldn't see. He comes every night for a week, staying later each time, and I sing for him and Daddy. Now, I've always loved a song—Mama said I could sing "Amazing Grace" before I could talk. Before I got to high school, everybody in town was asking me to sing at revivals and weddings and even to sing the National Anthem before the ball games. I loved it.

It's about nine o'clock one night and I just finished "Sweet Adeline," when Daddy gets up to chase a dog out of the yard and Galen leans over and whispers, "How's about meeting me at the fence out back when your mama and daddy turn in? I'd like to talk to you about something."

I couldn't believe my ears! I look at him and give a little nod, and he waves to Daddy and heads off toward Miss Pearlie's Boardinghouse as usual. My heart was beating so loud I was sure Daddy could hear it. I went into the bedroom and brushed my hair. Then I brushed my teeth. Then I brushed my hair again and pinched my cheeks and bit my lips so they'd be all pink. Then I thought that was stupid, 'cause even with the moon it was so dark he wouldn't be able to see 'em. After Mama and Daddy turned off the lights, I waited a few minutes, then sneaked out through the kitchen.

There's a good moon that night and the air is cool enough to keep the skeeters down. I see Galen waving at me and I run over to him. He's got a bundle under his arm and he takes my hand and whispers, "There you are!"

I don't know what to say. "Yeah," is all I come up with. I'm so dumb.

"Thanks for meeting me," he says. "I just wanted to have some time to talk to you."

"Um, okay," I say, standing there like a fool with my hand in his.

"Come on this way," he says, walking toward the woods. "Say, you got a boyfriend?"

"No."

"A girl pretty as you? I can't hardly believe that."

I know I'm blushing, but thank goodness he can't see it. "Aw," I say, "Mama keeps me real busy. I never had time for a boyfriend."

"Let's stop here," he says, unfolding the bundle from under his arm and spreading a blanket out in a little clearing. I pull my hand away and sit down beside him. Soon as I'm free, I want to put my hand back in his, but can't see no way to do it.

"You're so smart," I say. "You know so many things. What do you want to talk to me about?"

"Well, really, I just wanted to get to know you a little better," he says, taking my hand again. "I asked around to find out where you live; that's how I come to your house. You're as pretty as any gal I ever seen, and I seen a lot in my travels."

I got no idea what to say, so I just smile.

He scoots closer, leans over, and kisses me real soft on the cheek. "I've been dying to do that since the day I met you at the fair."

"Really?" I say.

"Really," he says. "You never left my mind since I saw you at the Ferris wheel."

"Really?" I say, remembering how surprised he was to see me and that he couldn't call up my name the first day he come by the house.

"Really," he says. He reaches over and this time kisses me on the mouth, and his breath smells like apples. His lips are soft and nice, but I don't see any stars or fireworks like Dancy said she did.

I pull back and touch my lips with my fingers. "That's the first time anybody ever kissed me," I say.

"Naw!" he says. "I don't believe that for a minute."

"It's true!"

"Did you like it?"

"Um, well . . . yeah, I liked it."

"Want another one?"

"Well, okay, I guess so."

This time he takes my face in his hands, and when he kisses me, his tongue tries to poke past my teeth. I pull back and wipe my mouth. "What are you doing?"

"That's a real kiss," he says. "The way they do it in France."

"They touch tongues?"

"They do more than just touch," he says, coming back at me for another kiss.

"I don't know about what they're doing in France," I say, pulling away and standing up. "I think I better go back now."

"Oh," Galen says. "I hope I didn't do nothing wrong. I wouldn't want to scare you off."

"No, no," I say. "I just want to go home."

"Sure," he says. "Whatever you want. That's fine." He gets up and folds the blanket and we head back.

"Can I hold your hand?" he asks.

"Sure," I say. I don't reach out, just let my hand hang there limp at the end of my arm, but he grabs it and when he gives it a squeeze, I squeeze back.

I sneak back in the house and when I crawl into bed, Dancy whispers, "Where you been?"

"Nowhere," I whisper back.

"Come on, Elsie Lou. Where you been?"

"Just went for a walk with Galen."

Dancy props up on her elbow. "No kidding. Ain't it kind of late for a walk?"

"Look who's talking," I say.

"Did he kiss you?"

I don't answer.

"He did! He kissed you!"

"Hush up. Somebody'll hear!"

Now she's sitting up and I see she's got her hair rolled up with rags. "Did you like it?"

"Well, I liked the first one," I says.

"What was wrong with all the other ones?"

"There wasn't but one other one."

"So what was wrong with it?"

"I just didn't like it."

"Why? What did he do? Did he feel your titties?"

I make a face. "*No!* Why would he do that?"

"Did he French kiss you?"

"You know about that?"

"Sure. I like French kissing. Me and Durhill do it all the time."

"But . . . but . . . It's so . . ."

"It's sexy, that's what it is."

"You mean other people do it?"

"Sure. Everybody does it. Well, maybe not everybody."

"Mama and Daddy don't do that!"

"Well, no. Probably not. But you should give it a chance, Elsie Lou. You might get to like it."

"I don't think so," I say.

"And you better be careful about sneaking out. Remember that time Mama caught me?"

"Yeah, that was bad."

"So, here's what you do. Daddy, once he's asleep, he's dead to the world. And Mama, she's near about as bad, except she wakes up every night to pee, right just about one o'clock in the morning. So long as you leave when they're asleep and don't come in around one o'clock, she won't hear nothing."

"That's good. I'll remember that."

"And Durhill just got me a new watch, so you can take the old one with you when you go out. It's on the dresser over there."

"Oh Dancy, thanks so much. You're such a good sister."

"Well, I don't know about that," she says.

I spend the whole next day thinking about what I'll say when Galen asks me to meet him in the woods that night. I want to go in the worst way, but I'm scared at the same time. In the end I decide I'll go.

After supper we're sitting on the porch and Galen is telling us there's lots of tombs in Egypt full of gold and some have ghosts inside that kill anybody who goes in. That night it seems to me he knows everything.

The whole evening goes by and he never says nothing about meeting me in the woods. My heart sinks when he just heads back to the rooming house. I tell myself I didn't want nothing to do with that French kissing, anyways, and that I don't care. Later on that night, when Dancy hears me sniffling in bed and asks what happened, I won't tell her. But she knows anyway. The next night I have to sing at the church and the night after that I'm singing at the ball game, so I don't even see him. Daddy asked him if he wanted to go hear me at the ball field, but he said he had something else he had to do.

The next Friday night Galen comes to supper, and afterward we're sitting on the porch again. Galen turns to Daddy and says, "Mr. Only, I was wondering if it would be all right for me to take Elsie Lou out on a ride to the beach tomorrow. A friend of mine said I could borrow his car."

"Hmmm," Daddy says.

"I won't be working and I thought we might have us a little picnic and maybe build a bonfire and watch the sunset. Even go for a swim."

Daddy looks at me and I smile back and nod my head. He looks at Galen and says, "Well, I reckon that'll be all right if Elsie Lou wants to go. But you got to have her home by eight o'clock. She's singing her solo at church Sunday morning."

"That sounds nice," I say to Galen with a big grin. "I'll bring a picnic basket. I'll show you where Indian Rocks Beach is. There's lots of good shells there."

Galen grins at me and stands up. "All right, folks," he says. "Guess I'll call it a night. Elsie Lou, I'll pick you up around nine in the morning."

"I'll be ready," I say.

That night I tell Dancy about going to the beach and she gets all excited. "You can borrow my new swimsuit," she says. "You'll look real good in it." I have to say I've never been real fond of Dancy, even if she is my sister, but she sure tried to help me with Galen.

Well, when that day at Indian Rocks was done I had a bucketful of seashells and I knew about a lot more than French kissing. Kissing was nothing! After that, things got out of hand, if you get my meaning, and me and Galen met in the woods every third or fourth night. We was so in love, there was just no stopping us. I really liked all the kissing and snuggling, and after a few times even got to liking the other part. I didn't want to do it the first time when we was at the beach, but Galen explained to me that once a man's ready, he ain't got no power to stop himself. Can't nothing be done about it. If he don't go on ahead, he could have a heart attack and die, and I sure didn't want to kill him.

Every night I talk to Dancy about Galen and she says that if I'm worried about having a baby all I have to do is to bury a clean dishrag out under the oak tree in the backyard after midnight, and that'll take care of it. It don't make a lotta sense but I figure it won't hurt, so I bury an old ratty one that Mama won't miss.

After I been meeting Galen for a while, besides worrying about having a baby I start to worry about going to hell. I knew what we were doing was a sin in God's eyes. And even though I know that Galen would never say nothing to them other fellas at the boardinghouse, I don't want to get a name for being one of them slutty girls. I didn't never feel like a tramp or nothing, 'cause we was really in love.

One Wednesday night when Galen and me was out in the woods and we're all through with you know what, I work up all my nerve and say, "Baby, I think there's something we need to talk about."

"What's that, sweetheart?" he says, taking a puff off his cigarette.

"What we're doing. You know. It's a sin."

He turns over on his side and looks at me. "Aw, it ain't no sin," he says. "It's natural. It's the way God made us."

"And besides that, Galen, I don't want to get no baby."

"Listen to me, honey," he says. "You don't need to worry your pretty little head about that. I can't have no kids, myself."

That stops me for a minute. "You sure? How do you know?"

"I had the mumps when I was ten and got all swole up. You know, down there. Doctor told my mama."

"Oh well, okay," I say, embarrassed, and at the same time thinking to myself that I want to have kids someday, but then maybe I don't. "But . . . but . . . it's still a sin. We could go to hell." I start to cry. "I'm telling you, Galen, I ain't gonna keep doing this unless we're gonna get married."

"Baby," he says, sitting up, "we ain't known each other long enough to get married, even though I truly love you with all my heart." He takes a puff of his cigarette and blows the smoke out slow. "And besides, I need to get back to Arkansas by the end of next month."

My heart bumps down to my feet. "You leaving? You never said nothing."

"Just for a while, baby. I'll be back."

"But . . . uh . . . I could go with you then, if we was married. I'd purely love to get outta Toad Springs. Ain't nothing ever gonna happen here. I hate this place."

"Let me think about it," he says, fastening his pants and sitting up. "We'll see. About time to be getting you back to the house, don't you think?"

"Galen," I say, with every little bit of courage I can muster, "I'm telling you I ain't gonna do this no more unless we're at least engaged."

"But, baby, I need to have some money before I make any plans like that. I need to be able to buy a house and a car. I need a—"

"Well, if you need them things more than you need me, I guess that tells me something, don't it?" Now I'm starting to get mad.

He reaches over and puts his hand behind my neck real tender-like. "You know I love you, Elsie Lou. You're my girl. And I'd like nothing better than to marry you right this minute."

"All right then," I say. I stand up to straighten my clothes. "You can just ask Daddy tomorrow night."

He blows some smoke rings, then says, "Well . . . Maybe. If it's just to be engaged. I guess that would be all right. But I ain't gonna be able to get married for a few years yet. Long as you see that. And I can't afford no ring or nothing. Not now."

"Oh Galen, that's okay. I love you so much." I lean down and kiss him on the mouth. He falls backward, pulling me over on him and we do it all again.

The next evening me and Galen and Daddy's sitting on the porch and I can hear *One Man's Family* playing on the radio inside. I take a deep breath and say, "Daddy?" I can still hear the quiver in my voice. I was so nervous. "Galen has something he wants to talk to you about." When Galen don't say nothing, I punch him in the side.

"That's right, Mr. Only," Galen says, leaning forward, his elbows on his knees, looking at the floor. "Umm . . . Elsie Lou and me, umm. . ." He takes a quick peek up at Daddy, then looks back down. "We been talking about maybe getting engaged."

Daddy puffs on his cigarette for a minute, looks up at the porch ceiling, then stares out at the front yard. I'm chewing my fingernails like I ain't done since was in the spelling bee in the fourth grade and come in second. Finally Daddy says, "Well, son, you seem like a smart young man and I seen you ain't afraid of hard work. It's a big responsibility, you know, taking a wife."

"We ain't gonna be getting married for a while," Galen says. "My job and all. I have to do a lot of traveling. In fact, I'll be leaving in a few days . . ."

Daddy lifts one of his eyebrows and stares at him. "What you saying, son?"

"Oh, I'll be back. For sure, I'll be back," Galen says. "Didn't mean to . . ."

"He told me he'd have to keep going on the road, Daddy. I'm thinking maybe I could even go with him sometimes." I glance over at Galen and he looks at me, surprised.

"Well . . ." Daddy gives me a smile and I can tell he's gonna say yes. I get up and kiss him on the cheek. "Oh, thank you, Daddy. Thank you. I do love him so much."

"One thing, though," Daddy says, and I sit back down. "Your mama, I don't think she's gonna be too happy about this."

"I know, Daddy. But you're the man of the house. It's up to you, ain't it?"

"Well, that's right," he says, leaning back and sticking his chest out a little. "It is up to me. When you two thinking of getting hitched?"

"Won't be too soon," Galen says real quick. "Next week I'll finish up here and go to Turkey Creek and Mango, then I got to be over to Bartow by a week from next Saturday, then to Zolfo Springs and Arcadia. End of next month I gotta be in Georgia."

"Why you got to go there?" I ask him, sitting up straight.

"Well, that's where my headquarters is," he says.

"What you got to do there?"

He looks at me, then down at the floor and kind of wrings his hands together. "I got lots of responsibilities. Lots."

"Hmmm," Daddy says. "When you reckon you'll be back?"

"Don't rightly know, sir," Galen says. "I just can't say for sure."

"Well now, don't you think your future wife needs to get some idea of when she's gonna see you again?"

"Well, sir, I just don't rightly know. Maybe in three months?"

"And you sure this is a good time to get engaged?"

Galen looks kind of blank. I say, "Yes, Daddy. It's a good time."

Daddy looks at me and takes a drag on his cigarette. "When you planning on telling Elsie Lou's mama?"

Me and Daddy both peer over at Galen, but he don't say nothing. "Well," I say, looking at Daddy, "I thought maybe you could tell her."

"Me?" Daddy says, laughing. "I ain't telling her. It's your news. You gotta tell her."

"Okay," I say. "Then we might as well do it now."

"Better get your back up real good, Galen," Daddy says, getting out of the rocker, "'cause you're gonna need all the backbone you can muster." Daddy goes inside, letting the screen door slam behind him, and hollers, "Sorrey May! Come out front for a minute. Young'uns want to talk to you."

"I'm busy," Mama calls back.

"Come on," Daddy says. "They got something to tell you."

Daddy comes back out and sits down. "She'll be here directly," he says. "She'll be wanting to see a ring."

Me and Galen just look at each other. Nobody says nothing, and by the time Mama finally comes out you'd need a hatchet to cut through the tension in the air. She sits in the other rocking chair and looks at me.

I turn my head sideways and lean forward, looking at Galen. "Well?"

He finally clears his throat. "Mrs. Only," he says, "I was telling your husband that Elsie Lou and me, well, uh, well, we been talking about maybe getting engaged. Ain't done it yet, mind you. We're just talking about it."

Mama shoots Daddy a look that would send a twelve-foot gator running for the swamp. Then she sits there for a minute, eyes down, not saying a word. Her lips are pulled tight like she does when things don't go her way. When she looks up at Galen, her face is all red.

"You ain't nothing but a goddamned carnie and a traveling salesman and I don't know which is worse. We bring you into our home and feed you; we try to be good Christian people, and this is what we get! And you ain't even a damn Christian. Folks around here know what sorts of things your kind is into. You think you can see a pretty face and take her off anywhere you want, then toss her aside when you're done with her. You ain't nothing but . . ."

"Sorrey May," Daddy says, reaching out and touching her arm. "Calm down, for heaven's sake."

She snatches her arm away from Daddy. "You don't know the kinds of things I hear down to the church," Mama says, "'cause you don't never set foot in a place of worship. You don't know what goes on in this world like I do."

"I understand . . ." Galen says.

"Understand?" Mama snarls, squinting her eyes at him. "You don't understand nothing! Just what you think I'm gonna do without my daughter?" she says. "She's the only one ever helps me around here. The others don't care."

Then she turns to me with tears in her eyes and says in this whiney voice, "Elsie Lou, you don't want to go off and leave your poor old mama, do you? What would I do without you? You gonna break my heart. And what about your singing? You're all lined up to sing at the—"

"I ain't going nowhere right now, Mama," I say, looking over at Galen. "We're just getting engaged."

"Engaged, huh? So where's the ring?"

"Well," I say, "We ain't . . ."

"If you're really engaged, you got to have a ring," Mama snaps. She leaps to her feet, making that big ugly frown, and me and Galen both jerk back in our seats. "You got singing responsibilities in this town," she says, "and now you just want to run off."

I look at Daddy, who's staring at the lit end of his cigarette.

Then Mama stomps inside, saying under her breath, "No ring . . . ain't engaged without a ring . . . sharper than a serpent's tooth . . ."

When time comes for Galen to leave, I'm so sad I can't hardly stand it. Looking back now, that last night out in the woods should of told me something. But it was a full moon, and I was in love. When I run out to meet him, he's glad to see me and all, but I know I'm more excited to see him. We sit on the blanket and he gives me a big grin, like it's just a regular night.

"I'm gonna miss you," I say.

"Honey, I'll miss you, too," he says. "You just don't know how much."

"You sad about leaving me?" I say. "You don't look sad."

"Sure, I'm sad," he says, unbuttoning my blouse. "I'm just used to traveling all the time, so it's not such a big thing."

"But you're leaving me," I say. "You ain't never done that before."

"Yeah," he says, pulling my blouse off. "That's right."

"Well, I can't hardly stand to see you go."

"You know," he says, "I was thinking, maybe we should do something different tonight. It being a special night and all."

"Ain't it kinda late to go somewhere?"

"Oh, I didn't mean go off somewhere. This is something we could do right here."

"What we gonna do right here?" I say.

"Here, baby. I'll show you."

He lies me down and slips off my skirt and panties, then he undresses himself and I don't know where to look. He never stood up buck naked in front of me before, so I try to act like I'm just looking up at the moon, but out of the corner of my eye I'm looking at him. His old thing is big and hard and it's sticking up straight—looks real funny, but I don't dare laugh. He don't get on top of me like he usually does. No sir, he has something nasty in mind that I don't like. I ain't never told nobody what it was, and I ain't never doing that again.

Well, a month later come to find out that Daddy and me, we're the only ones surprised when I ain't heard nothing from Galen. First couple a weeks I worry that something's happened to him, or that I'd done something made him mad. After that I knew that Mama was right, much as I hated it.

She kept telling me, "I knew that lowlife was no good. Could tell the minute I laid eyes on him. You can't trust no carnie, and you sure can't trust no traveling salesman, and that fella was a double whammy. Didn't even get you a ring out of it. But don't nobody ever want to listen to their mama. Oh no, mamas don't know nothing."

Took me a long time to get over my broken heart, but I was glad I didn't get a baby. That dish towel must of worked. But my love affair did change me. I threw out that new Kewpie doll, even

though it was the prettiest one I'd ever had. And I decided I'd never talk to somebody who says their *S*'s funny, I'd never go back to
the state fair, and I'd never be with somebody with wicked notions
like Galen had.

The next summer I started going out with Darnell Swigfel-
low; met him while he was visiting his aunt and uncle in Turkey
Creek. The next year we got married and I moved with him up to
Nashville, Tennessee, where we live to this very day. That's how I
got my career started up.

We found us a church and I started singing in the choir.
Me and two other girls put together a trio and we got so good
we thought we'd try to go professional. We named ourselves The
Swingin' Sisters and we all bleached our hair the same color
blonde and wore it styled just alike.

We start out performing at some clubs that wasn't too nice,
but gradually we got hired at some of the better places, even sung
at the Grand Ole Opry a few times and made ourselves two re-
cords. I wrote lots of our songs myself; you might have heard of
the most famous one, "Don't Never Trust a Travelin' Man." Why,
Patsy Montana was thinking about recording it herself, 'til she
found out that we'd just finished making our own record.

Darnell takes care of the twins while I'm out there performing, since we most always sing at night. He ain't too wild about
me being up on stage with all the men yelling and whistling at us,
but he don't say much about it anymore 'cause the money's good.

It's the life I always wanted from when I was a little kid, and
some days I still can't hardly believe how lucky I am.

Still, once in a while, when I look in my jewelry box and see
those three little seashells I saved from that day on the beach, I
wonder if maybe Galen's somewhere out in the audience watching me. And sometimes I wonder if he ever wishes he'd stayed
with me in Toad Springs.

The Lord Works in Mysterious Ways
by Buck Blander, Pastor

When I was thirteen, an angel from heaven named Lynette come to visit me one night. She had wings and everything, and she said, "Buck Blander, you're gonna be a pastor when you grow up." And that's just what I decided to do. Life don't always go along like you plan, but I'm living proof that the Lord works in mysterious ways, thank you, Jesus.

I ain't what you'd call a tall man, but I got a good bit of weight on me, and that helps when you get sent up the river to Raiford Prison for something you didn't do. I even grew a beard while I was there, thinking I'd look meaner, but I don't have it no more. I was sent there by mistake, you understand, God as my witness. It was all just a misunderstanding, I swear on the Bible. Praise Jesus. I was just trying to save a feller who got cheated out of what was rightfully his. But them crooked heathen lawyers led the jury into thinking I was guilty.

Now, I come from a good Christian home. My aunt J.B. raised me in Tampa after my folks left me with her one summer when I was three or four, and went to visit Mama's cousin out in Texas. Must of liked it there, 'cause they wrote Aunt J.B. a letter saying they wasn't never coming back and she had got herself a new son. She never had no young'uns of her own and she was real bossy;

thought cod liver oil or a switch from the orange tree out back would fix whatever was wrong with me, but at least she took me in.

I'm proud to say I graduated from high school and afterward Aunt J.B. had a friend who got me a good job being a fireman for the Seaboard Air Line Railroad. I really wanted to start preaching instead, but 'cause she raised me, I did what Aunt J.B. wanted. After a few years, when the diesel engine took over the steam engine, the railroad folks thought they didn't need firemen no more since nobody was gonna be stoking a fire.

But the unions wasn't about to get pushed around, so they said they had to have a fireman in case a fire broke out, even though, unless there was a fire, the fireman wouldn't have nothing to do. Well, the unions won so I got to keep my job, but the rest of the crew all hated us firemen 'cause we got the same pay as them when we was hardly working at all. Some of them fellers got real ugly; a couple was always trying to start fights but I ain't never been a fighting man.

Now, there I was, a fireman with a good bit of time on my hands, and one day it come to me that God wanted me to spread his word right there in the train yard. So that's what I done. Tried to, anyway. But them railroad men was more interested in drinking and fornicating with women who wasn't their wives than listening about how to live with Jesus, and they just laughed at me. Later on when I got to court, two of 'em said that half the time I wasn't at work, which was wasn't nothing but a bald-faced lie and come Judgment Day they'll be paying for it. Seems to me that in the end nobody really gets away with nothing 'cause the Lord is always watching, so you might just as well go on and be good to start with. Praise God.

Anyway, in my spare time I'd got to where I'd go around to the hobos who was hanging out in some of the empty train cars and give 'em a little uplifting. Lord knows, they needed it, even if they didn't want it much. I always carried around a peanut butter and jelly sandwich wrapped up in some waxed paper; give them something to eat and them fellers'll listen for a minute.

One of them, his name was Grunchon, Gunny Grunchon, they called him. I found him one day lying in a stinky old boxcar, and he wasn't smelling none too good hisself. "Hey there," I says, nice and friendly. "How you doing today?"

He looks up at me. "What the hell you want?" he says.

"I just come over here sometimes to visit and spread the word of Jesus," I say.

He turns over and faces the other way.

"Got a peanut butter and jelly sandwich here," I says, pulling it out of my pocket and holding it out.

He looks back over his shoulder. "Got any beer?"

"No. But I got something better than that."

He sits up. "Whiskey?"

"No, sir," I say. "Even better. I got the everlasting salvation. Praise God."

He grabs the sandwich out of my hand and takes a bite. "I ain't listening to none of that shit. Salvation ain't what I need. I need money. Jesus ain't been doing me no big favors lately."

I had him talking. That was a good sign. "And just what you been doing for Jesus?"

He don't answer; just give me the turtle eye.

"So," I say, "how'd you end up here?"

He takes another bite and spits some out when he talks. "That bastard Santino stole my money."

"Who's he?"

"Santino's Cigar Store. Over on Seventh Street. Son of a bitch took my money."

"You know, it says in the book of Timothy that money is the root of all evil. You heard that?"

"Whoever said that didn't live in an empty boxcar in Tampa."

I can see he's got a point there, so I decide to go along with him for a little. "How'd he get it? Your money?"

"Santino, that SOB, he's with the Mafia. Pulled a gun on me in the middle of five-card stud. Stole seventy-five dollars."

"Well, there you go. Playing cards is bad enough, but you're cussing and gambling at the same time. You're just asking for trouble, sinning like that."

"I'm sure they got it locked in the store safe and I got the combination. But I can't get it without a lookout and won't nobody help me. They catch me, I'm a dead man."

"Hmm," I say, thinking that right there could be a way to save his soul. "Maybe I can help you. Praise the Lord."

He stares at me. Even his eyeballs look to be covered in dirt. "Yeah?"

"If you promise to go to church with me and get saved," I say.

"I ain't getting saved. None of that shit. I was gonna use that money to go back up and see my poor mama." He looks at me, then wipes under his eyes like he's crying, but with all the dirt, I can't tell for sure. "She's bad sick, may even be dying for all I know, and I'm stuck down here without a goddamned penny."

The thought crosses my mind that he's just play-acting, but I give him the benefit of the doubt. "Your poor, poor mama," I say. "But listen to me, Gunny. You shouldn't be taking the name of the Lord in vain and you done it twice in just a few minutes. God'll help you if you pray for him to lead you. Praise Jesus. The Lord helps those who help—"

"Well, he ain't come up with nothing so far. How about you? You gonna be my lookout?"

The wheels started turning in my head. "Maybe I could help you . . . since it's really your own money you'd be taking. But only if, um . . . if you'll get saved. Praise God. You know, Gunny, Isaiah 40:31 says, 'Them what *wait upon the Lord* shall mount up with wings as eagles; they shall run and not be weary.' You need to take Jes—"

"I ain't getting saved. That crap ain't for me."

"Well, I ain't helping you, then."

He's quiet for a minute, just looks up at the sky. "Okay. Okay. But only if we get the money first. And you got to cut out that 'Praise God' shit."

The fact is, I prayed over this whole thing a lot, and by the end of the second day it come to me in a flash that there wasn't nothing more important than saving sinners. Now you understand, I wanted to help Gunny to save his soul, just out of the goodness of my heart. Not 'cause of what the law said later on, that he was gonna give me a cut of the take for my trouble. That was Gunny's idea, not mine. I never would of took it.

Anyway, we sneaked up to the back of Santino's Cigar Store about two in the morning and while Gunny jimmies the lock, I'm looking up and down the alley. When we get inside, Gunny unlocks the front door in case he needs to make a fast getaway, then props the flashlight up where he can see into the safe. He unlocks it in less than a minute and starts pulling stuff out. They got all kinds of junk in there besides money, and he's tossing stuff everywhere, making a lot of noise. "Quiet," I tell him, but he don't pay me no mind.

About that time I see a couple of guys staggering down the alley. I go inside and whisper to Gunny that a couple of drunks are coming, but he don't act like he hears me. He's got one sack full, hands it to me, and he's just filling up another one when all of a sudden them two guys I thought were drunks come crashing through the back door holding their guns out, yelling "Stop!! Police!! Put your hands up!!"

Gunny, he flips off the flashlight so it's all dark, and runs out the front door. Me, I'm so scared I just stand there holding the bag, saying, "Don't shoot! Don't shoot!"

God as my witness, I was just trying to save that poor man's soul. But I paid the price for his sin, and he got away scot-free. In the end he'll have to pay double, of course, once the Lord gets ahold of him. Everybody knows the Bible says in Leviticus, "If thou steals from thy neighbor the wrath of the Lord shall be upon thee."

I got six years, 'cause my lawyer must have just got his law papers about twenty minutes before we went up to see the judge and didn't have no idea what he was doing.

I was determined I was gonna follow the Lord's path even if I was in prison, so at every meal I called the other men to join me in saying the blessing—most I ever had was four. Then, when we went out in the prison yard every day, I'd give a little sermon to whoever would gather around. And I was sure to read a chapter of the Bible every night before I went to sleep, too. Got to where I could explain God and his will so that even the most ignorant man alive could understand it, and I'm real proud of that. But by the time I left I'd saved only three of 'em, and one was just 'cause that old feller was dying with consumption and said he didn't want to take no chances.

All along I studied my heart out and prayed to Jesus that when I was released, he'd put me in a church so I could spread the good news. But before I got out, the chaplain told me I had a problem.

He said I'd have to go to school and get ordinated before I could have a church, earn me a certificate and all, but that cost money and I didn't have none. By that time Aunt J.B. had gone on to her great reward and couldn't help me. Not to mention she quit talking to me when I went to Raiford and took me out of her will. Anyhow, I figured I really didn't need to go to school. I knew the whole Bible backward and forward and figured there couldn't be much left to learn.

One of the fellers two cells down, we called him Big Havana 'cause he was big as a giant and was always smoking Hav-A-Tampa cigars his mama sent him, he give me the name of a feller in Tampa who'd done a little time for counterfeiting, said he could fix me up a paper saying I was a preacher. 'Course, I prayed on it first, but God told me it was fine 'cause my heart was in the right place and I'd studied for so many years that more schooling wouldn't be no help, I already knew it all.

First thing when I got out, I looked up that feller and he fixed me a fancy paper with a gold seal on it, saying I was a real preacher. Then I started looking for a church where I could hang it up.

One night when I was at a revival in Tampa I heard that some folks over in Toad Springs needed a pastor, so I called 'em up and said I'd like to meet with 'em. The next Thursday morning I borrowed a car and drove over there. Met with the head deacon, Hank Plenty—a tall feller with a big purple birthmark on his face—and all their regular deacons, along with the church secretary. We met at the town hall 'cause they said the church needed cleaning up and they hadn't had time to do it.

I was nervous, so I said a long prayer before I got there. I'd already asked God about whether I should tell 'em about Raiford, but he agreed with me that it would be better to let them get to know me first, so that's what I done. They passed around my diploma so they could all get a good look at it, but they didn't ask no questions, thank goodness. I'm sure the Lord had a hand in that 'cause they hired me right off the bat.

I won't never forget how I felt when I moved to town on that Saturday afternoon all them years ago, carrying my bags up the road toward the church. Aunt J.B. would of been so proud.

I was a little disappointed when I seen that the church building was peeling down to the bare wood, one of the front windows was broke, and weeds was growing up everywhere. But I told myself the Lord had sent me to fix it. When I got closer I seen a sign around back that said Church Office and behind that was what was left of a little old frame house, more like a shack, where I was gonna be staying. I knocked on the church office door, then opened it and went in.

The walls was kind of puke green and even though the sun's shining in the windows it's kind of dark. A heavy-set lady in a purpledy flowered dress with her gray hair all piled on top of her head is sitting at a table behind a telephone and a typewriter—looks to be in her late fifties.

"Why, hello there, Pastor Blander," she says, standing up and touching her hair where it had come loose down on her neck. "I'm Sorrey May Only, your secretary." She comes around the table, folds her hands together at her waist, and says, "Welcome to our humble Church of Everlasting Liability, where we all look out for each other through good times and bad. I'm so pleased to meet you."

"Hello there, Mrs. Only," I say.

"Oh, please just call me Sorrey May. Now, I'm the secretary here. Just want you to know that this job's the only thing keeps food on my table. It's been a lot of work but I don't mind. Did I mention I ain't been paid the past few months? Why, if it wasn't for my daughter bringing me eggs and collard greens and a few dollars now and again I just don't know . . ."

"Nice to meet you," I say.

She clears her throat. "I'm gonna call Hank Plenty and he'll come over and show you around. He's the head deacon; 'course you already know that." I stand there looking around while she makes the call. After she hangs up she says, "I expect you'll want to get right to work. This job has a lot of heavy responsibilities, you know, there's so much to do. I got the week all laid out for you." She hands me the calendar and moves over beside me, pointing at it. "We got no time to waste. I marked it all down right here. Now, I'm here most days from eight in the morning 'til noon, and Tuesdays and Thursdays from one to four in the afternoon. I answer the phone and do whatever you want. Hank Plenty, he's the one pays for the phone for us."

She sits down at her desk and looks at me like she's in charge and I'd better listen if I know what's good for me, which I don't like too much. Puts me in mind of the way Aunt J.B. used to boss me around. Then she points to a chair in front of her desk and says, "Sit down."

I keep standing.

"Now here's what I got. On Monday mornings at ten o'clock, you drop in on the Ladies Circle Meeting, a lovely group if I do say so myself. I been holding meetings right along even when we didn't have no preacher—been doing my best to keep things running—without any pay, like I told you," she says, patting her hair. "And the last month or so it's been a strain but I love doing the work of the Lord." She gives me a great big smile.

"Then on Tuesday and Thursday afternoons, your Personal Meeting Time is from two to four o'clock. That's when anybody can come to you with their private family business. Now, Preacher Outlaw was always partial to them meetings. Had a steady stream of ladies coming in and out all afternoon. And that's all confidential, of course. Preacher was very strict about that.

"Then, the first Monday night of every month you got a Board of Deacons meeting at seven o'clock. There's one tomorrow night and all the deacons are real anxious to talk about the budget. I have to tell you it ain't in good shape. Like I said, I ain't been paid for months now. I already put the treasurer's report on your desk. Now for Tuesday—"

"Wait a just minute," I say. "You already got all this laid out? I ain't been in town for half an hour."

"Well," she says, tilting her chin up and looking down at me. "I just figured you'd want to pick up right where Preacher Outlaw left off. He did such a fine job."

I take out a handkerchief and wipe my nose. Then I say, "I'm taking over all right, but I need a while to settle in before all them meetings."

"You know your flock's been waiting lo these many—"

"I know they have," I say. "But the first thing I need to do is finish up my sermon for tomorrow."

"Well, I'll see can I change some of the regular plans for the week, but Monday's all set. Ain't no changing that. Like I said, I just figured you'd want to do what our wonderful Preacher Outlaw always done, since it worked so good."

I sneeze and wipe my nose again. "Where's my office?"

"Right there," Mrs. Only says, pointing to a door on her left and standing up. I can tell she ain't too pleased with me.

"Hank . . . uh, Mr. Plenty should be right along to meet you," she says, "so if you don't need me, I'll be on my way now, it being Saturday and all. I'll see you in church tomorrow. Starts at eleven sharp. But you should be there by ten."

She's gone before I can get my handkerchief back in my pocket. I walk around the church grounds, looking at all the work that needs doing, and it ain't long 'til Hank Plenty comes. He apologizes for the look of things and says the church building used to be somebody's house. They'd made the pastor's office out of the old kitchen—which was out back, connected to the house by a porch, probably to cut down on the heat from the stove in the summer. It's bigger than you'd think, but you can tell by the smell a lot of fish had been cooked in there.

Inside the main house they'd knocked down some of the walls and turned it into the sanctuary. White paint's peeling and there's old rusty buckets sitting around on the floors to catch the rain. They'd closed in the back porch and made it into a meeting room.

Then, behind the church he shows me the little two-room shack where I'll be living. Can't tell that it's ever been painted at all, but it has a woodstove and a sink, a bed and a table with two chairs, and an outhouse out back.

"Ain't too fancy," Hank says. "We just ain't got the money right now to paint nothing or make no repairs."

"That's okay," I say, thinking to myself, *I'm just glad to have a roof over my head that don't have bars all around it.*

Hank promises that they'll fix it up one of these days, then tells me that some ladies'll bring me supper around six o'clock.

When I go back inside my office I notice that Preacher Outlaw must have been a cigar smoker. I didn't smell it when I first come in, but after I'm inside for a while it's almost as bad as when Big Havana smoked his cigars up at Raiford. The room ain't very big, two chairs sitting across the other side of the desk, along with a cot up against the wall, I reckon to take naps on. There's an electric fan on the bookshelf so I take it over and set it in the window, facing out, and turn it on high, trying to get some of that smell outta there.

The cigar smell makes my nose run worse, but I reckon I'll get used to it. I hang up my diploma right behind my chair so when I'm talking to folks they can see it, and sit down across from my new desk and admire it. I can't hardly believe I got my own church, at last.

That's when I notice there's some beat-up hymnals, a frazzled old Bible, and a few other books on the shelf: *The Perils of the Preacher*, *The Road to Pentecost*, and *God's Cure for Worry*. After looking through 'em, I sit down at the desk.

There's the treasurer's report, and from what I can tell, the church ain't got a penny to its name. Wondering what I got myself into, I go to work on my very first sermon for the next morning. The title is "Follow God's Path."

Just before six o'clock, Carrie June Neal and Hester Brisco show up with a pot of stew and a loaf of bread for my supper, along with bed linens, some dishes and pots, and some canned goods. I thought I'd done died and gone to heaven. A pastor at last, with a house to live in, good food to eat, and a chance to save souls. God done answered all my prayers.

The next morning seemed like a miracle. I couldn't hardly believe I was standing in a real pulpit. When I look down on them seventeen souls, I know that finally I'm a real preacher. At first I was nervous, my voice even wobbled a little, then I think to myself, *I'm just saying God's word. Now, God wouldn't be nervous up here, would he?* The worst part was that I had to keep wiping my nose, but I don't think folks noticed much. Once I get going, I talk longer than I mean to, but what I'm saying is so good I just keep going. I outsing 'em all and shake every hand after the service.

I spend the rest of the day getting settled in and take me a nice long walk down to Lake Bass in the evening before I go to dinner at Hank Plenty's ranch. When I get back home my nose is running so bad I can't hardly sleep.

Monday morning the ladies at the circle meeting give me coffee and cookies and then Mrs. Brisco pulls me to the side and whispers that Sorrey May Only's daughters are little tramps who got themselves into all kinds of trouble; it was just one scandal after another. One of them even dresses like a man! Even though none of them live at home with her no more, Mrs. Brisco says, "You need to know what kind of person your secretary is since she's got her nose into all the church business. If she can't even—"

"Thank you, ma'am," I say, smiling. "I'll pray on it."

"Just trying to help," she says. "And, if it's all right, I'd like to come and see you at your office one day."

"Why yes, ma'am. You just do that."

That night, the board of directors talks about how to raise money to get the church cleaned up and painted, and no two of them fellers agreed on nothing. They come up with ideas all the way from Bingo—which I wouldn't never allow, but Halt Brisco thinks maybe we should make an exception just 'til we raise the money—to having a cake sale, which everybody says wouldn't bring in much. Other folks think we could put on a fair or hold a raffle with stuff folks could donate, but the board can't decide on nothing.

After that meeting, the bloom was off the rose, like Aunt J.B. used to say. By the time I said my nightly prayers, I was ready for a vacation.

The next morning was a Tuesday and Sorrey May beat me to the church, even though I got there at 8:00. "Good morning," I say.

She pours some coffee in a cup and hands it to me along with a big warm, buttery biscuit. "Good morning," she says. "Brought in some home-cooked breakfast to get you off to a good start. I know men live by theirselves don't eat right," she says, touching her hair.

I wipe my nose, thinking maybe this might could work out after all. "Thank you. That's right kind of you."

"There's something I'd like to talk to you about," she says. "When you get a minute, that is."

"All right. I've got a minute right now," I say, sitting down in one of the chairs across from her and taking a bite of the biscuit.

"Wanted to tell you that Flavey Stroudamore, you met him Sunday after church, the tall, skinny feller. Anyways, he's planning to put a great big hog pen on his property. It's looking to be so big he could put three hundred hogs in there."

"Is that so?"

"All the men think that's what he's building but he won't say. Childe, that's his wife, she told me he's got some papers about hog farming, but don't nobody really know what he's doing."

"Hmmm," I say, having no idea in the world what she's coming to.

"Now here's the thing. They live just down the road from the few little stores we got in this town, and if he does that the whole place'll stink to high heaven."

"So, anybody asked him outright what he's gonna do?"

"I ain't, but Hank has. That's Hank Plenty."

"Oh yes."

"Hank says Flavey told him he's give up strawberry farming and he's starting something new. But he wouldn't say what."

I finish the biscuit and wipe the crumbs off my mouth. "Well . . . I don't quite see what that's got to do with the Lord." My nose is running so I blow it again.

She touches her hair. "You're a man of the cloth. Flavey would have to listen to you."

"Me? But it ain't my place to tell him what he can build on his own land."

"Why, a hog farm will be the ruination of this town. If he does that, you won't have nobody to preach to," she says. "You stay here, you gonna have to learn a few things. We got big problems. Problems what need solving, and if church folks can't do it, who in heaven's name can?"

"But . . ."

"You gonna get along here, you got to get down off the fence and defend your flock or you ain't gonna have no sheep following you. You got to stand by the folks in your church."

She's beginning to rub me the wrong way. "Well, I ain't been here a week, and if you don't mind my saying so, Mr. Stroudamore came to church, too. Seems to me if I was to take sides, I might have to take his." I take my coffee cup into my office and shut the door. Don't know what's in the air but my nose sure don't like it.

Nobody told me I'd get dragged into something like this. I turn on the fan again to help with the smell, then sit there and mull it over for a while. Finally I send up a little prayer, and I'm looking at *The Perils of Preaching* when there's a knock at the door.

"Come in," I say. I shuffle a couple of papers around on my desk so it looks like I been busy.

Sorrey May opens it up and steps inside, closing the door behind her. "Hester Brisco's here to see you." She touches her hair and whispers, "It's not during your Personal Time hours. I can tell her she's got to make an appoint—"

"No, no, that's fine," I say to let her know she ain't telling me what to do. She frowns and walks out and Mrs. Brisco comes in, face all squinched up like a thundercloud.

I welcome her and she sits down across the desk from me. "Now I ain't normally one to go stirring up sand," she says, fiddling with her pocketbook, "but me and some of the other ladies think there's some things you need to know before you get in too deep here. We drew straws to see who'd come and talk to you. I lost."

"Oh?" I say, wiping my nose and putting my handkerchief away.

"We all think you need to do something about your secretary," Mrs. Brisco says in a quiet voice, opening her pocketbook and then snapping it shut over and over. "You need to fire her."

I try real hard to call up my patience and take a deep breath, like Aunt J.B. always told me. I don't much like Sorrey May myself, but then I don't want nobody telling me what to do. "Ain't she been the secretary here for a long time?" I say.

"That's just 'cause Preacher Outlaw was partial to her. And that was 'cause she kept his dirty little secrets about what he was doing with the ladies of this town."

Glancing toward the door, I see the shadow of two feet under the crack at the bottom. They stay there for a little bit, then move away.

"What are you talking about?" I ask, leaning back in my chair and near about toppling over. Turned out one of the legs was wobbly.

Mrs. Brisco says, "That Preacher Outlaw was a dirty old man. Took advantage of at least two ladies I know about, myself. He'd just lead them on and did you know what, then he'd pretend nothing never happened."

"Is that so?" I say. "And how do you know about this?"

"I got my ways," she says, snapping her pocketbook open and shut. "And Sorrey May would set things up for him. When I called to talk to him, she'd say he was out visiting somebody when he was really in here doing his visiting, if you want to call it that. That ain't what I call it."

"What do you mean?"

"See that?" she says, pointing to the cot. "Why you think that's in this office?"

"Well, I thought it was to take a little afternoon—"

"No sir-ree, it ain't," she says. "It's for fornicating on."

"Heavenly days, Mrs. Brisco!" I say, sitting up straight in my chair. "I heard Preacher Outlaw run off with one of the ladies but . . ."

"She wasn't no lady," she says, snapping away on her pocketbook. "She was a hussy. And a married woman! Nothing but a Jezebel."

I got no idea what to say, so I put my elbows on the desk, fold my hands together, and close my eyes, trying to look like I'm communing with the Lord.

"And he couldn't of gotten away with none of that if it wasn't for Sorrey May helping him out."

I open my eyes and stare at her with no idea at all what to say. Or do.

"That look you giving me," she says. "You think I'm not telling you God's honest truth? Why I got the best reputation of any God-fear—"

"I didn't say that."

"Well, I'm honest as the day is long," she says. "You just ask anybody."

"You talk to Sorrey May about this?"

"Talk to her? Me? That ain't my place. That's your place."

"My place?" I say, pushing back from the desk.

"She's your secretary, ain't she? She's privy to everything that goes on in this church."

Her snapping that damn pocketbook open and shut is getting on my nerves. "Well, she's the secretary, that's right."

"Well then, who else should handle it, I ask you," she says.

"I don't have no answer for you right at the minute," I say. "But I'll pray on it. And I appreciate your coming in here to see me. Praise God." I get to my feet, hoping she'll stand up. She don't.

"That ain't the only thing I'm here about now," she says. Then she starts touching her fingers to her thumbs over and over instead of snapping her pocketbook open and shut.

I wipe my nose and sit down but I feel the old temper starting to flare up.

"It's that crazy old Flavey Stroudamore."

I know what's coming next.

"He ain't gonna build no hog farm right smack in the middle of Toad Springs."

I lean back real careful. "Well, far as I understand, he ain't never said that's what he's gonna do."

"You got to act. You can't just sit around and wait for the devil to get a holt of this town."

"I'm just the pastor here, ma'am," I say. "I just come here to spread the good news . . ."

"That's the problem. Only one around here has any say is Hank Plenty, and he can't get Flavey to 'fess up, neither."

I need to get her out of here. I ain't felt like this since Ralphie Ponzer kept stealing my toothpaste up at Raiford. Ralphie said if he could get enough and eat it all at the same time it'd kill him. He was tired of being locked up; but he was still doing time when I left.

I take another deep breath and try to stir up a little kindness in my heart, but I can't find none. "You asked his wife?" I say.

"Childe?" she says, snapping away. "She don't know nothing. That man never says a word to her from morning to night. She might just as well be living there all by herself, except she has to clean up after him. She's nice enough away from home, but go over to visit her, she don't even offer you any sweet tea or invite you to sit out on the porch and visit of an afternoon. Wasn't like that when she was young. Turned into a different gal after her baby girl was born dead. But, you know, life goes on." She looks out the window.

I stand up again. "Well, Mrs. Brisco," I say, "I'll see can I ask around about the pig farm thing. I ain't making no promises, mind you, but I'll see if I can check into it."

She frowns a little and stands up. "Well, all right. Guess I took up enough of your time for one day. I'll be real anxious to hear what Flavey has to say. And by the way, looks like there's something in the air around here that's making your nose run. You want to fix that, try sniffing up some saltwater up your nose. If that don't work, try cod liver oil."

I open the door and she walks out. Then I close it again. I feel like I need to go wrestle a gator or chop some wood or something. Instead, I pull down another book, *God's Cure for Worry*.

That night I try sniffing that saltwater like she said, and I can tell you I ain't never doing that again. Maybe I put too much salt in it. Only thing it did was make my nose run worse, so I couldn't hardly sleep that night. And I ain't never taking cod liver oil again, not even on my death bed.

The next morning, Hank Plenty shows up and says he wants to get folks together at the church the next night to talk about passing an ordinance to keep livestock out of downtown. He's asking everybody but Flavey Stroudamore to come, which I don't think is right, but being as I'm new in town, I give in. I been told Flavey's been coming to the church meetings right along with everybody else and I tell Hank we ought'a be inviting him too, but Hank says no. He says the meeting ain't about Flavey, even though a blind possum could see that's exactly what it's about.

Hank brought some papers to the meeting about making a law, but nobody much listened to him. They just wanted to complain about Flavey. It was almost ten o'clock and I was sick and tired of the whining when I finally give in and say I'll go talk to him, even though I don't think it's my place to do it.

The next Friday morning I knock on the Stroudamores' front door. They live on a nice piece of farmland in a white frame house with a front porch, set back a little from the road. Childe comes up wiping her hands on her apron. Before I can say good morning, she points around the side of the house and says, "Flavey's out back."

I say thank you and head out there.

He's kneeling down by the pens and I walk up behind him. "Howdy," I say.

He don't move.

I go a little closer. "Hello there, Mr. Stroudamore," I say, and this time he looks over his shoulder, stands up, and turns my way, but don't say nothing. "Just come by to visit to one of my flock. Ain't been here very long and thought it would help me get to know folks." I reach out to shake hands but he don't reach back.

"Better idea to come when they ain't working, you ask me," he says.

"What you building back here?"

"What's it look like?"

"Some kind of pens."

"At's right."

I look all around. "What you gonna put in them?"

"What's it to you?"

"Just trying to be neighborly," I say. "Trying to get to know folks around here. Good seeing you up to the church."

"Harrumph."

"Folks tell me you give up strawberry farming."

"At's right."

"What made you decide to do that?"

"You ask a lot of questions."

This ain't getting nowhere, so I say, "Can I give you a hand with something?"

He looks at me. "Well, you might could help me get this beam moved over here." I take one end and he takes the other, and we move it up on some low struts.

"You putting hogs in here?" I ask.

"Hogs?"

"Looks like hog pens."

"Naw," he says.

"Goats?"

"Nope."

"Some kind of livestock?"

"Nope."

"Well what, then?"

"Guess I'd say that's my business."

I wipe my nose. "Didn't mean nothing by it, Mr. Stroudamore. It's just that people are starting to talk."

He moves to stand right in front of me, grabs the straps of his overalls, and leans back on his heels. "What you say? People talking?"

"That's right."

"What the hell do I care, people talking? They need to mind their own damn business."

I take a step back and just flat give up on the whole thing. "Well, guess I'll be on my way. See you in church."

"Harrumph," he says.

I head around to the front, glad to get out of there and back to the church where I can sit in my smelly office all by myself.

The next Monday I'm at my desk trying to figure out how to raise some money to fix up the building when Sorrey May comes in with a cup of coffee and a slice of pound cake.

"Brought you in a little something from the circle meeting," she says, putting them on my desk. "The ladies was real disappointed you didn't show up this morning."

"I told you I can't be doing that every week. I told all the ladies that."

"They was still hoping and praying you'd come. Why Preacher Outlaw, he never . . ."

"Did you need something, Sorrey May?"

She sits down and wiggles around, fussing with her hair and getting comfortable in the chair. "Was nice of Mrs. Brisco to stop by the other day," she says.

"Yes, it was."

"Sometimes I get the idea she don't think too highly of me."

"Really?"

"Did she say anything about me?"

"Why are you asking that?" I say.

"'Cause I want to know."

I lean back in my chair, wiping my nose with a clean handkerchief, and nearly wobble over again, so I come back down fast. I fold my hands on the desk so I'll look wise and say, "I couldn't tell you if she did. From my first day here, you been telling me about being confidential and how important it is. How Preacher Outlaw was always careful about things people told him."

"'Course he was careful," she says. "But he told me everything. I mean, I can keep everything confidential, too."

"Is that so?"

"That's so."

"Well, you won't need to do that no more."

She frowns. "Why, Pastor," she says, "you ain't never gonna be able to remember everything and keep it straight all on your own."

I stand up behind my desk. "Thank you, Sorrey May. But, like I said, I won't need your help with that."

She looks madder than a sack full of wet cats. She jumps up from that chair and stomps out of the office and I take a deep breath and ask God for help. He must of been out doing something else though, 'cause I don't feel one bit better.

I pull out my handkerchief again and try to get back on track, but all I can think of is how bad I want to fire that woman. She was right that she knew more about running the church than me. But on the other hand, it's just a matter of time before I snatch her baldheaded, the way things are going.

I get *The Perils of Preaching* off the bookshelf and open it up but can't find nothing about nosy secretaries. When I hear the door slam I walk out to her desk, but she must of gone home without telling me.

When I get there the next morning, she's typing away at her desk. I say, "Good morning." She nods, touches her hair, then keeps on typing. I go into my office and sit a couple of minutes—no coffee and pound cake for me today, I see. Then I call out, "Sorrey May, would you please come in here?"

She don't answer, but in a minute she comes to the door with a paper and pencil. "We need to get a few things straight around here," I say, wiping my nose and thinking maybe I should try that saltwater again.

She sits down but don't say a word.

"Now, I appreciate all you've done, being the secretary."

"I still ain't got the raise I need if I'm gonna keep on working here," she says.

Thank you, God, I think. *Maybe she'll quit.* "You're gonna have to change your attitude if you're planning to stay on here."

"You trying to fire me?" she cries out. "You firing me after all I done for this church?"

"Didn't say that. I just said you're gonna have to change your tune around here and do things my way."

"You can't fire me," she yells, face red as the hot end of the devil's pitchfork. "I'm on the board of deacons, in case you forgot."

"You ain't really on the board, Sorrey May. You go to meetings 'cause you're the secretary. Just calm down and listen to me. If you're gonna keep on working here, you got to start following my rules and forget about Preacher Outlaw. He ain't here no more."

"Bless his heart," she says. "That man really knew how to run a church."

I count to ten, like Aunt J.B. was always trying to get me to do, but the anger starts crawling up my backbone. I take a deep breath and say, "He might be a fine man and he might not, but he ain't here no more and I am. Now here's what you're gonna to have to do to keep this job."

Sorrey May looks out the window and taps her foot.

"First thing, don't you leave here without telling me first like you done yesterday. Number two, you got to realize that what goes on here is really confidential and that you got no right to try and listen in at the door when folks are talking to me."

She sits up straight and gasps. "Why, I never . . ."

"I seen your feet under the door the other day when Mrs. Brisco was here," I say. "So don't go telling me—"

"You calling me a liar? Is that what you're doing?"

"I ain't calling you nothing, but I'm about to if you don't shut your mouth. I said you ain't allowed to listen in on people's private conversations."

"Well, I never in my life!" she says, crossing her arms in front of her. "Nobody ain't never talked to me like this . . ."

"Number three, you can't go around telling people nothing about what goes on here. That means nobody. It's not your place to go nosing around in what don't concern you and if I hear you been doing that, I'll make sure you won't be able to do it no more."

"You threatening me, Pastor Blander? 'cause if you are . . ."

"No, ma'am, I ain't threatening you. I'm just telling you what's going to happen if you don't change your ways."

Her face has turned all blotchy and she's getting louder and louder. "Well, that's what I call a threat. And folks are gonna hear about this, mark my words. Why, I ain't never been so insulted in my whole life. If you think I'm going to let you treat me this way, you got another think coming."

"Fine, Sorrey May. Now, do you mind telling me what you were typing when I come in?"

"Typing? Me?" She wiggles around in the chair. "Was a letter, is what it was."

"Letter to who? I ain't asked you to type no letter."

"Well, Preacher Outlaw, that generous man, he always said if I had some time with nothing to do I could write to my cousin

Mildred who's a big important manager over in Tampa, so that's what I was doing. Wasn't keeping me from the Lord's work 'cause I still got time to do anything you want."

"From now on I want you to do your church work first and when you finished all of it, then you can write your cousin."

"But that letter needs to go out today. That's why I done it first."

"You being paid to work here, Sorrey May."

"Ain't getting paid much—can't hardly make it one week to the next."

"Do you understand me?"

"I got plenty of time to do it all. That's just stupid."

"Beg pardon," I say. "You calling me stupid?"

She strokes her hair. "Um . . . um . . . no. I was not. You trying to put words into my mouth! I said what you was saying was stupid."

"Might not be the smartest thing you ever done, calling your boss's ideas stupid, Sorrey May."

She stands up. "You ain't firing me. My granddaddy started this here town and my daddy was the first preacher we ever had. And I need this job. I'm just a poor old widow woman and it's the only money I got coming in. I've stuck with this church through thick and thin, good times and bad, and just so you know, I ain't giving it up. What you got for me do right now?"

"I already asked you to type up a list of church members and everybody in their families, along with their address and phone number if they got one. Them papers in the desk are all in a mess and you need to organize 'em. I can't make sense of nothing. And when you finish that you can clean out the meeting room and look through the hymnals to see which ones got so much mildew on 'em we need to toss 'em out."

She just stands there, glaring at me.

I lean back in my chair, but this time I catch myself before it gets too wobbly. "And I want you to get this chair fixed." She squints her eyes at me, then walks out of my office and slams the door behind her. That little talking-to held good for about two weeks but then we was right back where we started from.

By the end of the first year it seems to me that ministering to them folks is like trying to drink sand. They got so many troubles 'cause they get their noses out of joint over the littlest thing. Seems to me they bring most of it down on theirselves.

My angel, Lynette, was right. I grew up to be a pastor. But it ain't nothing like I'd figured it would be. I'm proud to say we're up to forty-seven members though, so I must be doing something right.

The Lord does indeed work in mysterious ways.

From Shipbuilder to Rancher
By Childe Stroudamore

FLAVEY STROUDAMORE

A shipbuilder who never went to sea,
A farmer who never tasted his crop,
A rancher who never roped a cow.
May he rest in peace.

I knew my husband, Flavey, since we was both knee-high to a grasshopper. He wasn't the most outgoing fella you'd ever meet and was happiest when he was making something with his hands or figuring something out. He didn't much like school; couldn't get the hang of reading—said he seen all the letters backward or something—couldn't hit a softball and couldn't carry a tune, but he was a whiz with his fingers.

When he was in the fourth grade he glued Popsicle sticks together and made a model of the United States White House that was so good they kept it just inside the main door of the school for nine years. He was smart, too—once he got to concentrating he could figure out the trickiest puzzles in a flash. He was tall and sandy-haired with freckles and real nice teeth and all the girls at school had an eye for him.

On the Christmas when he was thirteen years old, Flavey got a kit that showed you how to build a ship-in-a-bottle. First one he made was of the H.M.S. *Grasshopper,* and he loved doing that more than anything else in the whole world. Soon as he finished it he got him another kit right away, and when school let out every day he went straight to the garage and worked there 'til supper. The minute he finished one, he'd sell it and buy a kit to do another one. After a while he was so good at it, his daddy took him to Tampa and he bought all his own supplies so he could try out new ideas. Got to where folks from Turkey Creek and Bartow and even Tampa was putting in orders.

One day his daddy got dressed up in his Sunday best and went over to Maas Brothers Department Store in Tampa and got them to buy Flavey's ships-in-a-bottle for a pretty penny. His daddy took half the money and Flavey wasn't too crazy about that, so when he got out of high school he moved to Tampa where he could sell the ships and keep all the money hisself.

In the meantime, back in Toad Springs, I was thinking I was gonna get married to Tony Cisco. He was dark and kind of short, and him and my daddy spent long hours talking about how Tony was gonna take over the strawberry fields when Daddy retired. After we graduated he give me an engagement ring and I was so proud and happy; wanted to get married right away. But Tony wants to travel out west and spend the summer in Houston with his uncle, and says when he gets home we'll set the date.

While he's gone, Flavey moves back home 'cause Maas Brothers found someplace they could buy the ships-in-a-bottle cheaper, and he couldn't afford to stay there. He mopes around town and finally gets a job in one of the groves. I tried to cheer him up, and we went on picnics now and then and to dinner a few times, but I made sure he remembered that I was getting married soon.

When Tony gets home at the end of the summer I was so glad to see him I wanted to be with him every single minute of every day. Then, soon as we set the date, all of a sudden he's so busy working with his dad and going out with his friends that the only time I ever see him is on Saturday nights. And then, all he talked about was Texas. I should of seen what was right in front of me and just broke up with him, but I went the other way and did every single thing I could to keep him. But before the end of September, he was back in Houston.

That's when I start seeing Flavey again, 'cause I really want to get married. And I want to do it now. Don't take me long to convince him, and when I tell Daddy he has a fit; tells me my mama was probably spinning in her grave, that he's worked his whole life to build the strawberry farm into something he can be proud of and leave to his only child, and Flavey ain't no man to take it over. He's so mad he says he's taking me out of his will.

But that don't stop me. Me and Flavey run off to Lakeland and get married like we planned. Since Flavey's working in the groves, we stay in a little old house on the property. He sets up a table in the living room with all his shipbuilding stuff on it, which would be okay except it's always a mess and the glue and paint and stuff stinks to high heaven and makes me sick. I get him to move it out to the barn, but I don't feel no better.

Then it comes to me one day that it ain't just the glue and stuff, but that I'm gonna have a baby. Either that or I'm dying. When I tell Flavey he's happy as a lark, wants to go out and tell everybody but I remind him it's bad luck to do that too soon.

It ain't but a few weeks later that the preacher comes by and tells me that my daddy died in his sleep. I'm real sad even though he wasn't never gonna speak to me again, and now I'm an orphan. But it also comes to me that before long I'm gonna have my own little family.

Everybody knew Daddy was mad that I married Flavey and his blood was up; lots of folks figured that's what give him the heart attack. At his funeral, a couple of ladies went out of their way to say he died too young, then give me a sideways look, so I'd know they was blaming me.

Turned out Daddy didn't take me out of his will after all, so me and Flavey got the strawberry fields to tend to, and we moved into the old house. We looked into selling the farm but there was something wrong with the property deed and we give up trying to figure it all out. Since we had a baby coming, seemed like there was nothing to do but keep on growing strawberries.

Now, I have to say that Flavey hated everything about farming. Every single thing. And it didn't help that he was allergic to strawberries. If he ate even a little one, he'd blow up like a balloon in two minutes flat. And he had to give up building his ships, the one thing in this world he really loved. Instead he spent his time worrying about freezes in the winter and sap beetles and two-spotted spider mites in the summer.

After Willard was born we had Bubba, and then a little girl, but she was born dead. Like to of killed me, it did. I love my boys now, but every woman needs a daughter. For years, I was so sad about losing that child and Flavey was so unhappy farming that we hardly even spoke to each other. He done his job and I done mine and that was that.

Sometimes it seemed to me that Flavey just got meaner and meaner 'til nobody wanted to have nothing to do with him. He'd go to church, now mind you, but he'd just sit there looking mad, like he was cursing God for putting him on earth. Didn't never talk to nobody more than to say, "Harrumph."

Have to say I changed a lot during them years, too. Where I'd been so full of life and ready to have a good time when I was young, I just turned myself inside out and come to be so meek and sad I couldn't hardly recognize my ownself. They started calling me "Oh My, Childe," 'cause I'd say "Oh my," all the time. Life wouldn't of been worth living if it wasn't for my boys.

Willard was the quiet one, real smart but never said much. He looked like my daddy, not too tall with dark hair and him and Flavey never did get on. If Flavey said yes, Willard said no. If Willard said it was hot, Flavey said it was cold. Bubba, on the other hand, was big and blonde, the spitting image of his daddy and he never met a stranger. That boy was the apple of his daddy's eye, could do no wrong.

He worked both of them boys in the fields soon as they was old enough to help, and both of 'em hated strawberry farming as much as he did. Flavey'd always told them soon as they was grown he was turning the place over to them, but neither one wanted it.

Bubba was in high school when he got hit on the shin with a horseshoe and had to have one of his legs cut off below the knee. And it just so happened that Willard's the one who threw it. Now Willard wouldn't never have hurt his baby brother on purpose, but after that Flavey wouldn't hardly speak to the boy. When Willard come into a room, Flavey went out.

One evening Flavey and the boys was still out in the fields when the sun went down. It was the end of a long, hot day and Flavey told Willard he had to pick one more row of strawberries while Flavey and Bubba went back to the house. Willard said he wasn't gonna do it. Flavey come at him and Willard fought back—Bubba said they was in a real knock-down, drag-out.

In the end Flavey won and Willard moved out of the house the very next day. Quit school and got a job in the groves, and moved into that same place me and Flavey started out in. He never once come back to the house, but I'd go over and see him every week. After a while he married Sorrey May's daughter Mindy Sue and they moved off to Ft. Pierce. Broke my heart they went clear to the other side of the state.

But something changed in Flavey after that fight. He turned in on hisself and for a while he wouldn't talk to none of us. Finally, one day he told me the last twenty years of his life hadn't been nothing but a lie. All that time he'd been living a life he hated, fighting with a son who was a stranger to him, and he wasn't gonna do it no more. He was done with farming. Said he'd rent out the land if I didn't want to sell it outright, but he was done. Had some ideas of other work he could do but he wouldn't tell me or nobody else what he was planning. About the only thing he ever said to me was, "Gimme more coffee," or "Pass the salt."

Next thing I know he orders all this lumber and starts building some kind of pens out back. When I ask what they're for he won't tell me. When all the neighbors seen something going up, they come asking me about it, knowing they'd never get a word out of Flavey, but I can't tell 'em nothing. Finally, one day I go look through all his papers while he's out back working.

Come across some stuff on hog farming and ads from feed stores in Tampa, so looks like to me he's gonna build him a pig farm. I never should of done it but I say something to Sorrey May Only, and that woman's the biggest gossip around. She could wheedle anything out of you if she wanted to bad enough and she must have spread it all over town.

One hot summer evening we're sitting on the front porch and Flavey says, "Why does everybody think I'm building a hog pen?"

"Oh my," I say. "How would I know?"

"Harrumph," Flavey says, and he gets up and leaves.

It ain't a week later, Flavey says, "Heard there's a three-legged gator out at the lake."

"Ain't heard nothing about that," I say.

"A three-legged gator," he says, and wanders off.

Then one morning about two or three o'clock, I hear this real loud *gronk, gronk* sound and sit up straight in bed.

"Flavey! Flavey!" I whisper. "What's that?"

He turns over and says, "Hrmmph."

"Dammit, Flavey. Wake up!! Sounds like a big gator!" When he don't answer I shake his shoulder. "Flavey, you got to go look!"

"It's a gator."

"What?"

"The three-legged gator."

"What three-legged gator?"

"One I told you about. I caught him."

"What? What in hell you saying? Turn over here and talk to me."

Flavey don't move. "Gonna put him in my gator farm."

I get up and turn on the light. Flavey pulls his pillow over his head.

"Gator farm," I says. "Gator farm?"

Flavey mumbles from under the pillow, "Beats picking god-damned strawberries."

I sit down on the edge of the bed and stare at the floor, feeling like the whole world just fell out from under me. I put my head in my hands and start to cry. And I ain't one to cry. Then all of a sudden, while Flavey's lying there in the bed, playing possum, I crack wide open, like a watermelon falling off a truck.

At first I just cry. And the more I cry, the madder I get. Then I start thinking about how my life's been wrecked 'cause I married Flavey instead of Tony, and how my baby girl died, and how Willard left town, and the neighbors don't never ask us over 'cause Flavey won't talk to 'em. In my mind everything bad that had ever happened to me is all Flavey's fault.

Then I look over and see him still lying in bed with his head under a pillow. I get up, storm into the living room, and head for the only ship-in-a-bottle Flavey's got left, the H.M.S. *Grasshopper*, the first one he made. I snatch it down from the mantelpiece and stomp back to the bedroom with it.

"Flavey," I holler. "You look at me."

He just lies there, don't move.

"Flavey, I got your *Grasshopper*."

With that he lifts his head up, turns over, and looks at me like a dog caught sucking eggs.

I take a good aim and slam that bottle across the room as hard as I can into the wall right over his head; little pieces of glass and ship fly everywhere.

Flavey sits up, brushes the mess out of his hair onto the floor, and looks down at the broken pieces of his precious ship. I go into the living room.

When he follows me in there I start screaming my head off. "Goddamn you! I spent all these years cooking your meals and washing your clothes and raising your kids and now you come home with a damned alligator? What a hare-brained idea! You're crazy!"

Flavey just looks at me with his eyes bugging out and his mouth wide open.

"Don't you never come near me again! My daddy built this house and he left it to me. It's mine, not yours, and you're getting out of here!"

Flavey's still standing there, staring.

"I hate you and everything about you. I'm sorry I ever married you."

Flavey don't say nothing. Then he turns around and shuffles back to the bedroom. I sit down on the sofa and stare into the empty, black fireplace and listen to the quiet 'til my breathing calms down. When I hear him snoring a while later, I run in there and start beating on him. Finally he grabs a blanket and goes out to the front porch in his underwear and lies down on the swing. I clean up the mess and get back in bed feeling a lot better, but I can't sleep.

Finally I get up, fix me some fried eggs and bacon and grits and coffee, and leave the dirty dishes on the table for the first time in my life. When I'm done, I go out back to see the gator.

He's lying up alongside the side of the pen, covered with dried mud and dead lily pads. Don't know what I was thinking, 'cause everybody knows you never mess with a gator, but anyways, I grab a hose and start rinsing him down. I guess leaving the dishes on the table was just too much and I had to clean up the next thing I run across, even if it was a dirty old three-legged gator.

When all that goop come off, lo and behold, I can't believe my eyes! He has this patch on his side, like a birthmark or a scar or something. When I look close, it's a picture of Jesus' face, clear as day I tell you, right smack-dab on his side just above the stump where his leg was missing. Can you believe it? Clear as day, except Jesus' hair's a little short on the one side. But other than that, it's his spitting image.

Well, I just stand there with my mouth hanging open. Without even thinking I hear myself say out loud, "Precious Jesus. Oh, my dear Lord in heaven." I was so overtook I even forgot how mad I was. "Flavey," I holler, running toward the house. "Flavey, get out here!"

He come on out back, still in his underwear. "What is it, woman?"

"Look, look what I see here," I say, pointing.

Well, Flavey, he can't believe it neither. "I never seen that," he says. "I got him 'cause he was a three-legger."

"I'm getting Pastor Blander," I say.

"What about my breakfast?" Flavey says.

"You done ate your last breakfast cooked by me," I say. "Fix your own damned breakfast."

Pastor Blander, he come right over and declared that gator to be a marvelous gift from God for sure. Said it was a sign of things to come, but he couldn't rightly say what. And turned out he was right. That gator changed our little town.

After my nervous breakdown on that alligator night, something happened—and when Flavey told me his idea, I decided having a gator farm wouldn't be half bad. We started planning things together. First time we'd ever really worked together on something. And we started gettin' along.

I named that first gator "Precious" 'cause that was the first word come outta my mouth when I seen him. "Precious Jesus" is what I'd said. For sure, he was a gift from God. I went all the way to Tampa and talked to the *Tribune* newspaper people about Precious. They sent a feller out who took some pictures they put in the very next Sunday paper. The next weekend Mayor Chancey of Tampa come out with his son and took snapshots. His wife wouldn't come; said you seen one gator, you seen them all.

After that, folks come by the dozen. We charge a nickel for the kids and fifteen cents for the grown-ups. At first Flavey ain't too wild about talking to folks, but when he sees how much money he can make, he loosens up and starts smiling and enjoying himself. He starts reminding me of that good-looking feller he'd been in high school all them years ago.

He tells everybody that Precious is fourteen feet, three and a quarter inches long, even though he hadn't never measured him, and he's a rare "Green-speckled Shade Gator," only two others ever seen in the whole country—which he just flat made up out of the blue—and that Precious got his leg tore off by a panther when he was little; says he could tell by the marks on his stump.

One time, he tells everybody, a feller come over from Orlando with a little crippled boy. When that kid seen Precious, his leg healed right up, quick as a flash, and he walked away from the pen without his crutches. And all them scars from his six operations? They was gone! It was a miracle! And then there was the old lady who had an arm that hadn't never worked right, and when she left, she was waving at everybody and snapping her fingers.

When he tells his stories he still makes sure folks know to keep their distance, 'cause in spite of his holy ways, a gator is still a gator and the animal side of Precious could take over faster than a no-see-em can bite your ankle.

After a while, Flavey leases out the strawberry fields to some of the other farmers and puts a fence around five acres out through the swamp up north of the house. Next, he catches himself a whole bunch of regular gators and lets them live out there where they can have more babies, but they can't get away. Then he builds a walkway up on stilts so people can stroll along and look down at the gators and not have to worry about getting eaten up. And, of course, he'd already made that special pen for Precious so folks can walk all around him and see Jesus on his side. Even has pictures of him hung along a wall near the pen.

After the second year we build a covered entranceway to the pens and set up the front door so it looks like you're walking into a gator's mouth. It's so good some little kids was afraid to come in. After that, we get this feller to paint some big pictures of the gators and we set 'em along the front. One has his mouth wide open to show the pretty pink color inside, one is a mama gator holding babies in her mouth when she's taking them down to the water, and one is of Precious lying in the sun with a halo around his head.

With them gators fenced into the swamp, Flavey don't have to feed them, and after the Blue-Eyed Gator Restaurant got built, whenever they run outta gator meat, he'd just go out with his gun and shoot him one.

Early one spring he heard there was an albino gator up in the Okefenokee Swamp in Georgia, so he set his mind to finding him. Took three trips, but him and some fellas up there who knew a thing or two about roping gators, caught that sucker and Flavey brought him back down to home. Folks couldn't believe he'd caught him, but here's his secret: he come up with something no decent gator could resist.

He got an old dead possum and packed it in cow manure for two weeks, and it stunk so bad he couldn't hardly stand to take it with him up to the swamp, but that's what done the trick. No respectable gator could pass up that smelly mess. Named that gator White Lightning. He had eyes as pink as the inside of his mouth. Something to see.

Now White Lightning and Precious was both boy gators, and not too fond of each other. Flavey even had to keep them in separate pens, or they'd have eat each other up. Gators'll do that, you know. Cannibals is what they are. They don't care. So anyway, even though he knew gators don't mate for life, Flavey put a girl gator in with each one of them 'cause he thought it would look better to the tourists. White Lightning didn't much like the gal Flavey picked for him, name of Louise, but Precious and Mildred, they was real happy.

Next, Flavey heard about a blue-eyed gator from somebody come to see Precious and White Lightning. Said he'd seen it in a circus a few days before over in Orlando, and the feller was looking to sell. Was going down to Miami to work at the new Parrot Jungle and give up the traveling life. Well, Flavey found that feller and come home with the blue-eyed gator, name of Sampson.

By this time we had so many rare gators we got that same painter to come make us a big sign that said, Stroudamore's Rare Reptile Ranch, the Largest Assortment of Rare Alligators on Earth. Then we added on a real gift shop and even put out some signs along the road, like the Burma Shave people did, that said things like:

> "We're just up the road,
> So stop by our farm
> All the kids'll stop fussing.
> It'll work like a charm!
> Come to Stroudamore's Rare Reptile Ranch!"

And,

> "Our gator named Precious
> Won't give you a ride
> But a picture of Jesus
> Is right on his side.
> Come to Stroudamore's Rare Reptile Ranch!"

Wasn't too long before the folks in town started making stuff to sell at the Gator Gift Shop. The Ladies Circle Meeting at the Church of Everlasting Liability started making quilts to sell and some of the ladies was crocheting little alligator booties and baby sweaters and pot holders. Other ones was knitting gator sweaters and scarfs and making jewelry out of gator bones and selling 'em through the shop. And we put in a leather section where we had gator pocketbooks and briefcases, even some shoes, brought all the way from Atlanta.

I get business cards made up and advertise in newspapers as far away as Miami and Jacksonville and Tallahassee. Toad Springs grew up overnight; even got us a hotel, The Green Gator. At the Blue-Eyed Gator Restaurant they served gator fixed every way you could imagine: gator stew, gator steak, gator burgers, gator salad, gator gumbo, fried gator with grits and scrambled eggs, gator stroganoff, gator meat pie, barbecued gator, and even come up with a green limeade drink they called gator juice.

By that time we'd made enough money to buy us a new car and Flavey was actually talking to folks when he didn't have to. Seeing him change like that made me think it must of been spending all them years in strawberry fields in a job he hated, that turned him so sour.

After things are going along pretty good, Flavey loses interest in the business. I take over running it with Bubba helping me some, and Flavey goes back to building ships full-time. Never lost his touch for that, he didn't. The first one he made was of the H.M.S. *Grasshopper*, like the one I smashed, and he set it up on the mantelpiece at home right where the old one had sat all them years before.

Never made another one exactly like it. That was just for him. He sold his ships-in-a-bottle in the gift shop; once in a while he'd put some little tiny wooden gators in there with the ships even though any fool knows gators don't like the ocean. But them tourists from up north, they don't know squat.

In the end, Flavey got to be famous like he wanted 'cause the *Tampa Tribune* come out to visit again and wrote an article on his ships-in-a-bottle. They even put in a picture of him with some of his ships on the front page of the newspaper, and he was as proud as the president of the United States standing on a bear.

For his last ten or twelve years Flavey was a deacon in the church, who would a thunk it, and he run them a merry chase 'til he died at eighty-two. And I'm glad he got to be famous for his ships. He felt real good about the gator ranch, but them ships was his pride and joy. Since I figured it would of made him happy, I got a picture of the H.M.S. *Grasshopper* carved into his headstone.

The Only Murder
by Sorrey May Riley Only

A few years back, my dear, departed husband, Lucas, was murdered in cold blood by Gladys Heppner, who still lives right next door to me to this very day. It's the only murder we ever had here in Toad Springs, and she just done it 'cause she carried a grudge against me lo these many years. Jealous is what she was.

She couldn't stand it that my Lucas was tall and blond with blue eyes that could break your heart and her Orin was shorter than her and bald besides and grew this big, ugly, brown, warty-looking thing over his left eye. Why, Gladys was jealous and all puffed up at the same time, acting like she was so much better than the rest of us 'cause she's from Ohio and went to college. She don't even try to hide the fact she thinks we're all stupid. Which we ain't.

Now my Lucas worked down at Smitty's Hardware and Feed for twenty-one years; was manager there when he was killed. We'd had us four girls in four years, then quit trying for a boy. Lucas wasn't ready to stop having kids, but I told him, if you want to have a boy you'll just have to do it with somebody else, 'cause I've done all the birthin' I'm gonna do. And I didn't take no chances on that score. He turned a little sour after that. Men. They only think of one thing. Jeeeesus Lord! It's a wonder they can carry on a normal life with that thing hanging down between their legs always looking for something to do.

On the day he died, my Lucas had just gone over to Gladys's house to talk to her about our dog, Dirty Sally, that she claimed was killing the squirrels that come to her bird feeder. Now, everybody knew Dirty Sally was a sweet old thing who couldn't of caught a squirrel if she'd tried, which she never did. She had the arthritis, for heaven's sake. And my Lucas wouldn't never of said nothing ugly to Gladys; besides being such a good looker, he didn't have a mean bone in his body.

But I heard her yelling that he was lying and no good and our damned dog ought to be shot; heard it all the way from our porch. And that's what give him the heart attack. Made me a widow woman, she did, right there on her own front stoop. And I know she done it out of spite. I could tell by the little smile she had on her snooty face at the funeral.

I made sure Constable Grogan looked into everything, but it turned out he didn't have no idea what he was doing. He come over and looked around and decided that since I was way over on my front porch I couldn't of seen what was going on. And Gladys, of course, said she didn't never raise her voice at all, even though I heard her hollering. But since there wasn't nobody else around, it was just my word against hers and they wouldn't take her off to jail where she rightly belongs. Don't know myself how I stand living next door to her to this day, but I ain't moving. I was here first and I ain't getting pushed out of what's rightfully mine.

My granddaddy was Buford Riley and he started this town, him and Jam Stroudamore. And my daddy, Buford Jr., was our first preacher. We been the heart and soul of Toad Springs ever since it began. Then somebody like her moves in and thinks she can push us around when we're the ones who built this place to start with. Like I said, wasn't no way I was gonna move outta my house to get away from her. But I did get my third daughter, Bob, to put up a six-foot wood fence along that side of the house so I don't have to look at Gladys.

Now, I should tell you Bob's real name is Barbara Jean, but she's such a tomboy, she wanted us to call her Bob. So we did.

Anyway, Gladys and Orin had two boys, Rusty and Little Mike, and they was pretty nice kids. Don't know how, but they was; played cowboys with Bob all the time. And Gladys was a teacher over at the school when my girls was coming up. They was all in her classroom at one time or another and with all the tears and aggravation I still ain't sure how we managed to live through it. My sister Carrie June taught the kids up to sixth grade and Gladys taught the older ones. Now every one of my girls did just fine in Carrie June's class; after that's when the trouble started.

My oldest girl's named Dancy Lynn. Lucas picked that name, I'd never of called a child something like that, but he had an old girlfriend named Dancy, which I didn't find out 'til Dancy Lynn was about four and by then it was too late to change it, much as I wanted to. Anyway, Dancy said Gladys was always picking on her. If Dancy answered a question wrong, she had to go sit in the corner, when nobody else had to. When Gladys give a test she was real strict, said the kids had to sit up with their backs straight, and only look directly in front of them or at their papers. If they looked anywhere else they got a zero.

Well, it just so happened that Dancy was one of them young 'uns who'd go all to pieces over a test. Said her brain would stall out like her daddy's old truck and she couldn't remember nothing, but while she was trying to think her eyes just naturally wandered around the room. She couldn't help it. Besides that, she was born left-handed and Carrie June didn't care but Gladys made her use her right hand so all the kids made fun of her. Many an afternoon she come home in tears, crying about how she hated school.

I went to over to Gladys's house a few times and told her exactly what I thought of her but nothing good come of it. She just acted like I'd raised a little hooligan who wasn't never gonna do nothing right in her life and if I'd been a halfway decent mother Dancy'd be able to remember the answers for the tests just fine.

Personally, I blame that woman for Dancy quitting school and running off to get married early. She's got three young'uns now and they live out west so I don't hardly ever see 'em.

And everybody in town knew Gladys didn't like Bob. Bob said that woman went out of her way to call her Barbara Jean—both names—and made the other kids call her that, too. And she kept telling Bob she ought to at least try to look like a girl; that she needed to let her hair grow long and act like a lady and sit with her knees together, which Bob wasn't never gonna do. Truth be told, if I hadn't changed Bob's diaper myself I'd of thought Lucas had got his boy after all. But I'd never of told Gladys that.

My other two girls, Elsie Lou and Mindy Sue, did better in school, but they both said Gladys was always in a bad mood and if you ever asked her a question she didn't know the answer to, she'd get all bumfuzzled and just make something up.

Well, I have to tell you, Gladys is still a thorn in my side even though my girls are all grown up and gone. Now that she's quit teaching school, she's showing up at the church circle meetings and expecting everybody to let her join in just like nothing ever happened. And they're doing it, too. That there's almost too much of a cross the Lord give me to bear. I think the devil's got his hand in on this.

The old pastor we used to have, Preacher Outlaw, was my salvation when Lucas got killed. He give me a job helping him out two afternoons a week and I did that for almost a year. 'Course, that was before I got hired on to be the first secretary the church ever had. I swan, I just don't know what I would of done without that wonderful man.

I talked to him a lot about my Lucas. My dear husband's been gone eight years this May and I still worry about him rotting away in hell for never going to Sunday services. Our whole married life I told him to repent and come to the Lord, but no, there weren't no listening to me. He just went his own way and now I'm gonna have to pray for him for the rest of my life, along with praying for everybody else around here and Lord knows, they all need my help. I ain't hardly got room to add anybody to the list there's so much going on. As it is I'm on my knees every evening for near about half an hour and it don't do nothing good for my arthritis.

A while back we got us a new preacher name of Buck Blander and just between you and me and the barn cats I say he'll never be able to fill Preacher Outlaw's shoes, regardless of what you might have heard about that dear man. No, sirree. Pastor Blander knows as much about running a church as a wild hog knows about Sunday. Since he got hired on I been working with him real close. Trying to, anyway.

I see that it's my responsibility to keep things going the way Preacher Outlaw done all those years, but in all this time Pastor Blander still ain't caught on how to do things right. It's a good thing I'm blessed with a lot of patience and I got a gift for handling people. Those are talents I was born with and I don't intend to hide my light up under a bushel, but trying to teach that man a thing or two has been like trying to get a damp hanky to stand up and dance. He just lets me talk and then goes on and does whatever he wants.

When he got hired, didn't nobody know he had the hay fever. He didn't even sniff once at the interview and his nose wasn't red, like it always is now. I know, 'cause I was secretary and had to be there and write everything down. But that man sneezes and snuffles all year long, can't get through a sermon without wiping at his nose all the time. If he'd just stop and give her a good blow once in a while it might help, but he don't. One Sunday morning I counted thirty-three wipes in twenty minutes.

It's got to where after the service, some folks sneak out the back instead of going through the main door where he might want to touch their arm or take their hand. I notice lots of the men just pat him on the shoulder or wave at him from a ways off. Most of the ladies are wearing gloves, but they're still careful to be holding something so their hands are busy. And, 'course, I make sure he don't never touch me when we're at the office.

I told him more than once he's got to quit wiping his nose like that, but he just looks at me with them sad, watery eyes and wipes his nose and asks how my girls are. And I'd tell him about my young'uns if I thought he might have any good advice. But if I told him my troubles, he'd just say, "Hmmm," and tell me to pray on it and that'd be the end of that. Then he'd know my business and I'd have nothing to show for it. I sure as hell ain't telling him nothing.

My best friend, Ree, said her second cousin, who works over to the jail in Bartow, heard that Pastor Blander done a little time in the state prison. I wouldn't be a bit surprised, myself. He's got them beady criminal eyes. I knew he'd never admit it if I asked outright so I hinted around some and said things to him like, "You know I can keep a secret if there's something you'd like to tell me about. Anytime there's anything you want to get off your chest . . ." But he just looked at me like I was crazy.

Now, his sermons put fear into the hearts of those who love the Lord, which you gotta do if you think anybody's gonna listen to what God has to say, and Pastor does a fair job of that. But he don't know how to help folks with their troubles. He just stares at you with this blank face and before you're done talking, you can tell he ain't got no idea what to say back.

Seems to me if he was better at that we could bring in more lost souls. We already got more members than the Fiery Freedom Baptized Holiness Church, 'course they got that crazy Harold Mayfield for pastor over there, but our offerings been down lately and it's getting to where I'm afraid they ain't gonna be able to pay me what little tiny bit I get.

That other church was just thrown together by some of our old members who got mad 'cause we wouldn't allow sinful acts like dancing and playing cards or Bingo. Good riddance, I said at the time and I still say. We'll just see where them sinners end up in ten years, with all their wicked ways. But of course, all the best people still come to our church, you know, the important folks in town, and that's 'cause we remind people to obey the Ten Commandments, even when it ain't all that convenient. People need good strict rules to live by and without us and the Bible, this place would of gone to hell in a hand basket years ago.

After all, the name of our house of worship, The Church of Everlasting Liability, says it all. I'm liable for keeping my brothers and sisters walking down God's straight and narrow path. It don't matter that I've had to endure having my dearly beloved husband killed right under my nose—by my next-door neighbor—and watching the murderer go free as a bird. I still manage to be a loving, generous person. When people make mistakes, like we all do, I pray for 'em and I forgive 'em in my heart.

All except for Gladys Heppner.

Caught in the Middle and Sewing in Circles

by Carrie June Riley Neal

Back when I was little I'd sit at Granddaddy Riley's knee and listen to his stories about growing up in South Carolina and coming down here with his best friend, Jam Stroudamore. Before he'd start spinning his yarns, he'd light up his pipe and he always let me blow out the match. If my sisters, Sorrey May and Never, was there, he'd light two more for them to blow out, but then they always run off. I stayed, and that's how I got to know more about the way this town started up than anybody else around here; from my granddaddy, Buford Riley.

Granddaddy told me that the first night they was here, him and Jam set up camp out at Lake Bass but they only stayed there for the one night, 'cause soon as the sun went down about a million toads come, croaking real loud and jumping all over 'em the whole night long. So the next day they moved over to what's downtown Toad Springs now.

It's the exact spot where Smitty Mallet's Hardware and Feed sits today. A week or two later, Granddaddy found this little baby coyote that he raised up that was better than any dog. He named him Juniper and trained him to hunt turkeys. Said that coyote slept right at his feet every night and Granddaddy loved him like he never loved nothing else. Except me, of course.

The story goes that Jam's the one who picked the name "Toad Springs" even though the closest spring is in Lithia and that's a good piece off. To this day don't nobody know why he named it that. But that's a Stroudamore for you.

Granddaddy and Jam started up a cattle business, turned into real Florida crackers, matter of fact. In case you didn't know it, that's where "Florida Cracker" come from—them cowboys cracking their whips.

He talked about rounding up cows and branding 'em, then letting 'em loose again. Him and Jam got into fights with other cowboys who tried to steal their cows. One time he got shot in the arm. It was a hard life, Granddaddy said.

He told me all about the winter of 1894–'95, when that famous freeze that folks still talk about come through. By that time Toad Springs was built up and there was orange groves everywhere. What made it extra bad was that the weather had warmed up early that year, and the sap was rising. When it come a hard freeze, them trees split wide open—most of them killed dead. Granddaddy said it broke everybody's heart, women crying and men sitting around staring at nothing for weeks. Took years to get things back up to snuff.

And in 1921 a bad hurricane come through, a real gully-washer, blew the roofs off four houses and killed seven people. Everything was flooded, trees down everywhere, dead cows and armadillos all over the place. The smell was more than most folks could abide—everybody had to tie a handkerchief over their nose for a month.

Jam quit working when he was sixty-three 'cause he said it was too dangerous for an old man. Two weeks later he went on a fishing trip out off Indian Rocks Beach, over on the other side of Tampa, and got caught in a waterspout. He was sucked way up in the sky and folks on the beach said he never come down. That feller went straight up to God, is what everybody said.

On the other hand, Great-Granddaddy died from a heart attack at the age of ninety-two while he was hunting wild boar out by the Peace River. And you ask me, ain't nothing worth mentioning's happened around here since.

Today the cowboys are all gone. Instead we got citrus groves and strawberry and tomato farms; we also got the Stroudamore's Rare Reptile Ranch that Jam's grandson Flavey started, and that's what's made us famous.

On Main Street, there's the Toad Springs General Store, Smitty Mallet's Hardware and Feed where you can pump gas, and Andy's Barber Shop. The Green Gator Hotel and the Blue-Eyed Gator Restaurant both come along after we got the gator ranch. And, we got two churches and the school. At the last count there were three hundred and twelve people living here with two more on the way that I know of. And that's the history of our little town, where I was born and raised and lived my whole life.

I'm the middle girl, between my sisters Sorrey May, who thinks she has to run everything and Never, who was the town's first telephone operator and always has her nose in everybody else's business. And I'm here to tell you mine ain't been the easiest path God ever give a body to follow. Couldn't hardly get a word in edgewise between them two the whole time I was growing up and I reckon I just give up trying. Still, to this very day, I get all bumfuzzled if I have to be standing up in front of people.

I was glad to marry Tully and get away from my sisters, but he died only three years later. Three years, five months and sixteen days later. Got drowned in the Peace River while he was fishing. He always thought he had to wear these waders. They looked like overalls with boots attached to the feet so you could wade way out in the water and not get wet.

But Hank Plenty give him these waders and they was way too big. Besides that, the buckles on the shoulders was all rusted. What happened is he went in too deep and them waders filled up with water and he couldn't get out of 'em. So he drowned. And can't nobody say I didn't warn that man time and again. He didn't even need them waders, nobody else used 'em, but he wouldn't listen to me.

We didn't have no young'uns, and after he passed over to greener pastures, I didn't know what to do with myself. Was about that time the town decided we needed to have our own school, so I got to be the first schoolteacher we had here. All's I had to do was take this mail-order class and I got me a certificate to teach. I learned pretty quick and I'm proud to say I taught Worthy Perkins how to read, and he's the smartest person ever born here.

Gladys Heppner come to town a few years after we opened up the school and she took over the older kids. Things got harder after that 'cause she thought she knew everything in the whole world, just 'cause she'd been to college for a year. She was always complaining that I didn't teach the kids to talk right and said I wasn't strict enough, that children should be seen and not heard and there was way too much noise in my classroom. Took me a while, but finally I got to where I just ignored her whiney voice and how she was always sucking air through her teeth, and taught the way I wanted to.

Never did marry again and when I retired after twenty-five years, Preacher Outlaw says to me one day, "Carrie June, now that you've got time on your hands, reckon you could start up a Ladies Circle Meeting for us?"

Well, I can't even tell you how proud I was to be asked to be a church leader; but at the same time my stomach went into knots just thinking about it. It's one thing to stand up in front of a room full of young'uns but another thing to do it with a bunch of ladies. He announced during the Sunday service that the first Circle Meeting would be held at ten on Monday morning and I have to tell you he said some real nice things about me. 'Course I didn't let them go to my head, not for one minute.

The night before I baked up some sugar cookies and the next morning I was at the church thirty minutes early to tidy up. That meeting room used to be a back porch and they closed it in, but it's dark and kind of sad in there. I opened the curtains to lighten it up but it didn't help much. But really, my main problem was that I was nervous about being up in front of grown-ups so I said lots of prayers ahead of time.

Hester Brisco got there first, hugging her pocketbook like she always does, and helped me put some chairs around the table. There was six of us in all, a good turnout; Hester, then Gladys Heppner and Childe Stroudamore come in at the same time, talking about how Childe's husband had got so sick after he accidentally ate one of her strawberry biscuits and him so allergic and all. Then come my big sister, Sorrey May, along with Ree Perkins, her best friend.

When they showed up my heart sank down to the floor 'cause I knew Sorrey May was gonna make trouble. She never liked me from the minute I was born, always setting out to trip me up and make me look stupid. She'd go around telling the other girls that I'd wet my pants or I liked some boy who wouldn't have nothing to do with me and stuff like that. I sent God another prayer and carried on.

At ten o'clock sharp I stood up so I'd look real official and said what I'd practiced, "I want to thank you all for coming today. I think we'll be able to do a lot to help the church and spread the word of the Lord. Now, first thing is to get us a volunteer to bring the refreshments next week. I got sugar cookies for today."

It was quiet for a minute, then Childe Stroudamore says, "All right, I'll bring strawberry tarts."

"Thank you, Childe," I say. "That's right generous of you. Now, we're here to talk about raising money. I was thinking that some bake sales might be a good idea."

"All churches can ever think to do is have a bake sale," says Sorrey May, touching her hair in that irritating way of hers—trying to act like she's better than the rest of us. "Let's do something ain't done all the time." Since we was kids, Sorrey May ain't never gone along with nobody else's ideas. She could start an argument in an empty house.

"Oh my. What else could we do?" says Childe.

"How's about weaving baskets?" Sorrey May says.

I try to keep myself from rolling my eyes. "You know how to weave baskets?" I say.

"Well, no. But it don't look to be hard."

I sit down in my chair and look straight at her. "Maybe we should start out with something we know how to do since the idea here is to serve the Lord and not ourselves."

"Maybe . . ." says Hester. "Um . . . how's about sewing a quilt?"

"A quilt?" says Sorrey May. "That's no good. Everybody does that, too."

I look right at her and try to stay calm. "Everybody does it 'cause it's a good way to raise money."

"I got some scraps," says Hester and the others nod.

"Well, I don't," says Gladys. "I spent my life teaching school and I think we should do something where we can all contribute equally and it just so happens we don't all have scraps available." Then she sucks air between her front teeth like she always does— "*Thssst*"—sets my nerves on edge.

"I think most of us got some scraps, don't we, girls?" I say, and everybody nods their heads. "See Gladys? We all do."

"Well," she says, "I don't. I've always bought clothes ready-made, myself."

"That don't matter, honey," Ree says. "We can just put everything in a big pile and nobody'll know who brought what."

"If I can't participate equally, I just won't come," Gladys says.

Sorrey May turns to look her in the eye. "Look, Gladys, if you don't want to come you sure don't have to. As a matter of fact . . ."

Gladys starts clouding up, looking like her feelings are hurt. "I knew you all wouldn't want me here," she says, pushing her chair back. "All those years I was teaching school and I couldn't come to meetings—I got left out."

"Come on, Gladys," I say, at the same time I'm wishing she hadn't come. "I was teaching, too, and I'm here."

"You people have never made me feel welcome. I know you just want to get rid of me. What about the raisin muffins? Remember that?"

"Oh yes," says Sorrey May. "I sure do remember that."

"Oh honey, that was years ago," Ree said. "And we know it was just an accident. Come on now, don't leave."

A few ladies mumble something and Gladys sits back down, saying, "*Thssst.*" Hester pats her on the back.

"Quilting is too much work," Sorrey May whines, touching her hair again.

"Not if we cooperate," Childe says. "We could each one of us take some pieces home and stitch 'em up, then come here of a Monday morning and put 'em all together."

"I ain't got much time to sew at home," Sorrey May says.

"Me neither," says Ree. "I got a few scraps, but I'm awful busy."

Now I might of known this was gonna happen 'cause Ree is always on Sorrey May's side.

"Well, since most of us got scraps," I say, "looks like we're gonna be quilting." I smile real big at Sorrey May. "Now we got to pick out a pattern. I like the Double Wedding Ring, myself."

"I'm partial to the Pinwheel," Sorrey May says. I swear it's still like when we was kids; if I wanted to play paper dolls, she said we had to make mud pies.

"Oh, all them little tiny triangles can get to be a lot to keep track of," I say. "I think the Double Wedding Ring would be the best one to start with."

Hester lets go of her purse and raises her hand. "My sister-in-law's got the Charm."

"Reckon we're gonna have to vote on it," I say. "Anybody got any other ideas?"

Nobody says nothing.

"Okay, then. The Double Wedding Ring, the Charm, and the Pinwheel," I say. "Personally I don't think the Pinwheel is as pretty as the other two, but that's just my opinion. So, everybody in favor of—"

"This vote should be by secret ballot," says Gladys.

"Why you want to do that?" says Sorrey May. "That's just a waste of time."

"I think it's a good idea," I say, just to get her goat.

Ree smooths out her dress and glances over at Sorrey May, then sits up straight in her chair. "You want to make good money on it, you gonna have to make it fancy. Like the Pinwheel."

"This ain't gonna be the only quilt we're making," I say. "I just think we need to start with something simple. Let's go on and vote on what we got. What do the rest of you think?"

Nobody speaks up.

"We gonna have to vote on whether we want to vote or not?" I say.

Gladys takes a deep breath. "Yes . . . *thssst*, let's go ahead and vote."

I get some paper and pencils from the office, and when I come back Sorrey May's got a big frown on her face.

I write down the Double Wedding Ring on my paper and we all put our votes in a collection basket. Then me and Hester count them up together so, like Gladys says, nobody can accuse us of cheating. To my surprise, the Double Wedding Ring only gets one vote, one piece of paper is blank and all the rest are for the Pinwheel. I can't believe everybody went with Sorrey May's idea.

"Looks like somebody forgot to write down their vote," I says. "Maybe we should do it again."

Sorrey May gives me a great big grin and pats her hair. "Won't make no difference. Pinwheel's gonna win either way."

Guess I know when I'm beat. "All right," I say, "let's all bring some scraps next week."

"We ain't even elected no officers," Sorrey May says. "How come we're voting on something when we ain't even got no officers?"

"We got an officer," I say. "I'm the president."

"How'd you get elected? I don't remember voting on nothing."

"Preacher Outlaw asked me to start this meeting."

"But that don't mean you get to do whatever you want. This here's a free country and the rest of us got a say."

I look around at everybody but Sorrey May. "You ladies feel like there's something you want to say?"

They all glance at the ceiling or out the window or at each other and mumble and shake their heads. I look over at Sorrey May and she's trying to stare them down, one at a time.

Then Gladys says, "And I believe we'll need a secretary to take minutes during the meetings."

"Minutes?" Hester says.

"You know," Gladys says, "write down what we do each time."

"That's right," I say. "Almost forgot. Thank you, Gladys. Anybody want to volunteer?"

Nothing.

"How about you, Gladys?" I say, picking her on purpose to aggravate Sorrey May. "You got such nice handwriting."

Gladys looks surprised. "*Thssst*," she says, nodding her head. "All right."

I clap my hands and the others join in, glad not to have to do the job theirselves, I reckon. "Anything else we need to go over?" I ask.

Sorrey May says, "So you gonna be the president?"

"That's right," I say.

"You ever done anything like this before? 'cause I—"

"I'm the president," I say, raising my voice and staring her in the eye.

"So, how long you gonna be the president for?"

"Well, a year. A year sounds about right."

"I think it should be for three months," she says. "That way we can rotate around and give everybody a chance."

"I don't think—"

Gladys speaks up. "Should I write all this down?"

"Not every word," I say. "Just write down—"

"She's supposed to write down who says what, and like that," Sorrey May says. "I thought you knew how to run a meeting."

"We ain't down to the courthouse, Sorrey May. This here's a circle meeting."

Sorrey May leans back and crosses her arms. "There's a right way and a wrong way to do things. Personally, I always run meetings the right way. Saves time and aggravation."

She's trying to drive me into a hissy-fit like she did when we was little, but I ain't gonna give in. "Thank you for your comments, Sorrey May. I'll take 'em under consideration." I heard Hank Plenty say that once and it sounded pretty high-falutin' to me. That ought'a shut her up.

I turn back to the others. "Let's have some of the sugar cookies I brought. I'll pass the plate around and you ladies can visit for a while. Then next week we'll all bring our scraps and see what we got."

"As I've already told you, I don't have any scraps," says Gladys.

I look out at them all. "Let's just everybody bring what you got, or ask your neighbors if they'd like to give you some."

"And if we ain't got enough scraps, then what?" says Sorrey May.

Gladys says, "You had four girls, Sorrey May. You don't mean to tell me you don't have anything left . . ."

Sorrey May glares at her. "I got to squeeze every single penny since my Lucas died. On your front porch, I might add."

Gladys rolls her eyes.

"I like what Sorrey May said about weaving baskets," Ree says. "I'd like to learn how to do that."

"That's nice," I said. "But we ain't here to learn new things. We're here to do the Lord's work and raise money for the church. We can't be thinking of ourselves."

"No reason we can't be doing both things at once," says Sorrey May. "Ain't no reason in the world."

"Well, y'all want to learn to weave baskets," I say, "you just do that. When somebody else is president you can teach us all how. But for now, the meeting's over."

Before the next meeting, I'm careful to get plenty of scraps and have them stacked on the table when the others come in. Just to make sure Sorrey May understands I'm in charge, I keep standing 'til everybody pulls up a chair, then I sit down and say, "I want to thank you all for coming again."

"Now, first thing let's decide who's gonna bring refreshments next week. Sorrey May, how about you?"

She looks around the room, then says, "I reckon I can do that. I'll make a pound cake over the weekend. And maybe Childe can bring some strawberries to put on it."

"Now, Sorrey May," I say, "Childe's already brought her refreshments today. You're responsible—"

"It's okay," Childe says. "I can bring strawberries."

I give Sorrey May a dirty look, then go on. "All right, then the next thing is to decide which scraps we're gonna use. So if you'll all put your pieces up here with mine, we can see what we got."

They all do, and I'm happy to see we have enough for two or three quilts. "Now, anybody got ideas about what colors we want to use?"

"Looks like we got a lot of blue," Sorrey May says. "I say we just use them, nothing but blue."

I know she's just saying that 'cause I hate blue—it just ain't got no life to it. "Nothing but blue?" I say. "Hmmmm. We could dress it up with this nice pink cotton, with the little white flowers on it. Might be nice to mix the pink and the blue."

"That would look tacky," Sorrey May says. "Using all different colors of blue would look the best. You know men don't like sleeping under a pink quilt."

I look her dead in the eye. "Ain't no man I ever knew cared a fig what color the quilt was, long as it's warm."

She looks right back at me. "Look, Carrie June, I'm just saying it would be harder to sell with pink in it. And if the idea is to raise money . . ."

"What do the rest of you have to say about it?' I ask, looking around the room.

"I don't care," says Hester, snapping her damn pocketbook open and shut.

"Oh my. Either way," says Childe.

"It doesn't really make any difference to me," says Gladys.

"I like the blue," says Ree. "I think Sorrey May's got the right idea."

"Okay," I say, trying to look like I don't care. "We'll do the first one all blue. Next one we'll use the pink. Childe, would you figure out what size pieces we need, and who wants to start cutting 'em out?"

"I'll do it," says Gladys, reaching in her pocketbook. "I brought scissors."

"Me, too," says Hester.

"I ain't gonna be able to take but maybe three or four squares," says Sorrey May. I guess she's decided she can do a little work at home, now that she's got her way on both the quilt pattern and the colors.

"Fine," I say, looking at her. "If you can't contribute your fair share we'll make up for it."

The rest of the ladies get out their needles and thread, and as Gladys and Hester pass out the pieces, everybody starts stitching.

"I'm gonna have to get me a job," Sorrey May says to nobody in particular.

"What kind of work you thinking about?" asks Hester.

"The church here ain't got no secretary since Preacher Outlaw's wife went back to her mama," she says. "I'm thinking about working right here, just to bring in a little money. Remember I helped him out for a while after my Lucas died." She looks at Gladys. "The church is bigger now and he needs a real secretary."

My heart sinks down to my shoes. Why, she'd know every time anybody wanted to talk to him about something personal. And the walls in them offices is thin as the skin on sour milk.

"What makes you think he wants a secretary?" I say.

"Everybody knows he needs help," she says, "and I aim to ask him about it right after this meeting. Wouldn't have to pay me much at first, but once we get the membership up, I could earn enough to stay out of the poorhouse."

I break out in a sweat.

At the next meeting I'm just about to tell everybody to sit down so we can start when Ree speaks up, "Sorrey May said she was gonna be late today 'cause she's talking to Preacher Outlaw about the secretary job."

I put my hand on my heart. "Oh, my dear Lord in heaven." Everybody else looks like they've just been told Jesus ain't coming back after all.

Ree looks at me and takes a bite of one of her famous lemon drop cookies she brought to share, since Sorrey May said she was too busy to make the pound cake. I notice she don't offer one to nobody else.

I walk over to where I was sitting at the first meeting I was in charge of, and stand behind the chair. "I think it's time to get started. Why don't you all come over here to the table." I hold up some of my work. "Got my triangles all sewed into neat little squares, here."

"I got mine, too," says Hester, waving hers.

"Looks like we'll soon be ready to start putting it all together."

"Oh," says Gladys. "I believe I'm supposed to be taking notes. *Thssst.* I forgot to bring any paper."

I point over to a little table by the door. "There's some over there. Go on and get it."

Ree pipes up. "Sorrey May asked me to tell y'all if she was late, that she was thinking we could put a little strip of navy blue between all of them squares. You know, kinda make them stand out. Like a picture frame."

"Oh, that sounds like a lot of extra work," I say. "Was Sorrey May willing to do it herself?"

"She was thinking you could do it," Ree says. "Since you ain't teaching no more."

I can't hardly believe my ears. "Why now, I'm a busy woman, Ree. I do things you don't know nothing about. How's about you? Since Landis ain't around much on the weekends, you got the time, don't you?"

Ree gives me a blank look. I know I shouldn't of said nothing about him drinking, but it's too late now.

"No, I don't have the time," she snaps back.

I look around the room. "Anybody else want to volunteer?"

They all look at each other like they don't want to get in the middle of things.

"Well, if Sorrey May wants to think up extra work, then she should be the one to do it. And since she ain't even here we'll just talk about that another time." I look at Ree.

Just then Sorrey May walks in with a great big smile on her face. Everybody turns toward the door. Gladys looks over at me and rolls her eyes. "Sorry I'm late," she says. "Just had to get a few things straightened out with Preacher before I start work." You could of heard a pin drop.

"Looks like the church has got its first real secretary." She pulls out a chair and sits down, still grinning.

Ree jumps up and hugs Sorrey May while everybody else watches, glued to their seats in horror.

"It's such a wonderful way to serve the Lord," Sorrey May says. "But I told Preacher I'd need to keep coming to circle every week."

The other ladies nod their heads and Sorrey May touches her hair and smiles, pleased as blueberry punch. "'Course, I may have to miss meetings now and again. You know, if Preacher needs me for something important. I start working first thing Monday morning."

I stand up and clear my throat real loud. "All right. All right. We got work to do," I say. "Now, where were we?"

The rest of the meeting all I can think about is marching into Preacher Outlaw's office and telling him what he's doing to hisself. Not to mention the rest of us. But there ain't no use. What's done is done.

Finally we get all the pieces handed out and Sorrey May and Ree are the first ones out the door with their heads together, talking real low.

When I get home I'm all in a state. Have to make myself some chamomile tea and read through the Bible. "Yea, though I walk through the valley . . ."

At the next meeting I'm ready for whatever comes, Sorrey May or no. Ree and her are late but they're both carrying their quilt squares.

"All right," I say, "let's lay everything out on the table and see how they're gonna fit." Everybody starts mumbling and pulling theirs out.

"You done it wrong," Sorrey May says. "You were supposed to sew 'em end to end, not bunch 'em together like you're making a big square."

"You're the one who don't know what you're doing," I says. "I been quilting since I was four years old and I reckon I know how to lay out a quilt."

"Nope. You're wrong," she says again. "That ain't the way Mama taught us."

I stand up and look around the room, the hackles rising on my neck. I take a deep breath. "Well, let's see what everybody else did."

Turns out everybody else done them like mine, thank the Lord for small favors. I look at Sorrey May and I can't help smiling. "Well, since you done yours different from everybody else's, I reckon you're gonna have to rip yours out and do it over right. It's a shame."

"Ain't got time to do that," Sorrey May says in a nasty tone. "I got a job now, in case you forgot. I can't just sit on the front porch and drink sweet tea all day like some people."

This is worse than being back teaching school when it's been raining for a week and them kids are all acting up. I remind myself I'm the leader. I'm supposed to stay calm and hold my temper. I breathe in real deep. "If you want your squares to be in the quilt, they're gonna have to be fixed," I says. "They ain't gonna fit like that." I feel my temper sneaking up behind me.

"Then somebody else'll have to do it," she says, looking straight at me.

I squint my eyes at her, then look around the room. "Anybody got extra time on their hands they can fix Sorrey May's mistake?"

Everybody looks at each other but nobody says nothing.

It takes every single bit of willpower I can muster, but I hold my hand out to Sorrey May. "All right. Give it to me and I'll do the whole thing over."

"Don't need doing over," Sorrey May says. "Just make a couple of rips and stitch it back."

"If it's so simple, seems like you could do it your ownself." I reach for her squares but she pulls them back.

"You don't got to take the whole thing apart," she says. "No use to waste all that work."

"If I'm gonna do it, I'll do it any way I please, thank you," I say, reaching over and snatching it out of her hands.

She leans back and looks around the room, touching her hair and smiling.

When we meet the next week, Sorrey May and Ree get there early and stand in the corner talking real quiet while I move the chairs over to the table and lay out my quilting squares along the ones of Sorrey May's that I ripped out and re-sewed. Her stitches was all uneven like I knew they'd be, but I fixed everything.

Of course, I ain't trying to listen in on Sorrey May and Ree, but I just accidentally hear a few things while I'm straightening up, like Ethel Grogan just marches right into Preacher's office whenever she wants without even saying boo to Sorrey May—thinks she's something just 'cause she's the constable's wife, and Hester come in and talked to the preacher with the door closed but Sorrey May couldn't hear nothing but mumbling and her pocketbook snapping open and shut. Then I heard something about somebody drinking, but I reckon that was about Ree's husband, Landis. By that time, everybody else started coming in and Sorrey May and Ree quit talking.

Hester brought an orange cake, which was nice, I guess, but I just don't think it's right to eat cake before noon. Really, sweets like that are supposed to be for after supper, but then I'm sure she means well.

When everybody sits down and pulls out their work, I stand up again and start the meeting. "Ladies," I say, "I think we're gonna be able to get this quilt finished by the end of the month, if we get serious. Now that we got all the squares stitched together right," I say, looking at Sorrey May, "we can get to the batting."

"It's going be quite pretty," Gladys says, nodding her head.

"I think we'll be able to get a good price for it," I say. "If we keep doing this every week, before you know it, we'll be bringing in some real money for the Lord."

"Amen," says Sorrey May. "This church needs some fixing up, that's for sure. I know just where we can spend it."

Every time my sister opens her mouth I want to strangle her, but I just say, "Seems to me that's for Preacher to decide, ain't it?"

"He depends on me a lot," she says. "He's always asking me what to do about this and that."

Yeah, I think to myself. *I just bet he is.*

"Says he don't know how he ever managed without me all this time."

"What do you do there?" asks Hester.

"Why, I take care of everything for him. I usually start the morning off by making coffee—take it to him at his desk. He says it's the best he ever tasted." She pats her hair. "Then I leave him alone a while and type out whatever he wants, write letters and like that. And I take calls for him and give him messages. Anybody who wants to see him has to go through me."

"Is that so?" I say. This is just too awful to even believe. "What if somebody wants to see him and not have everybody know about it?" I say.

"Oh, everything there is confidential, very hush-hush," she says. "He's real strict about that."

"You mean you can't tell anybody what goes on there?"

"That's right." She looks me square in the eye and she knows damn well I heard her talking to Ree before the meeting. "I can't tell nobody nothing."

I grit my teeth and remember what Grandma Riley said about minding your P's and Q's, not that she ever did. Anyways, I just say, "Is that so? Hmmm." I wait a spell, then I just can't help myself. I say, "You seen Ethel Grogan lately?"

"Ethel Grogan?" Ree says, like she never heard of her. "You mean the constable's wife?"

"That's the only Ethel Grogan I know," I say.

Sorrey May touches her hair again. "Well, if I had I wouldn't be telling nobody about it."

"That's very interesting," I say. "Very interesting. But I think we'd better get back to our job here. We don't want to be wasting our time in idle gossip. That ain't the Christian way and it ain't ladylike, neither. I was thinking we should be planning what we're gonna do for our next quilt."

"Well," Sorrey May says, "I believe you was the one asking about Ethel Grogan now, wasn't you?"

By the time the meeting's over, we'd picked out the charm pattern for our second quilt and Gladys offered to bring some peanut butter cookies to the next meeting. Sorrey May said she'd take what's left of the orange cake to Preacher Outlaw, so there wasn't none for the rest of us to take home.

Sometimes running this circle meeting feels the same as running in circles. But since my great-granddaddy was one of the ones who started this town, I got a responsibility to set a good example for those who need to learn how to be a good citizen. And I don't know nobody who needs it more than my own sister.

If Sorrey May didn't want to take everything over so bad, I might have to just give it up. But I reckon I can be every bit as stubborn as she can.

Little Pitchers Have Big Ears

by Jolinda Stroudamore

I was six, so DeLoyd would of been three when Mama left Daddy and moved us from Ft. Pierce across the state to Grandma Sorrey May's house in Toad Springs. My daddy, name of Willard, had some bad secret about growing up over there but wouldn't tell nobody what it was. Guess Mama'd give up on finding out anything, but when I hear something's a secret, I just got to do whatever I it takes to find out what it is.

Mama told us all about Daddy's kin, 'cause they're our kin, too. Like she said, Granny and Grandpop Stroudamore had a place in Toad Springs called Stroudamore's Rare Reptile Ranch that had lots of famous alligators. Me and DeLoyd was dying to go there, but Daddy wouldn't let us. Whenever I asked why he'd always say the same thing: "Jolinda, there's a good reason we moved all the way over to Fort Pierce and that's all you need to know. I ain't never going back. Never."

The only relation ever come to visit us besides Grandma Sorrey May was Daddy's little brother, Uncle Bubba. And he come only the once and that was just 'cause he was on a fishing trip. Mama'd already told us about him having only the one leg and all, so we wouldn't have to stare. She said it happened when they was in high school. They was playing horseshoes and Daddy threw one real hard and it accidentally hit Uncle Bubba in the shin.

At first they thought he'd be okay, but then his leg got all full of pus and the doctors had to cut it off right below the knee and give him a wooden one. Daddy felt real bad about it but Mama said it didn't seem to bother Uncle Bubba all that much. He's got his own dairy farm now and that's real hard work, you ask anybody, and he's been married three times. 'Course he's got divorced three times, too, but didn't never have no kids.

Mama was all excited that he was coming 'cause we hadn't hardly ever had any visitors. She scrubbed the floors and washed the windows—even made me and DeLoyd rake the front yard. She squeezed a gallon of fresh orange juice, got an alligator pear for the salad, and made a chocolate cake for dessert—and we hadn't had chocolate for a long time.

Uncle Bubba pulled up in the driveway late in the afternoon, in an old black beat-up truck that had a bunch of fishing poles in the back. Mama run outside to meet him, and me and DeLoyd come out, too, but I hid behind the hibiscus bush where I could watch. Uncle Bubba hopped right out of that truck. He was a great big man, lots bigger than Daddy. He had light brown hair and a nice neat beard, a big old belly and the best smile I ever seen. I looked at his feet first thing, but all I could see was two shoes down at the bottom of his pants legs. I thought he'd just have a stump sticking out there—like a pirate. Only thing I could tell was that he limped a little bit.

"Hello there, Mindy Sue," he called out to Mama and she run over to him, looking happier than I ever seen her, maybe in my whole life. She just hugged and hugged him like he was her long-lost brother or something. And he hugged her right back.

When they started walking to the house, Daddy come outside and Uncle Bubba put out his hand to shake and said, "Hey there, Willard. Good to see you."

But Daddy turned around and said, "I'll go get us a beer."

Uncle Bubba just tilted his head a little and looked at Mama, then reached in his pocket and handed DeLoyd and me each a piece of peppermint candy. Mama even let us eat 'em right then and there.

Later on, DeLoyd got to sit with Daddy and Uncle Bubba out on the porch while I had to help Mama in the kitchen. I wanted to be out there listening to 'em talk, but she made me set the table.

Anyway, at supper Uncle Bubba told us about his milk cows, and Granny and Grandpop Stroudamore and the gator ranch, and the biggest snook he ever caught, and what was the best kind of bait to use, and where the best redfish holes were over off Indian Rocks Beach. Mama kept getting up to get more sweet tea or sourdough biscuits and she laughed at everything he said. Three different times he looked at me and winked, and that just made me feel good all over.

After everybody but Daddy'd eaten two helpings of chocolate cake, the men went back out in the living room and, of course, I had to help Mama clean up. At least she made DeLoyd dry the dishes. By the time we was finished, Daddy was snoring on the sofa like always and Mama made me and DeLoyd go to bed before it was even dark good.

After I heard Daddy go to bed, Mama and Uncle Bubba went out on the porch. Being real quiet, I sneaked up close to the front door so I could listen to them talking, but I couldn't tell what they was saying. Part of the time Mama was laughing, but two times it sounded like she was crying. I wanted to go put my arm around her, but I knew I better not. Next morning when we got up, Uncle Bubba was gone.

That night we was all in the living room listening to the radio when Mama said to Daddy, "Willard, I really want to go home and visit Mama. Wouldn't take much money to get over to Toad Springs. All we'd need is enough for gas."

Daddy didn't say nothing.

"Willard . . ."

Daddy started hollering, "I said no, Mindy Sue. Goddammit! I ain't going back there." Daddy's always saying bad words when he gets mad and Mama don't like it at all.

"Why?" Mama asked. "I been married to you for all these years and I got no idea why."

"I ain't telling you nothing," he said.

"Come on, Willard," Mama said, "If things don't change we gonna have to move back over there anyways. We ain't hardly got enough to get by."

Daddy stood up and headed out to the porch. "Found enough money to make a chocolate cake!" He slammed the screen door.

She hollered after him, "You spend a lot more than that on beer. And Bubba's the only one come to visit in years. I had to do something nice."

After that, they was yelling at each other every night 'cause Mama said he didn't work out in the groves unless he just felt like it and they was way overgrown and full of fruit rats and if Old Man Bickers ever come out to check on things, Daddy'd get fired. Every night Mama ended up in tears and Daddy went off down the road to Metzger's Bar.

Daddy wasn't always like that, though. When I was little sometimes he'd take us to the beach and a few times he borrowed a horse from one of the neighbors and let me and DeLoyd ride it. And I remember him sitting in his big old chair in the evening smoking a cigarette and listening to the radio. Sometimes I'd crawl up and sit in his lap for a while. I don't know why he turned so mean.

A week or two after Uncle Bubba come to visit, Daddy stopped coming home. We was used to him not coming back for one or two nights, but this time he was gone for a week. At first Mama said she worried that he might of got hurt, but the place was so peaceful without him that me and DeLoyd got used to it real quick. It was so nice to sit around at night without all that hollering.

Finally, Mama told us that she'd talked to Daddy and he was moving to Vero Beach, and that Uncle Bubba was going to come get us in his truck and carry us all to Toad Springs. We'd be staying with Grandma Sorrey May 'til we could get our own place. It made me sad to think we wouldn't be with Daddy, even if he was mean sometimes. He could still be nice, too, and I still loved him.

Uncle Bubba come over the next Saturday and we packed all our stuff up in his pickup. I thought it would be fun, riding back in the truck bed under the tarp all that way, and maybe it would of been if the road hadn't been so bumpy. I'd brought me some coloring books and paper dolls but DeLoyd didn't have nothing but a rusty old toy truck and he couldn't do much with it.

So, of course, he wanted to color in my coloring book but I wasn't about to let him mess up all my nice pictures. Sometimes I just hate him. Then he wanted to trade seats so he could sit where it was softer and I tried to share my space, but there just wasn't enough room and I wasn't gonna give it up all together. He started crying and when that didn't work, he pinched me. I hit him as hard as I could and he let out such a big long holler that Uncle Bubba stopped the truck. We was both yowling like wounded coyotes by the time Mama got out and come around. She was really, really mad.

"Stop it! Just stop it!" she hollered at us. "I ain't putting up with that all the way to Toad Springs."

"He started it," I said. "He pinched me." I held out my arm for her to see the red marks.

Then DeLoyd pointed to his leg and said in this whiney voice he always uses, "She hit me. Look! Right there!"

Me and DeLoyd both begged to get up in the front, but Mama says there ain't no room. I look through the back window of the cab and I was sure I could fit right in the middle, but I could see that she wasn't gonna let neither one of us in. While she was fussing, Uncle Bubba got out of the truck and started around to where we were, but halfway there he turned around and got back in the cab. After we was on the road again DeLoyd tried to pinch me one more time for spite but I pulled away. I started to yell and go after him, but decided I didn't want to have to listen to no more of Mama's fussing. The whole rest of the way me and DeLoyd didn't even talk.

Finally, after what seemed like three days, we pulled in at Grandma's house. She come out to the truck, a big lady with her gray hair piled up high on top of her head. "I'm so glad to see you," she said, leaning over and giving me and DeLoyd great big hugs.

When she stood up, she said, "Bubba, time you get the truck unloaded, I'll have supper on the table. You can put Mindy Sue's stuff in her old room. The kids can have the front bedroom and just leave the rest of the boxes in the dining room. We'll get to them later."

"Yes, ma'am," he said.

Mama and me and Uncle Bubba started taking stuff inside, but DeLoyd said his ear hurt from all the wind so Mama didn't make him help. He was just saying that 'cause he's lazy, but Mama was busy unpacking and didn't pay him no mind. When we got done, Grandma had fried chicken ready for us with mashed potatoes and gravy, green beans, and applesauce.

"And for everybody who eats all their green beans," she said, looking at me and DeLoyd, "there's lemon meringue pie for dessert."

Well, Uncle Bubba ate half the chicken all by himself and nobody said a word about it. I got the wings, my favorite, so I didn't care, but DeLoyd didn't get his drumstick 'cause Uncle Bubba ate 'em both and DeLoyd had to eat a thigh instead. He was all pouty and didn't smile once all night, but I thought Uncle Bubba was so funny that I laughed at him the whole time we were sitting there.

Soon as we finished supper, Mama said we was probably tired from the long trip so we had to go to sleep, just like she said the last time we seen Uncle Bubba. Since Grandma put me and DeLoyd in the bedroom that had a window onto the front porch, I was hoping the grown-ups would sit out there where I could listen to them talk, but they didn't.

When I got up the next morning, I went into the kitchen in my nightgown with the little purple violets on it. I was real proud of it—Mama had made it for me not long before Daddy ran off, and it made me feel so pretty. Anyways, DeLoyd was just leaving the kitchen when I come in and he stuck his tongue out at me.

I said, "I knew you was gonna do that."

He said, "You did not."

"Did, too."

"You couldn't."

"But I did, so there."

He makes a face like he's gonna cry and runs out of the room. Saying "I knew you . . ." always works with DeLoyd. Every single time. And he don't never think to do it back to me.

Grandma was stirring a pot of oatmeal at the stove while Mama was getting a bowl out of the cabinet. "Now, Mindy Sue," Grandma was saying, "I told you a thousand times not to marry Willard. Those black eyes of his should of told you something. It was always plain as the nose on your face that he was only gonna give you trouble."

Now, my daddy ain't perfect by a long shot, but I don't want nobody else talking bad about him. I clenched my fist and gave Grandma a dirty look, but she didn't see me.

"Willard's gone now," Mama said. "You don't need to be worrying about him no more." She scooped some oatmeal into a bowl and set it in front of me.

Grandma put the lid back on the pot of oatmeal. "I seen you making eyes at Bubba last night. That man's already been divorced three times. My lands, Mindy Sue, you sure don't want to get mixed up with another Stroudamore."

"Bubba is a perfectly nice man," Mama said, getting red in the face.

"Looks to me like you already got your cap set for him. Ain't you had enough?"

"I ain't got no cap set for him," Mama said. "But you got to admit it was awful nice of him to go all the way over to Ft. Pierce and carry us back here." I seen her looking down at the floor, smiling.

"You're a married woman, Mindy Sue. Married to his brother! What's the matter with you?"

Mama looked up at the ceiling, then closed her eyes tight. She got the milk out of the icebox and said, "I'm gonna be getting me a job. Figured maybe I could work over at the Gator Ranch."

Grandma turned around real slow.

Mama rolled her eyes. "Thought I'd take the kids over to see Childe and Flavey this morning," Mama said. "About time they met their grandkids." My heart jumped to hear that we were finally gonna get to see that gator ranch, but I didn't say a word. Mama poured milk on my oatmeal, shoved the sugar bowl over, and gave me a spoon. "You know they ain't never seen their own grandkids? 'Course you only come over to visit once yourself."

"I was thinking you might could work at the church," Grandma said. "You know I been the secretary there for a while, now. Maybe you could work with me."

Mama sat down beside me and said, "I don't think that would be a good idea."

"Mindy Sue, you don't know what's good for you, girl. You need to spend some time close to the Lord."

"Mama, you know I ain't never been one to go to church. Besides, I got to earn more than the church can pay."

"What you mean? You're staying here, so's all you'll need is a little something for groceries. We can plant us a nice garden."

Mama took a deep breath. "Tell you the truth, I was thinking me and the kids would get our own place."

Grandma looked real surprised. "Well, saints above, Mindy Sue. You don't need to worry about that, honey. Y'all can stay right here. That's what family's for."

"Well, Mama, that's real sweet of you. But I think we need to be out on our own."

Grandma's voice started sounding wobbly and she wiped her eyes like she was crying. "I been so lonesome all this time. I been looking forward to having the house like it used to be, all full of life."

Mama looked up at the ceiling again. "When we was all here you could hardly wait to get rid of us. Remember?"

Grandma pointed her finger at Mama. "Don't you roll your eyes at me, girl. And don't you think for one second I don't know what you're after neither. I know the reason you want to be off to yourself. And I'd tell you what it is, too, if little pitchers didn't have such big ears." She looked over at me but I just took another bite of oatmeal and then put some more sugar on top, so she wouldn't think I was listening.

Mama dried her hands on a dish towel and said, "I'm going to the bathroom."

Later on we got all dressed up to go see Granny Childe and Grandpop Flavey. Me and DeLoyd wanted to go straight to the Gator Ranch but Mama said, "Now, you two just listen here. You got to be on your best behavior today. I want you to sit there with your hands in your lap, and remember to always say, 'Yes, ma'am' and 'Yes, sir' when you answer 'em. And, if you're really good, maybe they'll take you over to see the gators."

Both me and DeLoyd jumped up and down and clapped our hands, we was so excited. I forgot to be mad at him, but I did notice that his earache was all gone.

Granny's a skinny little thing with dark brown hair and glasses, but she's real nice, give us some sugar cookies she'd made up special. Grandpop's tall and has a big old potbelly that looks just like Uncle Bubba's, and he just sat there at first, not saying a word. Granny asked me and DeLoyd how we like school. Why is it that's all grown-ups can think to ask kids? Anyways, then she asked about Daddy, but Mama just said, "We can get into that later, Childe. What with the kids here and all."

Me and DeLoyd thought the grown-ups would never stop talking, but when DeLoyd started wiggling all over the chair or I started swinging my legs back and forth, Mama'd give us the look so we'd get quiet and mind our manners.

After about fifty hours Grandpop said, "Well, would you young'uns like to see the gator farm?" We was standing up and ready to go before he got the words out of his mouth. We followed him over while Mama sat and talked to Granny.

The gator farm was right next to the house, a big old place. To get in we had to walk through a great big gator's mouth that was the front door, and at first DeLoyd was afraid it was gonna eat us up. He's such a baby! And Grandpop had to hold his hand when we went out back where the gators lived.

There was lots and lots of them and one opened his mouth real wide so we could see his big sharp teeth. There was three that was special. The most famous one was Precious, and he had a picture of Jesus' head on his side, just growing there. On part of his skin. Grandpop said that Precious had healed a boy who couldn't walk even after he'd had three operations. And that boy's scars disappeared! Right then and there. It was a miracle, he said.

Then they had White Lightning, who was a light gray color and had pink eyes. Grandpop said he was what they call an albino and he should have been all white, but down in the mud and all, he was always dirty. And then there was Sampson who had blue eyes, but he was way across the pen, and anyways his eyes were closed. Time come to go, me and DeLoyd didn't want to leave, so Grandpop took us in the gift shop and gave us a piece of candy.

Turned out they didn't need Mama to work at the gator farm, so she went to see if they needed a waitress at the Blue-Eyed Gator. She come home all down-in-the-mouth so I knew she didn't get a job. I took her a glass of sweet tea, hoping that would make her feel better, but I don't think it did.

She called Uncle Bubba after supper that night and I heard her asking him if he needed any help running things at the dairy, but when she got up from the phone she wasn't smiling. She saw me watching her and gave me a big hug and said not to worry, she'd find something.

Every morning at breakfast Grandma'd be telling Mama how she'd warned her not to marry my no-good daddy. And every morning I got mad at her. Finally I started eating my oatmeal out on the porch.

Me and DeLoyd had to go to church with Grandma on Sundays; she said it was bad enough Mama wouldn't go, but the devil would get us if we wasn't saved. Mama said the church was full of people who'd stab you in the back every chance they got, and it was all just hogwash, but she let Grandma take us anyway.

One Sunday afternoon after lunch I was lying on the dining room floor in the corner, coloring behind some cardboard boxes that we hadn't unpacked yet, when Mama went to answer a knock at the door. I looked over to see who it was.

"Hello there, I'm Buck Blander, the new pastor," the man says. "You must be Mindy Sue. How's the Lord treating you today?"

Mama didn't open the door like she usually did for people, just said, "Hello. I'm fine."

He took off his hat and held it in front of him. "It's been a glorious Sunday," he said. "Praise God. Missed you at church this morning."

I ducked down a little so they couldn't see me. Mama always said she hated preachers so for sure I didn't want to miss this.

"I had some things I needed to do," she said.

"Nothing on earth is more important than giving thanks to God."

"Wait just a minute and I'll get Mama." She'd already took three steps toward the kitchen when Pastor Blander pulled the door open. "All right if I come in and set a spell?"

Mama looked back and I scooched way down so I could look between the big box of pots and pans, and the littler one with the linens in it. I made sure they couldn't see me.

He come on in and said, "I'm not really here to see your mama. I thought I'd just pay you a visit."

"Me?" Mama stopped and looked at him. "Well, I might just as well tell you, I ain't going to no church. Mama should of told you that."

Pastor Blander sat down on the sofa, put his hat on his lap, and waved for her to sit beside him.

She squinted her eyes, then backed over to the rocker and sat down. I had to move over a tad so I could still see them both.

"I'm glad you're sending the young'uns, at least," he said. "But I ain't here to get you to come to church. Your mama told me how your husband treated you all."

Mama crossed her arms and stared at him.

"And I know things are hard right now. You must be struggling."

"I'm doing just fine, thank you," Mama said.

"Ain't no shame to be in spiritual need," he said, running his hand around the brim of his hat.

"I ain't in no spiritual need," Mama said. "I told you, I'm fine."

Pastor Blander sat back and smiled, put his hat on the sofa beside him, and blew his nose. "Well, that's not what your mama's been saying. She's worried about your soul."

"My soul ain't none of her business," Mama said. "She ought to be worrying about her own damn soul."

Pastor Blander raised his eyebrows, then he put his handkerchief in his pocket and folded his hands in his lap.

Mama crossed her legs, and stared at him.

"Sorrey May tells me you're looking for a job. And it just so happens we been needing a little temporary help at the church."

Mama looked down at the floor and started jiggling her foot. Then she looked up at him. "I appreciate your thinking of me, but I ain't interested."

"You know we can't always have everything we want," he said, putting his hands together like he was praying. "We don't always know what's best for us. Sometimes we struggle. But God . . ."

Mama stood up and about that time DeLoyd came running through the front door. When he seen Mama's face, he kept right on going into the kitchen.

"I'm just trying to help out . . ." Pastor started.

"I know who come up with this idea," she said, "and I already told Mama that I ain't working at the church. I don't believe all that hogwash, and I sure as hell ain't never gonna be working alongside her. I'll go back to Willard first."

Pastor Blander stood up, too, and put his hands together. "Maybe we should have a little prayer."

"You just go right on ahead. I'm going for a walk."

Just then I dropped a crayon on the floor and held my breath. Seemed to me that it made a loud noise but they didn't notice.

He closed his eyes, bowed his head, and said, "Dear heavenly Father . . ." as Mama headed for the front door. When it banged shut behind her, Pastor Blander opened his eyes and snapped his head up. About that time, Grandma came in from the kitchen with a big smile on her face. She said, "Why Pastor Blander! Didn't realize you was out here."

He looked over like he was surprised, and said, "Oh, hello there, Sorrey May."

"Let me get you some coffee," she said.

He moved his hands, from like he was praying to like he was pushing her away. "No, no, that's all right. I don't need no coffee."

"Oh, it's no trouble at all," she said. "Already got it perking. Sit down, sit down."

Seemed like he didn't want to, but he sat back down. He looked around at the walls 'til she come back in with two coffees and sat beside him.

"It's been almost two weeks now, and Mindy Sue needs a job bad. She ain't got two cents to rub together and it's putting a strain on me."

"I talked to her, Sorrey May," Pastor said, "and she ain't interested."

Grandma kept right on. "It ain't just the money. I'm afraid her no-good husband's gonna come back for her and she'll go with him."

I made my hand into a fist. *I hate her,* I thought, *even if she is my grandma. It's not right for her to talk about my daddy like that.*

"That Willard," she says. "He's got the devil in him. He don't like to work and he drinks too much. Why he even run off and left her and them kids."

"You already told me," Pastor Blander said. He sighed and blew his nose.

"When he was a young'un, seemed like he was all right," she goes on. "Went to church with his mama every Sunday, Willard did. I reckon he was sixteen or seventeen when something happened." Sorrey May patted her hair and took a drink of her coffee. "Get you a cookie or something?"

"No, no, thank you."

Grandma wriggles around 'til she's comfortable. "Don't know what happened for sure, but when Willard missed school for a whole week my oldest girl, Dancy, she was in the same class as him, she said she heard he'd got hurt, but she didn't know how. Naturally I baked me up a pound cake and went right over to the Stroudamores to see if there was something I could do to help, but Childe wouldn't even let me in the house. Just took the cake and said she didn't have no time to sit and drink tea."

"Hmmm."

"Then she said Willard accidentally stepped on a rake and it popped up and hit him in the jaw. But later on I heard that him and his daddy got into a fight. Anyways, after that Willard wasn't never the same."

"Is that so . . ."

I felt bad for my daddy, getting treated like that when he was just a boy. Then I remembered how he was always saying that he wasn't never coming back to Toad Springs. Maybe it was 'cause of that fight with Grandpop.

After Pastor Blander left, I kept thinking about what they'd said. Then it hit me. Uncle Bubba would know what happened!

When Mama came back from her walk I ran up and told her what I'd heard and that I thought maybe that's why Daddy wouldn't come back here.

She looked at me like I was a grown-up, and said, "Well, Jolinda. Maybe sometimes it's good that little pitchers have big ears." Then she gave me a big hug and smiled at me.

Well, it just so happened that Uncle Bubba was coming over for supper that night, and Mama said she'd ask him about Daddy and Grandpop after we done the dishes. I knew they'd be sitting out on the porch so they could talk away from Grandma, and I also knew that Mama would make me and DeLoyd go to bed early, like she always did when Uncle Bubba came to visit.

So, I dragged the rocking chairs on the front porch over close to my bedroom window, then ran inside and made sure the window was open all the way so I'd be able to hear them talking. When she sent us to bed after supper, I put on my nightgown real fast and snuggled down to listen. At first DeLoyd fussed about having to go to sleep so early, but I just shushed him and he finally got quiet.

When they come out on the porch, first Uncle Bubba was talking about his cows and how he'd found this new cream to use on their udders that worked real good, and Mama talked about how she still hadn't found a job.

Then she said, "Bubba, I want to ask you something about Willard."

I was so excited I held my breath.

"Willard? Well, all right."

"He always told me and the kids that he'd never come back over here, but he wouldn't tell me why. I tried everything I know to get it outta him, but he never told me."

"Oh," Uncle Bubba said.

"I know he had a fight with Flavey."

Uncle Bubba cleared his throat. "Well, it ain't nothing good to talk about. Nothing we can do about it now."

"But I want to know. He's still my husband. I got a right."

He didn't say nothing at first, then gave a big sigh. "Well, I reckon I could tell you. But it ain't a pretty story."

They got quiet and I scooched up in the bed so I was closer to the window.

"Please, Bubba," Mama said.

I heard Uncle Bubba strike a match, saw the light flickering on his face when he leaned down to light his cigarette. I could even smell that funny smell from the match.

"I ain't never talked about this to nobody. But I guess it's all right." He was quiet again for a minute. "Well, Pop always made us work in the strawberry fields after school every day. Even after I got my leg cut off, I worked right along with 'em. Now, Willard and Pop never got on too good. I always thought Pop was too hard on him, myself. Finally come the night when Willard had just had enough.

"Me and Willard and Pop, we'd been working since sunup and it was getting dark. We was all out in the field, and Pop told Willard he had to finish picking a row while me and Pop took a load up to the barn. When Willard told Pop he wasn't going to do it, Pop just blew a gasket. He hollered at him like he always did, then he said, 'You ain't no son of mine, talking to me like that.' Then Willard said, 'I wish I wasn't no son of yours. I hate your damned guts.' And Pop said, 'Well, you get your wish. 'cause you AIN'T my son. You got a different daddy.'" Bubba cleared his throat. "Me and Willard just stood there with our mouths hanging wide open."

I put my hands over my eyes and listened harder.

"Then Willard said, 'What you mean, I got a different daddy?'"

"Pop said, 'Nothing. I don't mean nothing.'"

"Then even though he was shorter than Pop, Willard went over and grabbed the front of his shirt and hollered right in his face, 'You lying to me?' That did it. Pop socked him hard as he could right in the jaw and Willard come right back at him. I'm bigger than both of them and maybe I could of stopped it. Maybe I should have. But I decided not to. All that arguing they done through the years, it was time to just let it all out. And it was some fight. Went on for a good while. But Pop finally won."

I started chewing my fingernails.

"Oh, my sweet Jesus," Mama says in a quivery voice. "So, what happened to Willard after that?"

Bubba coughed again. "Well, I don't want you to think bad of my mama now. And you have to swear you'll never tell nobody else about this."

"No, no, I won't tell," Mama says. "And I won't think anything bad about Childe, neither."

"Swear?"

"I swear."

He takes a deep breath. "Well, later on he told me that the next day Mama had a long talk with him and told him it was true. Said his real daddy was a feller, name of Tony Cisco. Before Willard was born, she didn't know if his daddy was Tony or Pop, but once he got born she said she knew for sure right away."

"Oh my," Mama said. "Poor Willard."

They were quiet for a minute and somebody lit a cigarette.

"Then what happened?" Mama said.

"Not long after that Willard went looking for his real daddy, but said he couldn't find no trace of him. Then all of a sudden he got to be a real loner. It was like he just didn't belong nowhere. He quit school outright, just a month or two before graduation, and got him that job with Hank Plenty, so he could move outta the house."

"Yeah, I remember," Mama said and I could tell she was crying.

"You know, I don't think he ever got over feeling bad about hitting me with that horseshoe. And Pop was always reminding him that it was all his fault I got this wooden leg."

I heard Mama sigh and could just barely see her wiping her tears with the hem of her skirt. Then it was quiet.

Uncle Bubba coughed. "After that the only thing he done right was to marry you."

It was quiet for a minute, then Mama said, "Oh Bubba."

"You know, Mindy Sue, I always felt bad about how unhappy Willard's been. Mama worries about him a lot. She was all the time wondering how you all were doing all the way over in Ft. Pierce. That's the real reason I went over to go fishing that time. Mama thought maybe I could talk to Willard, but there wasn't no way of doing that."

"I know," Mama said. "I give up on him, myself. Wish I'd a known all this before. Maybe it could of been different. But it's too late now. I ain't going back to living like that. I reckon I might be getting me a divorce."

I felt my eyes getting all watery when she said that. I knew they fought, but I didn't want 'em to get divorced.

Uncle Bubba coughed. "You be real sure before you do something like that, Mindy Sue. Unless you got somebody waiting for you, that is. A divorced woman don't get much respect these days."

Mama's voice turned a little mean, like when she was talking to Daddy. "I know that, Bubba. Look at you. You been married . . ."

"I know, I know. I didn't mean to say nothing wrong. But it's different for you girls when you're divorced. I seen it for myself."

It got quiet, then Mama said, "You reckon you'll ever get married again?"

"Nope. Nope. Nope. Never in my life. I struck out three times and I ain't never getting in that game again." It was quiet, then Uncle Bubba said, "I reckon I better call it a night."

Mama says, "Bubba. I really want to thank you for telling me about Willard."

I felt so sorry for my poor daddy. I felt my cheeks and they were wet with tears.

I heard Uncle Bubba stand up, then he said good night and went down the front steps. The door of his truck slammed, the engine started up, and he pulled off. When I couldn't hear it no more, Mama got up from the rocker and I heard the screen door bang shut as she come back inside.

Then all I could hear was her chair that was still rocking on the porch.

Citrus Secrets

by Ree Perkins

My husband, Landis, has always been an expert at keeping secrets, so I figured I could do it, too. Turned out it wasn't near so easy as it looked.

We got forty acres here in Toad Springs, out by Lake Winnie, and Landis planted it all with orange and grapefruit trees. He was one of the best ever at grafting citrus and had the sweetest oranges in the state 'til he had his stroke. He won more blue ribbons than anybody in the history of the Florida State Fair. Had this special fertilizer recipe he'd put out in the groves in the spring, always in the dead of night, but wouldn't never tell a living soul what was in it—not even me or the kids.

Running a grove ain't no easy way to make a living. You got to depend on the weather, and when there come a hard freeze, the whole town's out all night burning railroad ties and trying to keep the crops from getting ruined. It ain't nothing but cold and miserable. Then in the spring and summer, you got red spider mites and aphids and mealy bugs and six-spotted mites and scabs and root weevils, and lots more, not to even mention the fruit rats that want to move right inside the house with you.

Landis done good right from the start, but he's the kind of feller who always has to find a better way to do things. Whenever he seen a grove that looked good to him, he'd go right up to the owner and find out what he put in the soil when he planted, and what fertilizer he used and how often he tried to water and anything else he could wheedle out of him.

One year he'd try a new fertilizer mix and get a bigger crop but then he'd think they wasn't sweet enough. The next go-round he'd try a different mix and he'd like the taste better, but he wouldn't get as much fruit. It was always a constant battle with him. Nothing was ever good enough. He was like that in lots of ways.

Since he got some of his ideas from what other folks had told him, I always thought the least he could do was share what he'd learned, but Landis wasn't never one to give up his secrets. I have to say his work paid off. Every farmer around here knows the name of Landis Perkins and they all work hard to outdo him.

I met Landis at a church social when I was nineteen, and was real taken by his big brown eyes and thick black hair he wore all slicked down. He's the one started calling me Ree and after a while everybody else did, too. He didn't like the name Marie 'cause it was his mama's name, and all I'm gonna say about that is that he had good reasons. He said at least I had blonde hair and green eyes, just the opposite of the way she looked. Anyways, we had us two young'uns, first a girl we named Ginger, then, our boy, Worthy.

Now, I'm a good cook, and I always took real pride in keeping my house just so. A place for everything and everything in its place, I always say. I even ask folks to leave their shoes at the front door, and if somebody moves an ashtray or one of my little whatnots, I'll pick it up and wipe it off and put it right back the way I want it.

When Ginger got to high school, she started doing things just to aggravate me, like not drying the iron skillet before she put it away so it'd get rusty, or leaving the butter out to go rancid; or she wouldn't make her bed. She knew how to get me all fired up. Worthy, on the other hand, was quiet as a mouse on duck feathers; always had his nose in a book, hated to argue, and every time he heard me starting up with Ginger, he headed for the door.

Now, Landis has been a good provider. My only complaint is that he's always liked the drink. Me, I don't think nobody should ever let liquor pass their lips, and I won't stand for having no alcohol in my house. That's the one thing we used to argue about a lot, but finally he got to where he'd only drink on the weekends, and he'd go to Schniticker's Tavern over near Turkey Creek to do it.

At first he just went on Saturday afternoon and come home that evening, but after a while he got to where he didn't come home 'til Sunday. In the beginning that near about run me crazy, but I finally decided that in the long run it was easier than having to put up with him here, all drunk and dirty, messing up the house. After a while we just went our separate ways on weekends.

There's been a time or two when I thought I could of done better than marrying Landis. Way back in high school Hank Plenty had an eye for me, but I never give him the time of day. Hank's mama and daddy was dirt poor and he had this purple birthmark on his cheek that made you want to look at him longer than you should, so he was shy back then.

But when the cash started rolling in he come outta his shell, so to speak, and I thought to myself more than once that maybe I should of looked past that birthmark. Now he's one of the richest fellers around. He invented a way to clean oranges faster using this special conveyor belt, and near about every grove in Florida is using it.

From the time we got married Landis always kept a close eye on me when Hank was around—'cause Hank hadn't never gotten married. I could tell Landis was worried maybe I'd change my mind and run off, but of course he never said nothing about it.

Anyhow, when Landis went to Schnitickers, sometimes he run into Hank there. I heard this story from Sorrey May, who heard it from somebody at church—Landis wouldn't of told me. Seems this one Saturday him and Hank had been playing pool and drinking all afternoon and since they was both good players it was nip and tuck the whole time. They'd never liked each other so that made it pretty exciting, and everybody in the bar's taking sides and yelling and cheering. Then, right near the end of the last game Hank lets out a big loud sneeze just when Landis is making a shot, and Landis says that made his ball miss the corner pocket and he would of won the game.

'Course Hank says he never meant to sneeze; just got the hay fever once in a while. But since he hadn't sneezed all afternoon, Landis wasn't about to believe him. Landis grabs Hank by the shirt and slams him up against the wall, but Hank just stands there and won't fight back. When Landis pulls back to hit him, Hank ducks and Landis near about breaks his hand hitting the wood planks. While Landis leans over and yells about his hand, Hank goes out the door. After hearing that story, I remembered when Landis hurt his hand, but he'd told me he done it on the tractor.

Now Landis always give me an allowance and outta that I had to buy groceries and all the clothes and everything for me and the kids. And he made sure to give me just a little bit less than I'd need so I was all the time coming up short.

I'd started crocheting alligator baby booties and pot holders and the like to sell up at the Stroudamore's Gator Ranch for a little extra money. Done it while Landis was over at Schniticker's of a weekend. Now, I never felt right about doing it behind his back, but he was so stingy I didn't have no choice. And maybe it wasn't really a lie, since I wasn't actually telling him nothing that wasn't true. Just kept the money up on the top shelf in the pantry.

One morning after Landis leaves for the grove, I finish up the breakfast dishes and go in the pantry to get some flour to bake a strawberry pie. Like I did every so often, I got the sock down just to look at my money, but as soon as I have it in my hand I know something's wrong. I always tied a real tight knot in the end of it, and the knot was loose. I near about faint when I see two dollars is missing.

Then I remember Landis asking about where to find the pickled okra a few days before and he went in there. It must of been him. Wouldn't have been neither one of the kids. Ginger never set foot near the kitchen without being dragged in by the ear and Worthy wouldn't have no reason to go poking around in there.

I sit down at the table to think about what to do. If I move the sock somewheres else, Landis'll know that I found out the money was gone, but if I leave it there, he'll take more of it. I'm sitting at the kitchen table, moving the salt and pepper shakers so that they're facing the exact right way in the exact right spot when Ginger, who must have been about sixteen, come flouncin' in. After taking one look at me she says, "What's wrong? You look like the butter done slid off your biscuit."

"Just lost something," I says.

Ginger looked interested. She knew I never lost nothing. "What'd you lose?"

"Just a sock."

"You getting that cross over losing a sock?"

I give her a blank stare, then looked away.

"Want me to help look for it?"

"No, honey, that's okay."

Ginger's almost to the living room when she calls back, "It ain't that sock you keep up in the pantry, is it?"

My mouth drops open. "What?"

Ginger comes back in the kitchen and stands there, her right hand on her hip. "That sock with the money. The one that's always in the pantry."

"How do you know about that sock?" I ask.

"Oh Mama. Me and Worthy always known about it."

"What? How did you . . . There's two dollars missing. Did you take it?"

"No, ma'am," she says, putting her hand on her heart. "I did not! I ain't no thief."

"I know, honey. I didn't think you'd steal," I say. "But who?"

Ginger sits down next to me. "Wasn't Worthy or me. He'd have told me. And . . . if somebody was gonna take it, why not take it all?" She's quiet for a minute, then looks straight at me. "Daddy. I bet it was Daddy."

"Maybe. I don't know."

"Mama," Ginger whines. "That money's for my wedding dress!!"

I just look at her. "What?"

"What else would you be saving it for?"

I slam my hand on the table, which makes the salt shaker tip over and the top comes off. Salt spills out, which is bad luck, everybody knows. While I'm putting the salt back in, I toss a little over my left shoulder and say to Ginger, "That money's for emergencies, that's what it's for." Then I grab a wet rag and get down on the floor to clean up the salt.

"But my wedding's an emergency," Ginger whines.

I look up. "What are you talking about, girl? You ain't even got no boyfriend. Do you?"

Ginger gives me a dirty look and stomps out of the room.

"Wedding dress. Humph," I say out loud. I think and think— *how can I get back at Landis?*

The next morning I come up with an idea. After Landis leaves for the grove, I check the sock. All the money but the two dollars is still there. I get me a piece of paper and write a note in this real fancy handwriting. "My Darling Marie, I'm praying you'll change your mind and meet me soon, All My Love," and then I sign it with a line scrawled across the bottom that looks a little like an *H* for Hank Plenty, but not so's you could tell for sure.

I scrunch it all up, then smooth it out and sprinkle some water on it so the ink smears a little, like maybe some tears fell on it. Then I rub it on the back steps so it'll look like somebody had been carrying it around for a while. Then I fold it up real careful, stuff it in the sock, and tie it up tight. That very day I start keeping the new money I earn in a little cloth bag pinned underneath my apron.

There wasn't no more money missing for a couple of weeks and I was going crazy as a Betsy bug, waiting for Landis to say something. At any minute he could storm in the house and accuse me of all kinds of things. I didn't know when it would happen.

It was a Friday morning when I checked the sock and found the knot was loose again. *Figures*, I think, *he'd take it just before the weekend.* I look inside and one more dollar is gone, but the note was still there, just like I'd left it. *Had he seen it? He must of seen it. But did he bother to read it?* I can't tell. I started sweating. Not knowing give me the willies, but I knew I'd have to act normal or I'd give it all away. Then, when I think about how to act normal, I realize I'd never thought about what normal was, I'd always just been me. And now, since I ain't really myself . . . Well, you see what I mean.

At supper that night Landis grumbles that the pork chops are burned and the mashed potatoes are full of lumps, but that wasn't nothing new, really. He yelled at Ginger for spilling a glass of buttermilk and he didn't hardly ever fuss at her, but I just couldn't tell nothing for sure. I think maybe he's watching me a little more than usual, but maybe not. But for sure I'm watching his every move for a hint about what he knows. And it's wearing me flat out.

That night when we go to bed Landis don't reach over for me like he does almost every Friday, so that was a little off, but then maybe he was just tired. He's up early Saturday and by noon he's headed over to Schniticker's. After he left, I checked the sock, but it looked just like it had the morning before—nothing else was missing. I put it back.

Two more weeks pass and I'm ready for the booby hatch. I scrubbed and bleached and swept and mopped and polished that house to within an inch of its life, and then did it again. How could I figure out if Landis had read the note? By this time I decided something had to happen, even if it was bad, so I come up with a plan.

Monday night when he comes in from the groves I look up from the pot of mustard greens I'm stirring on the stove and say, "Landis, remember them socks you liked so much—the gray ones you got in Tallahassee—I found one of them behind the dresser. You seen the other one?"

He's sitting by the back door, pulling off one of his filthy old boots on my shiny kitchen floor. "Huh? What'cha say?"

I turn toward him to see if I can tell anything by looking at him. "Your socks. I'm missing one of your socks. Those gray ones you like."

He looks up with a blank face. Then he looks down and pulls off the other boot. "Naw. I ain't seen nothing," he says.

I stand there watching him. Waiting for a sign. I can't tell a damn thing.

He glances up at me. "What you looking at?"

I turn back to the stove. I'd have to think of something else.

That night I moved the sock to the other end of the pantry shelf. A week later it was still sitting there. I hated Landis Perkins and everything about him. I knew he just loved watching me go through this torture. I was jumping all over the young'uns for the least little thing and snapping at Landis every time he walked in the door, but it didn't seem to bother him even a little bit. I took everything out of the sock but three dollars and the note and waited another week.

Nothing happened.

Meantime, Landis is still going off on weekends, like always. And I'm crocheting them scarves and booties faster and faster. I finally can't stand it no more, so I take the money and the note out and throw the damned sock away.

Not too long after, late one Friday afternoon I'm sitting in a rocking chair out on the porch with a pot in my lap and a paper bag on my knees, shelling black-eyed peas, when Landis come out and sat on the swing. Neither one of us said a word; the only sounds were the swing creaking and the black-eyed peas hitting the bottom of the pot when I scraped them out of the pod, then a rustling sound when I put the pod in the paper bag. Landis lights up a cigarette, then blows the smoke out, hard. "Ree," he says. "You been lying to me."

I keep on shelling peas. "Huh? What you talking about?"

"I'm talking about the money. The money in the sock."

I look up at him with my mouth open, then shut it quick hoping he hadn't seen my face, and kept on shelling away. "What money's that?"

"You tell me."

More black-eyed peas plink down into the pot but I don't say nothing.

"Where'd you get that money you been hiding up in the pantry? Where'd it come from?" He takes another puff off his cigarette and blows the smoke out the side of his mouth.

"Ain't no money in the pantry."

"Ain't no more, there ain't. But it was there before."

I don't say nothing.

"Where'd it come from? You save it outta what I give you?"

I don't answer 'cause if I say yes, he'll give me less money than I get now.

"You rob a bank?"

Nothing.

He stands up, walks over, and points his finger in my face. "Dammit, Ree, I'm your husband. You got to tell me."

Well, by this time I've been worrying about the whole thing for so long that I'm beside myself; my hands are shaking and I knock the bag of pea pods off my lap and they spill all over the floor.

He leans over me and grabs hold of the arms of the rocker. "Ree, you tell me right now what the hell's going on. This is my house and I got a right to know. If you're stealing money from me . . ."

"I ain't stole nothing from you, you stingy old bastard," I yell, kicking him in the shin. "You stole money from me!"

He jerks back and grabs hold of his leg.

"I ain't never took one penny of your money," I say. "It's got nothing to do with you."

He's madder than I've ever seen him. "Woman, don't you ever kick me like that again. You hear?"

I glare at him. "Then don't shake your finger in my face," I holler.

He stands up straight. "So, where'd you get the money? Who give it to you?"

"Now just who do you think would be giving me any money?" I yell at him. "Ain't nobody give me a plug nickel."

"Not even one of your old boyfriends?" he says, curling his lip.

That's when I knew. He *had* seen the note.

"Dammit, Ree," Landis says, "I'm responsible to take care of you and the kids and every cent we got is my money. I'm the man of this house. And don't you forget it."

"You don't give me enough to make ends meet," I say. "I got no money for decent clothes or Sunday shoes for the kids. Me and Ginger, we'd like to have a little powder or perfume once in a while. We deserve stuff like that. And that ain't asking much."

"I give you plenty," he said. "And if you'd just be more careful where you spend it . . ."

I take a hold of the pot handle, jump up, and start yelling. "You think you're such a big shot, making all that money, winning all them prizes at the fair. Then you take what you earn and keep it all to your own self. You spend more every weekend at Schniticker's than me and the kids spend on clothes in a year."

His face gets real red and he points his finger in my face and yells, "What I do with my money is my business, woman. I give you enough to get by."

I start crying, which makes me madder than I already am. "I been selling crocheting down to Stroudamore's. 'Cause without that extra money ain't no way I can run this house. And I'm gonna keep doing it. No matter what you say."

"No wife of mine is gonna work!" he shouts, shaking his finger in my face. "I told you that already! You got no business gallivanting around town. You need to be home. Besides, folks'll think I can't take care of my own."

I never been so mad in my whole life. "Goddamn you, Landis Perkins," I scream. "You *ain't* taking care of your own." I throw the pot of peas at him but he holds his hands up and ducks, and the pot and them peas I'd shelled fall into the crocus bushes behind him.

"Stop it, woman. Get a hold of yourself."

I go inside and slam the screen door behind me but he follows me, yelling. "Who do you think you are, throwing that pot at me? I ain't about to put up with no woman treating me like that. No sir."

I stop and turn around to face him. "Landis Perkins, I been married to you for almost twenty years. I took care of you when you was sick, cooked you three meals a day, seven days a week, washed your clothes, kept your house, and raised your babies."

He just looks at me through squinty eyes.

I start shaking my finger at him. "Damn it! You don't give me and the kids enough to be able to hold our heads up in this town. I ain't got but three dresses I dare to wear outta this house. And I ain't gonna live like this no more. I ain't."

"Oh, you ain't, huh?" he says, in a low voice.

"No, I ain't. This is my money and you ain't taking it away from me."

He wipes his brow and leans back against the counter.

"Ain't no way you're stopping me from selling my crocheting and if you even try to I'll take Ginger and Worthy and go stay with Doris out in Lutz. You just see if I don't."

Landis don't say another word, just walks out of that kitchen. I know he went straight to Schniticker's; didn't come home 'til Sunday evening. I was glad to have him gone and I crocheted all day Saturday and after church on Sunday, so fast them needles was smoking. When he gets home Sunday evening, we both pretend none of that ever happened. I'm kind of nervous the first time I start crocheting in the living room while he's listening to the radio, and but I'm determined I'm gonna be able live like I want to in my own house.

The very next day I go out and buy me a little metal money box that locks up tight, and hide it down under the kitchen sink behind a big old sack of Borax. Then I put the key to the money box between the pages of the Bible where Landis'll never find it.

Before long I'm crocheting alligator toys and knitting af-ghans right out in the open, in my own living room, even when Landis is home. Another thing I done was to go over to Sweetie Mooney's beauty shop one afternoon and get myself a flapper haircut, which don't make Landis none too happy. And I buy me and the kids some new clothes and got me and Ginger some nice toilet water.

Years later, after the young'uns left home and Landis was retired, I turned Ginger's bedroom into a sewing room where I could keep everything just so; Landis put shelves on the wall where I could keep all the different colors of yarn and knitting needles and such, lined up neat as a pin. After I got me a brand-new Singer sewing machine so I could make dolls to sell, I put my thread and patterns and scraps up there, just the way I want-ed them.

Landis never did ask where that letter in the sock really come from.

And I never give up my secret.

The Beauty Shop at Carrie June's
by Sweetie Mooney

The only plan I ever had for my life was to marry Rusty Heppner and have babies, even though his snooty mama never liked me. Then the week after we graduated high school, he found hisself another gal over in Mango, so I was dragging around the house like I'd missed the second coming. Late one hot afternoon I was sitting on the back stoop, staring at the tangerine tree and feeling sorry for myself when Mama come and sat down beside me.

"Sweetie," she says, that's what everybody calls me, Sweetie, "that boy ain't no good—ain't worth his salt, treating you like that."

"Oh Mama, I just don't know what I'm—"

"Hah!" she says. "He ain't nothing but a fool. But don't you worry now. There's lots more frogs in the pond."

I give her a sad look. "Not around here, there ain't."

"Now, just listen to me for a minute. You're a pretty girl, lucky you got your daddy's hair, that pretty auburn color with that little bit of natural curl. And you've always been good at cutting hair. I was thinking you could start up a little beauty parlor. We ain't never had no beauty shop in Toad Springs, but the ladies here want to look nice, just like the ladies do everywhere."

Now, normally I wouldn't of listened to my mama, but when she said that, I quit thinking about Rusty for the first time in days and my heart felt a little lighter. "Why, that's a good idea, Mama," I say. "I could wash their hair right here in the kitchen and . . ."

"Well, you know, Sweetie," she says, looking over at me, "I was thinking you might could do it at your aunt Carrie June's. She's right in town, and she's got that great big kitchen. I hear she's been lonely since she quit teaching school, and with Tully gone so long now and them not having any kids, she's there by herself a lot. You could pay her a little somethin' for rent; I figure she could use a few extra dollars."

The more we talked, the better it sounded. Finally we decided I should go visit Carrie June by myself, 'cause her and Mama didn't get along too good since that big argument over who was gonna get Grandma's wedding ring. Mama thought it should be hers 'cause she was the only daughter, but instead Grandma give it to her son, my uncle Tully, and he give it to Carrie June 'cause she was his wife. And after Tully died, Carrie June said she was keeping it. She said it nice, like she always says everything, but the way she does it just makes you want to slap her.

Anyway, when I called her she seemed kind of interested in the beauty parlor idea, but said she'd have to talk it over with Sorrey May and Aunt Never first and for me to come see her in a couple of days. Now, neither one of her sisters ever had a forward-thinking idea in their whole lives so it didn't seem too likely that they'd cotton to it. Me and Mama talked about all the reasons they'd find to tell her not to do it and come up with some good answers I could give 'em right back.

The day I went back to see her I wore my blue dress with the little yellow flowers that looked so fresh, and curled my hair in the latest style so I'd look responsible. She invited me in, sat me down at the kitchen table, then poured two cups of coffee. After she put the coffeepot back on the stove, she sat down herself and tumped four spoons of sugar into her cup. When she finished stirring it, she looked at me, and said, "Well, Sweetie, I talked to

Sorrey May and Never, and neither one of 'em thought I ought'a let you run a business here."

I was ready. "But remember, you could be earning money without doing nothing at all, yourself," I said. "I'm just trying to help you out."

"I know, dear, I know. But both of them thought it was a bad idea to rent out part of my house to anybody."

"What are they talking about? Aunt Never used to rent out a room in her house. To a man!"

"I know, dear. I know. But that's just one person. Like Never said, you're talking about having people coming in and out of my house any time they please, at all hours of the day and night. Why they'd feel like they could just come strolling in, any old time they took a mind to."

Just like Aunt Never, I think, *to say something like that.* "Well," I say, "people wouldn't just drop in. We'd have regular hours, so they'd only be coming in when they had an appointment."

She took a sip of her coffee and went on like I hadn't said a word. "And I'd have to keep the house all cleaned up all the time. Couldn't relax or nothing. Five days a week."

"Wouldn't be five days a week," I said.

"Well, Sweetie, I don't know. Sorrey May and Never both thought—"

"And I know you need some money coming in, Aunt Carrie June. What with you not teaching school and Uncle Tully gone and all."

Right away she looks down, like she always done when anybody said Tully's name. "I know. I know." She's real quiet. "I just don't know what to do."

I take a sip of my coffee. "Well, that's what he'd want for you. Don't you think?"

I sit there 'til she looks up at me. Then I say, "Well, how's about this? How's about if we just try it for a little while and then you can decide. I mean, it couldn't hurt nothing."

"Well, I, um . . ."

"Please? Please? If you don't like it, I'll quit. I promise."

Carrie June looks down at the table. "It's really against my better . . ."

"Please?"

She sips her coffee again and thinks for a minute. I sit there quiet—the hardest thing I ever done in my life. Then she says, "Well, all right. Just for a little while."

"Oh, thank you!" I say, jumping up and giving her a hug.

"But everybody has to stay in the kitchen or the dining room. They can't go into the rest of the house. And you gotta let everybody know the rules; I ain't telling 'em."

"I will! I'll do it!" I jumped up and hugged her, then headed for the door. "You won't be sorry, I promise!"

As the screen door shut behind me, I heard her saying, "But, Sweetie, do you know anything about cutting . . ." but I didn't stop. I ran right to our little library and it was nothing short of a miracle that there was a book in there on how to fix hair. I knew I was good at the cutting part, but I needed to know more about styling and like that if I was gonna be an expert at it. I read the whole book that same night and made myself a list of what I'd need: combs, brushes, and scissors, of course.

The book says you have to sterilize everything and use a clean utensil, that's a brush or a comb and like that, for every lady coming in, so I thought I'd need three each of those, some Breck shampoo—so I'd look like a real professional—some hair nets, curlers and curling fluid, towels, a bunch of lemons to lighten the color and vinegar to help with the tangles. Figured I'd get some of that Mrs. Stewart's Bluing they talked about in that book to get that nasty yellow color outta the old ladies' hair. Then I'd need a box of hairpins and one of them little hot air drying machines you can hold in your hand—the big ones cost way too much.

I decided I could have the ladies bend over the kitchen sink to wash their hair and rinse it there, then sit them at the dining room table while I rolled it up and dried it. That way I'd have all my pins and stuff right there on the table. Had a little hand mirror that they could look into after I was all done.

Mama said I could use her curling iron and crimper and we could set up some extra barrels at Carrie June's to catch the rain-water to use to rinse the shampoo out. And Mama let me use some of her savings to buy supplies, but I'd have to pay her back.

On Friday we went out and bought all the supplies and when we took 'em over to Carrie June's she put up a big fuss about where to set everything up, and I had to promise to put every single thing away every day before I left. Just between you and me, I think she got her back up 'cause Mama was there.

That night I practiced cutting on Mama's hair. It was pretty long and she wore it tied back so I snipped off the ends, then kept trimming and practicing getting it all even 'til she didn't want it to go no shorter. Then I curled it and she looked real good.

I put up signs at the grocery and the hardware that said Toad Springs Beauty Shop Opening Up at Carrie June's House. Lady's haircut, washed and set for fifty cents on Wednesdays, Fridays, and Saturdays. Call Sweetie Mooney. And me and Mama showed off our hair at church on Sunday and told everybody what I was doing.

Then I made up the rules for my customers:

Call Sweetie to make an appointment.

Come by only on the days the Beauty Parlor is open—Wednes-days, Fridays, and Saturdays.

Come in through Carrie June's kitchen door, not the front door.

Stay in the kitchen and the dining room 'cause they're the only part of the house that's the official Beauty Parlor.

Wouldn't you know, my first customer was Ree Perkins. I have to say, I wouldn't never have picked her to be my first one, she's so persnickety about everything, but I didn't have no choice. Ree always wore her hair braided up around her head, and I figured getting her braid to look real nice wouldn't be hard to do. Maybe even put it in a French twist.

Things was going like I planned—I got her all washed and rinsed out in the kitchen and was standing behind her, drying her hair with a towel at the dining room table, when she says, "Sweetie, I decided to cut my hair."

"Sure," I say. "I can even up them split ends."

"No, Sweetie. I want it short. Like the flappers."

I walk around to look her in the face. "Like the flappers? You sure?"

"Yep. I'm sure."

"But what will Landis . . ."

"I told you, Sweetie. It's my hair and I want it short."

"Well, okay," I say, with a knot in my stomach. "If you're sure." But I'm thinking, should I let her know I never did such a short haircut before? She might go around telling everybody I don't know what I'm doing and ruin my business before it gets going. 'Course, if I mess it up, everybody'll know anyway. But on the other hand if I do a good job, it'll help me advertise. I take a deep breath and send up a prayer, and decide to keep my mouth shut.

"I've always had long hair 'cause that's the way Landis likes it," she said, "but I'm burnt out on trying to please that man. It's time to do what I want."

Well, you better believe I was as nervous as frog legs in a frying pan about taking off so much. I tie her hair back in a ponytail and cut it off at the neck, then I figure out where to start trimming. Takes a while, and when I get that done, I use Mama's crimping iron. It turns out pretty good, I'm glad to say. Not perfect, but the two little tiny mistakes was in the back so she can't see them.

When Ree looked in the mirror she said, "Who is that? My, oh my, oh my. What a pretty woman you are, Ree Perkins!" Then she calls out, "Carrie June, honey. Come in here and look at this!"

Carrie June comes to the door, lets out a squeal, then puts both hands over her mouth. "Lordy mercy," she says. "Landis know you're doing this?"

"No. No, he does not," Ree said, still grinning. "It's a surprise."

"Oh, my heavenly days," Carrie June said. "You look just beautiful."

I'm real proud I made it through my first haircut and think to myself, I'd like to be a fly on the wall at the Perkins house tonight.

By Saturday afternoon I'd done six more and paid Carrie June the rent money, and she said she reckoned it was okay for me to keep doing hair there. I think she liked having the company. Every week more ladies come in and it only took me two months to pay Mama back.

Along the way I figured out just how much lemon juice to use when they wanted to lighten their hair up a little, and how long to sit them out in the sun. I used Mrs. Stewart's Bluing on Sorrey May's hair after she finally come around to giving me a try, and she even had to admit that it looked good. Of course, being Sorrey May, she had to say it had just a little too much blue tinge to it.

Childe Stroudamore had the straightest hair I near about ever seen so I mixed up some egg whites and a few drops of olive oil and combed them in to hold the set. Worked better than I thought it would.

Hester Brisco come in one day all in a state 'cause she had some kind of rash on her head and her hair was falling out. She said she'd tried wearing hats but it's way too hot to do that in the summer when you don't have to. She'd been combing it over to the side and tying it so the braid come over her shoulder instead of down her back, but it was getting worse.

She was especially worried about it 'cause Halt's brother, Karl, was staying with them and she didn't want him to know. Since he was so much taller than her and Halt, she knew he was forever looking down on her and could see right to the skin on her head. Poor nervous thing always had a hankie in her hand to dab away the tears when she talked about it.

Well, I went back to the library and got me some ideas. The first thing we tried was that every single day she had to cut a

Vidalia onion in half and rub it on her head 'til the skin turned red. For sure it didn't smell too good, but what are you gonna do? Then after that she had to smear honey all over it and leave that on for two hours. It wasn't no easy trick for her, living in the house with two men she was trying to hide it from, and she said she had to cook onions every single meal, even breakfast, to cover up the smell.

After she did that for a week and couldn't see no difference I checked the book again and the next time we made a paste out of ground-up collard leaves, lemon juice, and smushed-up mango. She said it was harder to keep all that on the top of her head—every time she looked down to wash the dishes or sweep the floor, some of it fell off. But at least it didn't smell as bad. A week later we tried ground up lime seeds and black pepper and lard—and that one even smelled kind of good, she said, but the flies was a little bothersome.

In the end, what done the trick was honey and egg. Either that or the rash just finally went away by itself and her hair started growing back on its own. She was so happy you'd think I'd saved her life or something and she sent me more customers.

One thing about fixing hair is that you're always up on the latest gossip. I heard how Bubba Stroudamore had brought his third wife to meet his people and his mama thought the gal was snooty, and how Sorrey May was worrying about Elsie Lou's singing career up in Tennessee and the fact that she hardly ever come down to visit her mama, and how Hank Plenty was getting the county to pave the road out to his place when people thought he ought'a be paying for it himself since he had so much money. The county needed to be doing things for the rest of us.

Had my little beauty shop for seven months and eight days and if two awful accidents hadn't of happened so close together, I might still be there.

The first bad thing was when Ree's baby sister, Iona, come over from Tampa on a Saturday morning to get her hair tinted a little darker. Iona was pale herself, and her hair was a kind of a dirty dishwater blonde. She didn't have no more color to her than beach sand; even all her clothes was some shade of tan.

Anyway, it was the first time I tried using the dye that's made from henna leaves. The night before, you mix the ground-up leaves with lemon juice 'til it's about as thick as mashed potatoes, then let it sit overnight. Next day you're ready to go.

Iona come in that morning with her nose in the air like always and says, "Now, Sweetie, I never colored my hair before and I want it just a little bit darker. Not so much as people would notice right off, just something to liven it up a little bit. My hair's so very fine, you know . . ."

"Okay," I say. "I can do that. This henna stuff is supposed to be the very best. The longer you let it sit, the richer the color, and you can keep it on up to four hours. I figure we should try it for about thirty minutes."

"All right," she says.

Well, after I got her washed and combed out, I rubbed the henna in real good and put an oilcloth scarf over it. That's to keep the heat in and help the color set. While Iona sat at the dining room table drinking coffee and trading lies with Carrie June, I went to rinse my hands and clean up the kitchen. I knew I was in trouble when I washed off the brown goop and seen my fingers was dyed bright orange. I scrubbed really hard with Carrie June's Old Dutch Cleanser I found under the sink but it wouldn't come off.

I felt like a raccoon trapped in a garbage can. Oh, dear Lord, what was I gonna do? I waited another two minutes—longest two minutes of my life—and went back in the dining room. I peeked under the oilcloth scarf and said, "I think you might be ready to rinse already, Iona."

She was right in the middle of telling Carrie June a story about somebody at her office, and looked up at me. "I thought you said thirty minutes."

"Well, that's right. I did. I just want to check on how it's coming along since it's my first time doing this color and all."

She let out a big sigh. "Oh, all right." Then she looked at Carrie June. "Don't forget what I was telling you."

Soon as I started getting the goop off I seen her hair was the same bright orange as my fingers. She was gonna look like a Sarasota circus clown.

"Looks like we can go on and rinse it out now," I say. "I think it's been on long enough."

"Oh, goodie," she said. "I can hardly wait to see."

I washed it with shampoo again to see if that would help but it didn't. When I dried her hair off, the towel turned a brownish-orange. I hid it behind my back.

"How does it look?" she said. "Can you tell a difference?"

"Well, yes, ma'am," I said. "For sure you can tell a difference."

"Let's see," she said, leaning her head over so her hair fell forward. She pulled a strand in front of her face. She looked at it, then back at me, then back at her hair. "What in the hell is this?" she screamed. "What in the name of God have you done to me?"

"Well," I said, "it turned out a little brighter than I'd figured it would on the first time. I think maybe when it's dry—"

"Aghhhhh!!" She was screaming like she'd caught her hand in the meat grinder. "What have you done to me, Sweetie Mooney?" She got up and started pacing the kitchen. "This isn't brown!! It's ORANGE!! Where's a mirror? Oh, my Lord in heaven. Oh Jesus, God! What have you done to me?"

Carrie June come running into the kitchen. "What's wrong? What hap—" She stopped and covered her mouth with her hands.

"I'm ruined," Iona screamed. "She's killed me!! Get me a mirror!"

Carrie June says, "I don't think you want a mirror, Iona."

That's when I saw the little brown splotches on her face. "Now, Iona," I say, "I wonder if putting more lemon juice on it would help. That might change the color some. And the directions say it may get darker over the next few days, too."

"Oh my God!! I can't go back to work looking like this. I work at City Hall!! I'm a supervisor!! I'd be the laughingstock . . ."

"I'm so sorry," I said, backing away from her. "I really am. It's the first time I ever used henna . . ."

Iona sat down in a chair, fanned her face with one hand, and clenched her chest with the other. "I'm having a heart attack!!"

"I'll get you some water," Carrie June said, hurrying over to the sink. "You'll be all right."

"I'm gonna die! Sweetie Mooney, you're gonna be a murderer!!"

"Come on, Iona," I say. "Henna don't last forever. It'll fade."

"I'll have to quit my job," Iona said. "I'll wind up in the poorhouse. I can't face the world like this." She looks at me real hard.

"Now, Iona," I said. "I mean, it isn't . . ."

"Don't you dare say one more word to me! You've ruined my life. I can't work . . ."

"It'll grow out," I said.

She put her face in her hands and boo-hooed.

I picked up a clean towel. "Let's see if drying won't help. The directions say the color should darken some . . ."

She sat up straight and pushed me away from her. "*Don't you touch me! Not ever again!*" She held her hands to her heart and rocked back and forth in the chair. "Oh, why did I let Ree talk me into this? And Carrie June! You let this . . . this . . . this fool . . ."

She stopped, then looked at me and squinted her eyes. "You're a goddamned fool!" She yowled and cried a while longer, then blew her nose and took a deep breath. "Sweetie," she said, "on Monday morning I'm going downtown to the fanciest hairdresser in Tampa and get this mess fixed."

"Yes, ma'am," I said.

"And you're going to pay for every penny of it."

"Yes, ma'am. I will. Yes, ma'am."

By the time Iona walked out the door she sure enough looked like a clown, with a purple flowerdy scarf over her wet hair and Carrie June's bright yellow gardening hat on top. But I was ready to strangle her. I mean, I knew I'd done wrong and I told her I was sorry. I know I should have tried it out on Mama or the dog or something first. But she didn't have to be so awful.

Before she left, Iona made me and Carrie June promise not to ever tell a living soul what happened, which I was happy to do. She swore she'd never breathe a word about it to anybody. When she got to Tampa she had to get it dyed real dark brown, which wasn't her natural color and she said looked just awful, so she wore a hat all the time—even at work—'til it grew out. And I ended up paying her the seven dollars she said it cost to get her hair fixed even though I'll bet it didn't cost half that.

Of course, after that Carrie June was gonna kick me out until I cried and begged and swore I'd never dye nobody else's hair again. I think what really changed her mind was when I said I'd pay her more in rent money every week.

The second bad thing that happened was really Carrie June's fault. I found out I was in trouble again when Gladys Heppner—that's Rusty's mom—and Sorrey May Only showed up at our house late one evening. Soon as I opened the door I knew I was in for it. Any time them two agree on something, you know it's bad.

"Sweetie Mooney!!!" Sorrey May howled before they even got through the door. "This here is a scandal!"

"What? What?" I said. "What are you talking about?"

"Head lice! Head lice is what I'm talking about! Lord only knows what else you been spreading around."

"Head lice?"

Well, they explained they was both scratching their heads in church and noticed each other, and it was just a few days after they'd both got their hair done so they figured they'd got it from me. Wouldn't listen to a word I had to say, so I just told them to meet me at Carrie June's in the morning and I'd give them a free treatment that was guaranteed to work a hundred percent, even though I was sure I didn't give 'em them damn bugs.

Now, the whole subject of head lice is something we don't take lightly around here 'cause everybody thinks only the trashy folks from Georgia get 'em. And if you get 'em, you sure don't never tell nobody.

After they finally left, I was talking to Mama and much as I hated it, we figured out where the lice could of come from.

Mama reminded me about that bad summer storm we'd had the Wednesday before and when I come home that evening I'd told her that it was so dark inside Carrie June's that I couldn't hardly see what I was doing.

Just so happened that Carrie June didn't have but one weak little old lightbulb in the dining room that kept flickering on and off. I asked her could she change it but she said she was too busy and besides she didn't think she had another lightbulb. Maybe it could have been somebody who'd come in that day and I couldn't see the head lice. Probably somebody young. Then I remembered Jolinda Stroudamore. She'd just got her hair cut for the school dance.

I went right over to the Stroudamore's and talked to Jolinda and her mama. And sure enough, her head had been itching the day she come in, and later on her and her mama seen she had the lice for sure. But, of course, she'd never told nobody about it. They'd got rid of 'em by pouring kerosene all over her head.

Truth be told, I hadn't been cleaning my brushes and combs real good like they said you always should in that book. But I didn't tell 'em about that. All in all, it seemed to me they was making too big a fuss about it. I know head lice is hard to get rid of, but they won't kill you or nothing.

That night Mama and me made a great big jar of mayonnaise, and the next morning at Carrie June's I put it all over the ladies' hair, nice and thick, and wrapped their heads up in pieces of oilcloth. That stuff has to stay on for at least four hours so it can smother them little buggers. So them two ladies, who never had no use for each other in the first place, sat around Carrie June's dining room table drinking coffee and whining that they had lots of important things they needed to be doing and how was they ever gonna get rid of all the nits and lice in their houses and all the terrible, wicked things that church folks was getting into. I noticed Carrie June wasn't smiling neither.

I tried to get the ladies to play cards to make the time pass faster, but no, that's a sin. Then I tried to get them to talk about

New Deal stuff and the president, but they didn't care about that. Wouldn't sing no hymns, neither. Truth be told, all they wanted to do was gossip and complain. So that's what they done. For four hours. I tried to sneak out once, but Carrie June caught me on the porch and brought me back inside.

When the time finally come to get the mayonnaise out, I had to wash their hair so many times I used up all that nice expensive shampoo. Then I had to pull all them little tiny lice and nits outta their hair. You didn't dare leave any on, not even one, just in case they hadn't suffocated yet.

I wanted the ladies to sit out on the back porch while I did it, where the sun was good and I could see better, but they was afraid somebody might see 'em and know what we were doing. So I set 'em by the dining room window. I thought we looked like a bunch of monkeys, but to tell the truth, there was something kinda calming about it all, to be paying attention to just that one little thing, finding the nits and lice, and didn't nothing else matter. They was both feeling a little better when they left and they swore they wasn't gonna tell a living soul 'cause it was so humiliating. But I wasn't counting on them to be true to their word. Especially Sorrey May.

Naturally, that was the end of my hair-fixing career.

A few months after I closed up shop, so to speak, Rusty decided that gal in Turkey Creek wasn't all she was cracked up to be and, like Mama said, he come crawling back with his tail between his legs. Well, by that time I was seeing a feller who'd just moved to town, and wasn't so sure that Rusty was the one anymore. At least that's what I told him.

Now his mama had started talking bad about me all over town, but didn't never tell nobody about the head lice. Just said I was irresponsible and she didn't want nothing to do with me. Of course, she told Rusty, but he didn't care and said he wanted to settle down with me and raise a family anyhow. When we was together he'd talk about all them good times we'd had in high school. Said he should of seen it all along, that folks told him what a mistake he was making when he dumped me and now he's so sorry he didn't listen.

Well, I kind of strung him along for a while, making out like my new feller was more than he really was. Rusty was working at the barbershop by then, and turned out we had a lot to talk about, with the hair cutting and all. And he's one person who understood how the terrible accident that ended my career could of happened and me be completely, totally innocent. Along with that, the new feller was really starting to get on my nerves.

I finally told Rusty I'd marry him but I wanted a nice house with a garden out back and a brand-new stove and the best icebox we could find. He found a way we could get all them things 'cause he wanted 'em, too, and the next Valentine's Day we got married. The wedding was kind of tense, due to the fact that Mama still hadn't forgive Rusty for going off after that other gal and Gladys hadn't got over that thing at the beauty shop. Everybody could tell neither one of 'em wanted to be there.

But my Rusty's a good man, he is, and I'm lucky to have got him. He don't drink much and he'll even go to church sometimes, which my daddy never done. He still works with Andy down at the barbershop, and after hearing some of his stories, sometimes I think it might be fun to go back and fix hair again. These days they got new stuff out for dyeing hair and giving permanents and such. But I won't be doing that anytime soon, 'cause now we got us two pretty little girls and a boy and another young'un on the way.

Still, I'm always giving Rusty advice about the hair-cutting business and he could learn a lot from me if he listened better. He says men don't want their hair colored and curled. They just want a shave and a haircut and don't much care how they look, and he don't need my two cents' worth. I still tell him what I think, anyhow.

And two or three times a year he admits I'm right.

Worthy of Praise

by Rusty Heppner

I ain't never done nothing worth talking about except to be best friends with Worthy Perkins, the smartest person ever born in Toad Springs. We was always together—Rusty Heppner and Worthy Perkins. Fact is, they used to call us by the one name, RustWorthy. We was both tall and skinny and had real wavy brown hair. And even though we wasn't blood relatives, we looked so much alike that three times somebody thought we was twins.

My mama was his schoolteacher and she was always bragging on Worthy, especially after the thing with that big old gator. Then he was smartest *and* bravest. It's a wonder, having to listen to that day in and day out, that me and him stayed friends. You'd think somebody with all that going for them would have an easy life, but that don't necessarily follow.

We was both fourteen when we took my baby brother, Little Mike, on a fishing trip. We was rowing down the Peace River that Saturday when we heard some baby gators—you know them *cheep, cheep* sounds they make, like little birds. We turned around and pulled the boat up on the shore, with Little Mike fussing the whole way. We knew we ought'a stay away from gators, but Worthy and me figured this time it was okay 'cause we couldn't find no trace of the mama—figured it wouldn't hurt to wade over and take a look at the hatchlings, maybe even take a couple home. Little Mike was too scared to come with us so he waited in the boat.

Me and Worthy found a hole in the bank, right near the roots of a big old cypress and saw one of the little ones crawl inside. So him and me sneaked right up to it and could see a bunch of them little fellers, but they wasn't cheeping no more, was all still as death. I was just reaching out to grab me one when we heard a loud splash. Little Mike hollered once, and then there come the sound of something real big and mean in the river.

Worthy looked at me, then jumped up and run full speed toward the sound. I headed out behind him and when we got to the bank I could see Little Mike's shirt moving around in the water, but all the rest of him was underneath. The gator had him in its jaws! And 'cause the boat was jerking around this way and that, I knew Little Mike was still holding on to the line.

I ain't never forgive myself for it, but I just froze in my tracks, couldn't move. But Worthy went like lightning. While he was slogging toward Little Mike through water that come up to his waist, he pulled out his fishing knife. That gator must of been ten or twelve feet long and it was thrashing back and forth, this way and that, throwing water everywhere. Big sucker. And Worthy ran right at it, yelling his head off and stabbing that thing everywhere he could reach but it wasn't making no difference.

Finally when Worthy seen the eye, he stabbed it, and the gator let go and swam off. By that time I was down into the water, too, and Worthy and me pulled Little Mike up on the shore, all bloody and sputtering and crying, but still holding tight to the line—had to pry it outta his hand. He had big gashes on both his legs and was bleeding pretty good. Me and Worthy pulled off our shirts and wrapped them around the worst bites, then got us all in the boat and Worthy started rowing for dear life while I tried to keep Little Mike from bleeding to death.

"What happened?" I asked him. "You was in the boat. How'd she get you?"

When he tried to talk he'd start crying again, but finally he got it out, "The boat . . . uh, uh, was sliding back . . . in the water . . .

uh, uh, and I didn't want to float off. So . . . uh . . . I grabbed the line . . . And then . . ." He started crying again.

When we got him home and Mama seen him, she like to of passed out. Had to sit right down on the floor. Her and Daddy took him over to the doc in Bartow and got him all sewed up, and he was okay but he had nightmares for a long time. He's still got big scars on his legs and to this day he can tell when it's coming up a cloud. He ain't been fishing since; won't even eat fish, but one time after he was grown he took a few bites of fried gator.

'Course, after that Worthy was a hero. And he was a good friend to me besides, 'cause he never said nothing about when I froze up like a sissy. They give him a certificate at the next town hall meeting for being so brave, but Worthy said he only done what anybody else would of done and didn't know what all the fuss was about.

Now, besides being a hero, like I said, Worthy was the smartest kid in the school. Nobody ever mixed us up when it come to the brain department. He was always reading books trying to figure out stuff, like how do birds know where to land when they fly south for the winter, and why grease and water won't mix together, and if God's so good, how can he be so mean at the same time. Me, I'm thinking about what size cricket catches the biggest bass.

Anyways, like I was saying, when we got out of high school Worthy got this scholarship to go to Tampa College, which didn't surprise nobody in town. And they even got him a place where he could live over there for free. I ain't never in my life seen nobody happier than Worthy was the day he found out about that. But he told me he was worried about what his daddy would say—and he didn't have to tell me why.

Worthy got Pastor Blander to go with him to talk to his daddy, but it didn't do no good. Landis just said Worthy had to work the groves and that was that. He was the best worker Landis had, and he couldn't do without him. Wouldn't hear of nothing else.

I can just see Landis now, in his overalls, sitting in one of their white rocking chairs on the front porch, looking out at his groves a hundred yards off, a sneer on his face and needing a shave and a haircut. He always needed a shave and a haircut. Maybe that's why Worthy was always careful to look so clean and neat. 'Course, the girls liked Worthy looking so nice, too, not that he ever took much notice.

So here we are, the smartest person ever born in this town, and instead of being proud, his daddy just wants him to work the groves. I swear, some people ain't got the sense God give a chicken. Landis just kept saying he didn't get past the fourth grade hisself, and he was doing fine.

Ree, that's Worthy's mama, she wanted Worthy to go to school and tried everything she could think of to get Landis to change his mind. But this one time, when she said Worthy was gonna need to know more than Landis could teach him, that pretty much put the sugar in the gas tank, if you know what I mean.

The whole town got mad at Landis, but it didn't make no difference. We all felt like maybe Worthy could of been a United States president or found a cure for the consumption or something like that there. Instead he was getting stuck with mowing groves and fighting red citrus mites and winter freezes.

I said, "Worthy, you ought'a go on and go to school anyhow. Your mama wants you to. And your daddy can't stop you 'cause it's free."

But Worthy just looked away and said in a wobbly voice, "I can't go. Not right now."

"You gone crazy? Why not?"

"Well, 'cause this is the first time that my daddy's ever said he wanted me around. Maybe he thinks I can help him improve the grove. I can always go to school later."

I'm telling you right now, if Landis Perkins was my daddy, I'd of gone to Tampa just to show him I could. He's just a mean old drunk. I know the Bible and my mama say you're always supposed to turn the other cheek. But when I try to be nice to some jerk, and don't nothing change, I just wind up hating him. And that's a sin. But then if I get mad and holler back, I'm being mean, and that's a sin. Either way I'm in trouble with the Lord, so I say just stay away. Seems to me, mostly, folks are pretty good to each other, but when you get down to the coffee grounds, I reckon everybody's out for their ownselves.

Me, I started working at the barbershop right out of high school—Old Man Barber's place. That's his real name, Andy Barber, but he says that ain't why he went into hair cutting. Anyway, he was gonna retire in a few years and wanted somebody to turn the business over to. Sounded easier to me than working out in the fields, so I took him up on it. But I learned the hard way that standing around all day, six days a week, inside the same four walls, cutting hair and trimming beards and shaving faces for next to nothing, it ain't as easy as you'd think.

The minute them customers walk in the door they start arguing about whether we ought'a be getting into that war overseas, and what the president's done now—some think he's no-count and is ruining the country and others say look at all the good he's done, 'til you'd never know they was talking about the same man. Listening to politics can get old real fast. Especially when you got some loud-mouth New-Dealer Democrat in your chair, like Bubba Stroudamore. Sometimes, when I'm standing there with that razor in my hand, I think it's a good thing he don't know what's going through my head.

While I'm doing that, I'm watching Worthy trying to work alongside his daddy in the groves. At night Worthy's studying all his books, coming up with different ways to graft the trees, finding new-fangled equipment, and special fertilizers and the like. 'Course, his daddy's dragging his feet and won't change nothing. Says what's good enough for him is good enough for his son. Says his secret formula was all he needed.

We all knew that Landis had this concoction he put out in the groves that he said made his oranges so good. Every year, he made it up in secret. All by himself. He'd go buy some of the fixin's over in Tampa and the rest in Turkey Creek so nobody'd know what he had, then he'd mix it up and put it underneath the trees out in the grove all by himself. Wouldn't let nobody help him.

Cost him a pretty penny, Worthy said, and was lots of extra work, but every year he won the prize for the biggest, juiciest oranges at the Florida State Fair. I never liked the man, myself, but I have to say he was always a hard worker. Trouble is, he was expecting everybody else to work as hard as him, and he never thought they did.

My mama told me once that Landis grew up real poor with a mama and a daddy who both liked the bottle and was real free with the belt buckle. Said Landis has the scars to prove it. Him and his brothers and sisters went hungry lots of times. Landis run off when he was thirteen and never went back—was hell-bent that he was gonna prove himself, and he done it, too. But he's so tight with a penny that he couldn't never sit back and enjoy what he worked so hard for.

Now that's all well and good. A man's gotta respect somebody who pulled theirselves up outta the muck like he done, but he don't have to be so mean to his only boy. Worthy told me that Landis wouldn't even give him—his own son—the secret formula he used in the groves. And he wouldn't write it down nowhere, neither. Scared somebody might find it. Worthy said he told Landis that when he died, all them prize-winning oranges would die with him, but Landis said he'd tell Worthy the recipe when he was on his deathbed and not one minute before.

That's what finally made Worthy decide to leave. After three years of being treated no better than a hired hand, one day he just broke. We was out fishing on Bass Lake one Sunday afternoon and he was real quiet, so I knew something was cooking. He hooked what must of been a ten-pound bass. Lost it when he jerked too hard on the fishing line and he let out a string of curses longer than a rainy Sunday. And Worthy, he wasn't never much for cussing. He threw his favorite fishing pole into the water, sat down in the boat, and started crying; you could hear it echo all around the lake.

Man, I didn't have no idea at all what to do—ain't never in my life seen a grown man cry. I was careful not to look at him or nothing, poked around in the water with my pole 'til I finally reached his that was floating off a little ways, and pulled it back into the boat. He was still crying, so I put a new worm on my hook—even though the old one was still there—and tossed it back out. Jesus, God! I didn't have no idea what to do.

I just sat there staring at the end of my pole like I was waiting for a bite, and after a while he settled down and started talking. Said he hated his daddy, couldn't hardly bear to even look at him, didn't know how the man could stand being with himself, he was so mean. Said if he ever ended up being like that, he'd go deep-sea fishing in a rowboat and throw away the oars.

Worthy said he'd been thinking about it for a long time, and he'd decided to move away. Got him a job over at the phosphate plant in Bartow. He said that he picked a time to tell Ree when he knew his daddy wouldn't be around. Said she was on the front porch in a rocking chair, embroidering some tea towels for his sister's hope chest when he sat down in the rocker beside her.

"Mama," he said, "I got something to tell you."

She looked at him, put her work down in her lap, and stuck the needle in the cloth real careful, like she always done every-thing just so; used to drive Worthy nuts.

"I'm gonna move to Bartow."

Tears come to her eyes but she didn't say nothing.

"Got on at the phosphate plant, and I can live in a rooming house."

"When did you decide this?" she said.

He leaned forward, resting his elbows on his knees, and looked down at his hands. "Been thinking about it for a long time. I got to get out on my own."

"Oh, honey," Ree said, rocking back in her chair. "Oh my."

"I'm sorry, Mama. But you know he don't trust me. He ain't never listened to the first thing I said. He pays more mind to what to the hired hands think."

"Oh, hon, I know. I watched you give up the chance of a life-time to go to school and instead you done what your daddy wanted. And that's something I can't never forgive him for." She wiped her eyes with the hem of her apron.

"I know when Ginger and Grady get married, she'll be leav-ing, too, " Worthy said. "I feel bad . . ."

"Oh, that's six months off," Ree said. "And she's just moving down the road. It'll be all right."

"You sure, Mama?"

She reached out and took his hand. "I'm sure, sugar. Bartow ain't so far away."

A few days later Worthy worked up the nerve to tell Landis. He picked Saturday morning, 'cause Landis always went over to Schniticker's Tavern in Turkey Creek on Saturday afternoons and never come home 'til late Sunday. That way Worthy figured he could leave town while Landis was gone. He asked me to come over and be there when he talked to his daddy, just in case. Landis hadn't never hit him harder than a swat when he was little, but Worthy just wasn't sure what he might do.

I got there early and they was still at the breakfast table. They'd just finished eating, or I should say everybody else finished eating but Worthy's plate was still full of pancakes. I paid my respects and told Worthy that I come to take him fishing. When Landis pushed his chair back, Worthy took a deep breath and said, "I need to talk to you, Daddy."

That's when I headed out to sit on the bottom porch step, kinda out of the way but close enough to see what was going on, like me and Worthy planned.

"Don't you start on me again," Landis says. "I ain't gonna give you . . ."

"No, it ain't that. I don't want your damn secret."

"What, then?" Landis sounds mad.

"Let's talk on the porch."

"I ain't got all day, boy. What you want?"

"Come outside, Daddy. Please." Worthy comes out the door and after a minute Landis follows him.

"What the hell . . ."

"This'll only take a minute."

Landis sits in a rocker, the same one Ree sat in when Worthy told her, lights up a cigarette, and blows the smoke out the side of his mouth.

Worthy's half-sitting, leaning back on the porch railing that him and me whitewashed every year, and takes another deep breath. "I'm leaving."

"Well, you gotta be back by ten. I'm gonna need the truck."

"No, Daddy. I'm leaving for good. I'm moving out."

"What the hell you talking about?"

"I'm moving to Bartow. Got me a job at the phosphate plant."

Landis leans forward with a mean look in his eye. "You ain't going nowhere, boy."

"I'm leaving Daddy. It's all set."

Landis looks out into the grove. He takes another draw on his cigarette and looks back at Worthy. "Well, that's just too goddamn bad. I said you ain't going."

"I'm a grown man," Worthy says. "I'm twenty-one now. I don't need your permission."

Landis starts yelling. "I can't run this place by myself!"

Worthy hollers back, "You do run this place by yourself! In three years you ain't never once listened to one goddamn word I said. Ain't never took my first idea. I ain't never been nothing but a hired hand to you. I give up a chance to go to college for free, 'cause you said you wanted me helping you here. I was dumb enough to think you needed me. You can just hire somebody else."

"Don't be a fool, boy. I can't trust the half-wits around here. And besides that I can't afford . . ."

"Don't tell me that," Worthy says, a little calmer. "You can afford whatever you want. I seen the books."

Now, Landis is an ugly SOB when he's mad, goes all blowed up like a puffer-fish. He gets up and walks over to Worthy. When Worthy stands up straight, Landis has to look up to see him eye-to-eye. I'd be willing to bet my granddaddy's gold watch that Landis hadn't never noticed, before that minute, how Worthy was a good four inches taller than him.

Landis shakes his fist in Worthy's face and Worthy don't even blink. Then Landis yells, "You don't know shit. Them books don't show the whole thing. You ain't as goddamn smart as you think."

Worthy stands his ground and looks down at Landis. He don't say nothing.

Lands lowers his fist. "You told your mama about this?"

Worthy don't answer him, just looks toward the screen door where his mama and sister are watching from inside the house. He looks back to Landis. "I'm leaving tomorrow. Got me a ride over there and a place to stay. I'm starting out at the plant making twice what you give me. And besides that, I got a chance to move into the part that does research. Might even could end up going to college after all."

Landis throws his cigarette down on the porch, stomps on it, and storms right past me out into the grove. I don't think he seen me sitting there and I sure as hell wasn't gonna say nothing.

Worthy goes back into the house where his mama and Ginger are standing near the door crying, and I head up and sit on the porch. "I'm sorry," Worthy says. "I didn't mean for you all to hear that."

"Wasn't as bad as I thought, honey," Ree says. "I expected worse."

Worthy hugs her. "Mama, I'm sorry."

She pulls back and wipes her eyes with her apron. "I'll do a load of wash. Can't have you leaving with dirty laundry."

"Thanks, Mom."

Then he hugs Ginger. "I'm gonna miss my baby brother," she says.

Well, after church the next day I drive Worthy over to Bartow, while his daddy's down at Schniticker's drinking hisself blind.

As time went by, I'd go over to see Worthy now and again and he told me all about how phosphate comes from old bones and stuff from millions of years ago when Florida was down under the ocean. Matter of fact, they call this part of the state "Bone Valley." He showed me the big old cranes they use to dig up the phosphate rocks, then how they knock off the mud and sand before they send them away.

Worthy said that everything that's alive needs phosphorus, I mean that's people and animals and plants, everything. Can't live without it. The stuff they dig out of the ground here, some of it's put into food, and with some of it they make fertilizer. That gives you something to think about, don't it? Like we're eating fertilizer? Guess, in a way, that's what food is. Too bad I thought of that.

When the time come for Ginger to get married, Worthy'd already got a raise. He come in town on Saturday morning for the wedding that afternoon, and him and Landis didn't speak the whole time. Ree tried to get them together, but neither one of them was having none of that and she had plenty of other stuff to keep her busy since everything always has to be just exactly right or she'll throw a hissy fit. Pastor Blander married Ginger and Grady at the Church of Everlasting Liability, and everybody in town was there. Worthy stayed at my house that night and went back to Bartow early the next morning.

After that, every time I talked to Worthy, he'd ask me about Landis's groves, and I'd tell him everything seemed to be doing okay, far as I knew. He didn't never ask about Landis, so I never said nothing, but down at the barbershop I'd heard Landis wasn't working as much as he used to and was ornery as a rattlesnake with chickenpox. Folks even said he was having trouble keeping the hired help.

Then I didn't see Worthy for a while, 'cause Andy got the lumbago real bad and I had to cut hair for the both of us. And Sweetie, that was my girlfriend, she was always after me to do stuff with her on the weekends.

About six months after Ginger's wedding we had a real bad freeze that wiped out most of that year's crop. All the men in town was out burning railroad ties in the groves to try and keep the trees from freezing, and that helped some. I even went and worked all night in Landis's grove, and I guess he was glad to have me there, even if he never said so. That man never knew how to say the words, "Thank you," I swear he didn't. He ended up losing more than half his fruit and had a rough time that year. Really missed Worthy, I bet.

Every time Landis come in for a haircut, which wasn't all that often, he's griping about the same old things—nobody knows how to put in a hard day's work no more; everybody's out to cheat you anytime you turn your back, especially the government; and everything costs too much. It gets to where Andy and me, we both roll our eyes and shake our heads when he walks in the door.

The next few years was good to Worthy, and he did finally make it to college and got a couple of degrees. Got to be a chemist working at one of the big phosphate companies figuring out ways to make plants grow bigger and healthier. Even won him some awards for the work he done coming up with new kinds of fertilizer.

Was a few years after that big freeze that Landis had a stroke. He was out mowing the grove in July, and it was damn hot. He was by hisself, so nobody knew what happened 'til he didn't come home that night and Ree went looking for him. Turned out it was real bad, he couldn't talk and couldn't hardly move. Worthy come down to see him, but Landis was just lying in the bed, looking up at the ceiling.

Worthy come back a month later to stay for a week, and by that time they'd put Landis in one of them rolling chairs and rode him out to the front porch. Worthy talked to him about what he'd been doing at the plant, which he figured Landis probably didn't want to hear, but he couldn't think of nothing else. And course, Landis couldn't say nothing. Didn't even nod his head to show you that he'd heard anything.

Ree said that once or twice seemed like Landis was trying to say something but her and Ginger couldn't make no sense out of the sounds he made. Worthy said it was like talking to a scarecrow, 'cause that's what Landis looked like, and along with not being able to talk at all . . . well, you can see what I mean. 'Course, Ree come out and sat with them off and on, fussing with Landis and trying to make everything all right.

Worthy went over the books with Ree that week and showed her what she needed to do to keep the place going. She knew a lot of it but he taught her the details. Worthy even said that if she needed him to, he could leave his job and come back home for a while, but she wouldn't hear none of it. She said he'd already give up his dreams for his daddy once and she wouldn't have him do it again.

One afternoon, me and him went to the barn to take stock of what all was out there. I reckon Landis never give away one thing in his whole life, 'cause that ratty old barn was cram-packed full of cobwebs and junk. There was plows from forty years ago, harnesses that hadn't been used since Worthy was born, five blowed-out tractor tires, two rusty kitchen sinks, a big old rolltop desk beat all to hell, and lots of broken furniture they accumulated through the years, stuff that wasn't worth fixing. Me, I'd have throwed it out long ago. Or never saved it in the first place.

Took us three days, but we finally got all the trash piled up that we were gonna throw out. Afterward we was sitting on the porch with Landis, while Ree fixed supper. Worthy was talking about how much old Rydel was gonna charge to come and get the stuff, and Landis started making noise, saying, "Graulmph, uhhhh, roaah." Me and Worthy was both surprised, and looked at him. His eyes was open real wide. He hadn't made this much noise since the stroke. "Grauullem!"

Worthy went over to him. "You want to tell us something, Daddy?"

"Uhhhhh."

"Okay. Try it again."

"Greeuummph!"

"Okay, Daddy. Okay. We'll figure this out." Worthy looked over at me. "Let's see, what was we was talking about? Oh yeah, about Rydel picking up the junk." He turned and looked back at Landis. "Is that it? Something about Rydel?"

"Uhhhhhhhh."

"Okay now. It was something about Rydel. You don't want him to haul off your stuff? Is that it?"

"Uhhhhhh."

"But it's all just trash! It's been sitting out there for twenty years and you never used none of it."

Landis looked at Worthy, then squeezed his eyes shut tight. A little tear run down the side of his face. When Worthy seen that tear, he said, "Okay, okay, Daddy. We won't have it hauled off just yet, if it's that important to you."

Landis stared at him. "Uhnnhhnn."

Worthy looked over at me, then back to Landis. "Seems crazy to me, but if that's what you want."

Landis kept on staring at him.

After supper, I said to Worthy, "You think he'd know if we had Rydel haul it all off anyway? I mean, none of that crap is worth keeping."

"I know, I know," Worthy said. "But if it'll make him happy, it can't hurt to wait a few months. Doc don't think he'll last much longer than that."

But Doc was wrong. Landis lived another three years. Never could talk again, but he got to where he could move his one hand some, enough to write a little bit. Most of it was just scribbles, but one word we finally figured out. It looked like *FRZL*. It was fertilizer.

Turned out that Landis didn't want us to throw out all that junk 'cause he'd put his special recipe out there. He'd wrote it down after all. So then me and Worthy had to go back out to the barn and start going through all that crap, still piled up where we'd left it three years before. When we started moving stuff, rats and mice and snakes come out of everywhere. What hadn't been full of varmints before, was by that time. There was cobwebs enough they could hide a whole house and I felt like I needed an umbrella to get through 'em.

Took us three days, looking in every nook and cranny where he might have stuck it, and I'm telling you, poking your hand down into some dark corner, you didn't know what you'd pull back. All it would have took is one black widow spider to bite you and it would all be over. Well, around three o'clock on the third day we was ready to give up the ghost. Figured maybe something had ate the paper. We were headed back to the house when Worthy says, "Wait a minute. Did you look in every one of them drawers in that old rolltop desk?"

"Yep. Every single one."

"Did you pull them out to see if it could have been jammed back underneath one of 'em?"

"Yeah. I think so."

"Let's look just one more time."

"Aw, Worthy, ain't nothing there. We already looked." But I followed him back inside. We pulled out every drawer again and Worthy run his hand in and felt around besides.

Finally, Worthy said, "Wait. I feel something."

"What? Ain't nothing there."

He pushed on something and a little drawer come open around on the side of the desk. "What's that?" I asked.

He pulled the little drawer all the way out, and there was a piece of paper. It was the recipe. Worthy was so happy he was almost crying. And I was so happy to be able to go home, I almost cried, too.

Later on, Worthy told me he felt that when his daddy wanted him to have the recipe, it was like he was saying that he finally trusted him after all them years. But even crazier than that, it turned out that the ingredients was almost exactly the same as what Worthy had won a great big award for, just a few months before.

After that, Worthy got married to a pretty little gal from Bartow, Rebecca's her name, and she looks a lot like Ree. Had two boys and a sweet little girl. And he did make a lot of money, bought a brand-new car and a nice house. It seemed like he settled down some, even come over to visit once in a while. He'd sit on the front porch with Landis and look out at the groves—he'd talk a little, but since his daddy couldn't answer or nothing, they mostly just sat. Sometimes I'd come by and talk to Worthy to where Landis could listen.

Wish I could tell you that after Landis died five years later, Worthy lived a happy and prosperous life. It wasn't too long after that, Worthy took to the drink. Couldn't ever figure that out, 'cause he wouldn't never touch alcohol before then. But all that drinking turned him into a different man—working all the time, always looking over his shoulder to see who might be trying to outdo him, never paying attention to his young'uns or visiting his mama.

From what I heard at the barber shop, Ree worried about him and was always calling and writing him that he ought'a stop drinking and move back to Toad Springs. But it never did no good. I'll tell you, offhand I don't know nobody who listens to their mama.

I think in the end Ree finally give up on him herself, but then she had enough to keep her busy with the five grandkids Ginger give her—had to make sure Ginger was doing everything just exactly right, you know.

Sometimes when Sweetie and the girls—did I tell you I ended up marrying Sweetie? Anyways, sometimes when her and the girls are washing dishes after supper, I sit on the front porch and think about Worthy. You know, him and his daddy turned out to be just alike—both smart, hard workers; always out to prove themselves; and big drinkers. But to me, the strangest thing was how them two come up with the same fertilizer recipe.

Worthy died in a bad fall over at the plant when he was forty-three. Even though it had been a few years since I'd seen him, I felt like something was missing, knowing he's gone. I still feel that way. His wife said he'd been real unhappy but she didn't know why, and she thought he'd been drinking at the time. It's downright odd you know, how in the end, as much as Worthy didn't want to be nothing like his daddy, he ended up just like him.

Myself, I always wondered if one day he looked in the mirror and seen Landis looking back, and that was just more than he could stand.

Cats and Dogs
by Never Riley

Some folks think if you gonna live a happy life you got to get married and have a bunch of young'uns like my sister Sorrey May done. But that ain't true. When I look at the way my nieces turned out, I just pet my sweet cats and count my blessings. They never give me no sass, don't make bad grades in school, and don't sneak off with fellers they got no business being with. They just stroll around minding their own business while I'm operating the switchboard. None of 'em was a minute's trouble 'til Old Man Peevy started renting house next door.

I'm Neva Birdo Riley but everybody calls me Never. Got my nickname from my daddy who said I never done nothing I was supposed to without putting up a hissy-fit and I have to say, being the youngest, behind Sorrey May and Carrie June, I didn't have no choice but to learn how to fend for myself.

I was the town's very first telephone operator and that's a big responsibility. Did it for forty-two years; dedicated my whole life to serving the folks here in Toad Springs. I ran the phone service out of my house, back in the day when to call somebody, you had to pick up the earpiece and just listen 'til I said, "Operator."

Then I'd connect you to whoever you wanted. I could tell everybody's voice right off, even when they was trying to disguise it, and I knew all the numbers by heart—could plug them in with my eyes closed. Whenever I got somebody on the line being mean or ugly I straightened them out in a flash. People learned fast that they wasn't getting past me without being polite.

When I first started being the operator I was afraid to leave the house in case somebody needed me, but that got old real fast. After a while I let folks know that I'd be working most days, but they shouldn't call between one and two in the afternoons or late at night unless it was an emergency—'cause I need my rest like everybody else. And I told 'em sometimes I'd have emergencies myself when I'd have to leave. But I took my responsibilities real serious.

Just between you and me and the fence post, it never hurts to know who's talking to who in a town this size and sometimes, even when you're following the Telephone Operator's Code of Honor and trying not to listen in, you might catch a few words. Why, I was the first one to hear about when Little Mike Heppner got bit by that gator and almost lost his leg, and when old Flavey Stroudamore died.

Why, when Willard Stroudamore left Mindy Sue and them kids way over in Fort Pierce, she called his brother, Bubba, to come and carry 'em back here. Then after that she was calling Bubba every time I turned around. Pretended like she wanted to get a job with him, she did, but I could tell what she really wanted. And married to his brother!! You'd think she'd had enough trouble with the one Stroudamore running off like he done. I'm telling you, some people never learn!

Then Rusty Heppner at the barbershop was always talking to this Cuban feller over in Tampa—I could tell by the accent it was a Cuban. I think Rusty was gambling by the way they was talking, but I couldn't tell for sure. That man's got no business spending money on something like that when he's got all them young'uns to feed.

And Sorrey May's favorite daughter, Elsie Lou, who married and moved up to Nashville—she's a singer up there now—told her mama some of the places she sings ain't really nothing but a bar, but Sorrey May told her not to tell that to nobody else.

Makes me uneasy sometimes, knowing all this stuff. When I see folks at church and the grocery I have to pretend I don't know nothing. Have to watch every word comes out of my mouth, and it ain't easy, I'm telling you.

Like I said, everything was fine 'til this short little fat guy name of Peevy moves in next door. Him and his dog show up one Saturday afternoon in an old beat-up pickup truck and I ain't never seen so much junk as he hauled into that house. There was lots of cardboard boxes and a bunch of furniture that was so ratty he must of picked it up at the dump on his way into town. Why, I'm willing to bet that man hadn't never seen the inside of a barbershop and I ain't sure he'd ever took a bath neither. Right off, his hound dog starts barking his fool head off and chasing my cats. With all that ruckus I couldn't hardly even hear when folks called in.

By the second day, all three of my kitties, that's Punkin and Lydia and Tom, they're looking nervous and one of them starts peeing in the house. Now I ain't having none of that. They got to go outside like nature intended. Just let me tell you, though, my Punkin's a beautiful cat who looks for all the world like a Siamese, with his dark brown face and blue eyes. He's my favorite. I know you ain't supposed to have favorites, at least not admit it if you do, but I just can't help it.

Anyway, that afternoon I decide to pay my new neighbor a visit, you know, trying to act friendly. I take half a loaf of banana bread over and knock on the front door. When he comes up I say, "How do? I'm your neighbor, Never Riley." He opens the screen door just wide enough to take the plate and pulls it inside.

"I live next door," I say. I try to look around him into the house but it's too dark in there to see anything.

"Hummph."

"What's your name?"

"John Peevy."

"Well, Mr. Peevy, I want to talk to you about your dog," I say, but he closes the door in my face. I knock on it again. "Hey, Peevy.

I want to talk to you." He don't come back so I knock a couple more times, then go down the front steps and head home. Well, that feller didn't know who he'd just insulted.

When folks called in on the switchboard I just happened to mention Old Man Peevy to 'em. That's how I found out he'd moved here from Alabama—probably running from the law, if you ask me. After three days of complaining, I got a couple of neighbor men to go over and make Peevy tie up that damned dog so he couldn't chase my cats. Problem was, though, he tied him to a tree just outside my bedroom window and seems like every night when my head hits the pillow, that hound starts up barking. I can't sleep at all and I'm here to tell you that not getting enough rest don't leave you in a mood where you can act too professional at work.

Wasn't no time at all before my kitty, Punkin, starts throwing up again. The first time he done that was right after I started being a telephone operator and all that buzzing and ringing must have upset his little stomach, bless his heart. Got to where he wouldn't hardly eat, so I finally had to take an emergency day off from work so I could get him over to the horse doctor in Bartow 'cause I was scared he was gonna die. Folks wasn't too happy about me missing work but I couldn't help that.

Well, first, the doctor says he don't know nothing about cats and they ain't worth fooling with anyhow, but after I told him loud and clear what I thought of a doctor who wouldn't help one of God's creatures who was sick, maybe even dying, he looked through some books. He tells me to feed Punkin some lard—thinks maybe he has a hairball. Then he charges me seventy-five cents. Can you imagine! Says he'd have charged the same for a cow since folks pay by the animal, but I think he was just taking advantage. Wasn't nothing I could do, though. It was Punkin.

Well, you ever tried to get a cat to eat something he don't want? It ain't a pretty sight. First I give him some of my biscuit lard to taste, which he didn't want no part of. Then I fried up some ham and took the grease off that—guess it was too salty for Mr. Persnickety. 'Course, he'll eat a rat's been dead for two days.

Finally I figured it out—sneaked up on him when he was asleep and dropped a towel over him. Then real quick I scooped him up with only his head sticking out, pulled the towel tight and pinned him down on the kitchen table, all the time him hissing and howling and scratching for all he was worth. Wasn't no easy task but finally I pried his mouth open with a spoon and stuck in some biscuit lard, then held on 'til he swallowed a little bit down. After I done that a couple of times and was covered with scratches from head to toe, he started eating good again.

Anyhow, to get back to Old Man Peevy—he comes over one afternoon and says for me to keep my cat out of his yard; says it vexes his hound dog and makes him bark. Now, I have to admit that Punkin's in the habit of sleeping out under a big old hibiscus bush next door, just past where that dog's rope reaches. It's always been his favorite spot since he was a baby. You know how cats are.

"Well, now," I says to Old Man Peevy, "nice to see you, too, and you just might be interested to know that my granddaddy was Buford Riley and he's the one started this here town and you better talk to me with a little respect if you know what's good for you. And if you just keep your damned dog in the house we won't have no trouble."

Then he says dogs ain't meant to ever set foot in a house and that hound's staying outside. Says if I don't keep Punkin off his property he'll shoot him.

And I tell him if he shoots my cat he'd goddamn well better be ready to have a dead dog lying in his yard, and I want my banana bread plate back. Then I slam the door in his ugly red face.

I have a cup of coffee to calm down and finish polishing Aunt Bixie's silver-headed Buddha that she got on a trip to Siam when she was bringing souls to the Lord with the Salvation Army. That silver tarnishes real fast if you don't keep right to it. While I'm rubbing away this thought in the back of my head gets bigger and bigger—that old coot really would kill Punkin.

Now, all the other neighbors love Punkin like I do, except for Gladys Heppner. A few years back, three little baby blue jays was in a nest right next to her kitchen window and her and her husband, Orin, used to watch them getting bigger every morning when they had breakfast. But one day while they was sitting there Punkin run up that tree and got them babies and Gladys ain't been able to eat potato pancakes since.

Anyhow, the next morning when I get up I feel like I actually had a decent night's sleep for a change. And then it comes to me that I hadn't heard that damn dog barking all night. Lifted my heart, I'll tell you, to think that old man must have put the dog in the house after all and we can all go back to our normal lives. I'm just getting ready to take my first sip of coffee when I hear somebody pound on the front door. I peek through the blinds and see it's Old Man Peevy. He don't look too happy.

I open up the door and give him a big smile so's he'll know how much I appreciate him doing the right thing. I say, "Why, good morning, Mr. Peevy."

And he says, "You killed my dog."

"What?" My mouth flies open and I put my hand on my heart.

"My dog's dead," he says. "You give him rat poison."

I am shocked down to my toes. I say, "Why, I did no such thing. I would never . . ."

"Oh, ho!" he says, shaking his finger in my face. "You said I'd have a dead dog lying in my yard and that's just what I got. Your cats are living on borrowed time. Just remember you fool with a Peevy, you're gonna wish you hadn't of."

He takes a couple of steps backward and says, "I'm going to the law, right now and I'm taking my dog with me. They can cut his belly open and see it's all burned up with poison." He turns on his heel and waddles off and I'm just too bumfoozled to say a thing.

Just to be on the safe side, though, I see Punkin out under the hibiscus and bring him in. Takes me a while to find Lydia; she's so black it's hard to see her in the in the shadows under the plumbago bush. The big yellow Tom's under the front porch and he gets ugly when I drag him out by the tail and he scratches me on the cheek, right near the scar from when I got bit by a dog when I was eight years old and run away from home 'cause Mama wouldn't let me wear my ballerina shoes to church.

I decide I'll just keep the cats in the house for a while. Problem is, I've always had a very sensitive nose so there's no way I'm having a sandbox inside my house. I figure I'll just take the kitties out a couple of times a day so they can do their duty.

I fix me up some collars out of twine but putting them on the cats is something else again. I grab Lydia first, sit her in my lap, and pet her real nice. Then when I wrap the twine around her neck she just backs up and pulls her head out of it, then jumps down on the floor and stares at me. I don't give up, though, chase her 'til I get her cornered in the bathroom and finally get her done. Punkin don't put up much of a fuss, which ain't no surprise, but then Tom, he gives me fits. He wiggles around so much I lose my balance and end up on the floor. Got a big old bruise on my backside, but the important thing is that I won the battle.

After lunch I put my feet up for my regular rest time, then at two o'clock I think we'll all go out in the yard—close by the house, of course, where I can hear if somebody calls on the switchboard. I tie one end of a string to Lydia's collar, and the other end to a leg of the kitchen table. Have to leave her there while I'm getting another cat hooked up or she'll run off somewhere, but I finally get 'em done and we head out the door.

Well, that is, some of us head out the door. Punkin decides he wants to stay inside, so I have to carry him out. Once they're all on the porch they freeze up like they've just come back from the taxidermist. Anyways, I walk over to the steps and talk real nice but they just hunker down more. I tug on the strings and they lie there and squint their eyes at me.

Just then the switchboard starts going off, but as much trouble as all this is, there ain't no way I'm stopping to answer it. Since I have to keep holding on to all the strings, I only have one hand free. So I pick the cats up, one at a time, and move them across the porch as close to the stairs as the strings'll reach. Then when I get them all lined up, I go down at the bottom and drag them down the stairs and by that time they're goddamned lucky I don't just snatch their fool heads right off.

That's when they decide they've been nice long enough—Tom starts growling and the other two join in. "Come on," I say, "I just want you to pee." I pull them toward the grass, but if they move at all, it's to try and go the other way. And no way in hell anybody's gonna pee. I can tell by their snippy little faces and the way they flatten their ears that even if they wanted to, they wouldn't do it now just to spite me.

Patience is what I need, so I set myself down on the grass and act like I have all the time in the world and don't have to get over to the Church of Everlasting Liability by three o'clock for an emergency prayer meeting for Gussie Simpson's aunt, and I ain't even ironed my dress yet. I just look at 'em and every damned one of them cats is lying as far away as the string will go, staring at me with the evil eye.

When I only have fifteen minutes left to get to the church, I stand up and that takes a minute or so in itself; funny how fast your legs freeze up once you hit sixty. When I'm up, I pull on the strings, but by then they've all decided they like it there and want to stay where they are. I'm about ready to kill them myself when Punkin finally stands up and starts to come along and the others follow. You can see why Punkin's my favorite.

But now I'm gonna be late and I have to wear that dress with the red and orange flowers that I wore last Sunday and Gladys is gonna make another smart remark 'cause it was left over from the church rummage sale and it used to belong to her rich cousin over in Tampa who looks down her nose at everybody and Gladys tries to be just like her.

When I get back home from the meeting, where Gladys acts just like I knew she would, I smell cat pee before I get the front door open good. And before I can take care of that, switchboard's buzzing and it's Mr. Big Important Hank Plenty as mad as a one-winged hornet, saying he needed to get through to Tampa right away, and 'cause I didn't answer his whole day got messed up. I told him I was sorry but I had an emergency of my own to take care of and he'd better be careful about how he talks to me even if he is the richest feller in town.

The next morning I cave in and fix up a damned sandbox 'cause by then the whole house is turning into one anyway. P.U! It never once crossed my mind that the cats wouldn't all use the same box, but before the week is out they're scattered from one end of the house to the other. God forbid those flea-brained cats have to be near each other when they do their duty. Must be like when I was little and had to wait 'til everybody else was finished and left the privy before I could pee 'cause the world would end if they heard me.

A week later I get a letter in the mail from Schick and Schick, Attorneys at Law, over in Bartow. It's most always bad luck to get a letter from a lawyer and I feel my blood rising when I open it. It says that they couldn't tell for sure if Old Man Peevy's dog was poisoned but he's filing a civil suit to make me pay for that damn mutt.

The next day I have to take an emergency day off from the switchboard. I get Halt Brisco to drive me over to Plant City in that old rattletrap he's so proud of, and I march right into Calvin McAlley's office. McAlley was our family lawyer before Daddy died and he promised he'd always take good care of us girls. Well, after he makes me sit in the waiting room for an hour just to show me who's boss, he says he'll call Schick and Schick and see what they can work out and that'll be five dollars for the visit today. And I say I thought you was supposed to take care of me after Daddy died and he said he is taking care of me but I just have to pay him.

Well, that ain't what I had in mind but I couldn't do nothing about it. And when all was said and done I ended up paying him twenty-two dollars, but it was worth it 'cause the Lord was definitely on the side of the righteous. The judge threw the case out and I never paid Old Man Peevy so much as one red cent. Not long after, that hateful old man moved off to Orlando—left my broken banana bread plate on my front porch.

I don't like to think about the thirty-four dollars it cost me to buy new rugs for the house but they do look real nice. And the smell only gets bad when it rains.

Broken Hearts and Gator Bones
by Hester Brisco

Life can give you lots you ain't expecting, and if you're a nervous person like me, it can make a damned fool out of you.

I was born in Tampa, and as a child I was always high strung, everybody says so. Scared of my own shadow and mousey-looking besides. And if that wasn't bad enough, what happened to me in the fifth grade made everything worse. My teacher was Miss Grimly, and she didn't have no toes, she didn't. Long time before she come to Toad Springs she was a missionary overseas and caught some kind of foot rot and they had to cut all her toes off when she got home. She could walk, but she had to take little tiny steps and you was always thinking she was gonna tip right over.

Sometimes, when she was writing on the blackboard with her back to us, the boys made fun of her. Once in a while she'd catch 'em and when she did, she'd hit 'em with a yardstick. Truth be told, she hit them boys whenever she felt like it, even when they wasn't doing nothing wrong. There was always broken yardsticks all over the classroom. Didn't never hit the girls, but then she didn't like us, neither.

The day my life got ruined was the day she made the class write a story about what we did during the summer vacation and I hadn't done nothing. There wasn't one thing for me to write and she picked me first to get up in front of the class and read. I told her I didn't have nothing interesting to say but she made me stand up there anyway. I was so scared, I fainted.

She was bending down over me when I come to, and I threw up my fried eggs and grits all over her. Well, she screamed bloody murder and jerked back and that made her lose her balance and sit down real hard on the floor. Right away she was yelling at me. "Oh Hester, look what you've done!! Oh, sweet Jesus on the waves!" She said that, I swear she did.

All the kids was standing there, looking down at us, laughing. It took Miss Grimly a good while to drag herself up by holding on to the desk and get back to standing, and after she did, she shuffled off to get cleaned up. Never mind me, of course.

From that day on, all the boys and some of the girls called me Heavin' Hester. And that's where my big troubles started. Ever since that day there are these little things I have to do when I get nervous. When I'm around somebody who's bossy, like Sorrey May Only, I need to do it more.

Sometimes I look down and see I'm wringing my hands when I didn't even know it, thought they was just lying in my lap behaving theirselves. Or I snap my pocketbook open and shut. Or I touch my fingers to my thumb one at a time, over and over. Sometimes it makes people look at me longer than they want to, but it makes me feel better when I do it. Been doing it so long now, I couldn't stop if I wanted to.

We moved to Toad Springs when I was thirteen and my husband, Halt, and his family come here from Okeechobee the next year. Halt—his real first name is Haltendorfen, so you can see why he goes by Halt. His brother, Karl, was two years older and I fell in love with him right off the bat. Whenever I was anywhere close to him I'd start wringing my hands.

He was so tall and handsome, great big shoulders, and always talking about how he was gonna grow up and be the governor of Florida someday. 'Course, all the popular girls in town was after him and he didn't even know I was alive. I started making up to

Halt, so I could get him to talk about Karl. I figured that was the best I was gonna be able to do.

Now, Halt wasn't no big prize, kinda scrawny and bow-legged, and his hair always stuck up in the back. Still does. But he took right to me. Never seemed to notice that all I wanted to talk about was his brother. Then, when Karl got out of the tenth grade he run off to Tampa and there I was, stuck with Halt and a great big broken heart.

In those days Halt could be real nice, I have to say. Once in a while he'd bring me a flower he'd pulled up from somewhere, or get me a piece of peppermint candy. A few times I seen his temper flare up real fast but I didn't think nothing of it at the time. Just goes to show that when I was young I didn't have no sense.

Halt made a pretty good living—owned the Toad Springs General Store for over twenty years, but he finally give it up when he pulled his back out trying to lift two cases of pickled okra at once. He was just fifty-one then but said 'cause he couldn't stand up for very long at a time, he had to retire from the store.

After a few weeks he started thinking about how the Stroudamore's Gator Ranch was bringing tourists into Toad Springs and he says, "Hester, we can make us some money off that place, too." Couldn't tell you why he thought Flavey Stroudamore was gonna let him in on the business—Flavey ain't the friendliest feller around—but I didn't say nothing. Wouldn't have done no good anyway, 'cause Halt ain't never heard a thing I got to say.

After we got married twenty-eight years ago I tried to put in my two cents' worth now and again, but he'd turn ugly real quick and still to this day it makes me nervous to cross him. You know, you grow up saying you ain't gonna marry a man like your daddy, you're gonna find a kindhearted feller who'll listen to you now and again and even give you a little peck on the check once in a while when he don't have to, then hell's bells, you end up just like your mama. I finally got better at speaking up with other folks, but still not so much at home.

Wasn't 'til after the kids was born that Halt got so ornery all the time. There was always something going wrong at the store, canned goods didn't get delivered on time, weevils in the flour, folks not paying their bills. He didn't have no patience at all. That man would argue with a croaking tree frog just to pass the time of day. 'Course, he'd never hit us or nothing like that, but it got to where me and the young'uns would just go along with whatever he wanted, 'cause he always ended up getting his way anyhow. I think that's why the both of the kids moved to Tampa soon as they got old enough to leave home.

But like I was saying, Halt was flat determined he was gonna make some extra money off of Flavey's gator ranch, so he figured he could come up with something to sell in the gift shop. "Them tourists from up north got money to burn," he'd say. "Everybody knows that."

He got the idea to whittle little toy gators outta wood, but I told him I already seen some in the gift shop. He thought about stuffing baby gators but he couldn't go hunting with his back hurt, and besides it was too dangerous. Finally, he come up with something nobody had ever seen before. Not anywhere on God's green earth.

In his younger days Halt used to go gator hunting all the time. He hated them things 'cause one of 'em had killed his dog when he was a kid. When he'd catch one, he'd clean it and throw the bones into the shed out back—had a whole pile of them in there but I never went near the place. I don't want to be near a gator even if it's just bones. Them nasty things give me the all-overs. Even to this day, when I'm at the gator ranch I go straight to the gift shop, never even been out back to see them big old ugly things.

Anyway, when Halt and our boy was out fishing or hunting, if Halt seen some bones lying there, he'd bring them home and throw them out back with the gator bones. I asked him one time why he'd pick up them old dead things, but he just give me a look like I was some kind of fool, that anybody smart enough to eat with a spoon saved old bones.

Anyway, his great idea was to clean up some of them gator skulls and paint a Florida sunset on it, right across the forehead.

Then he put little palm trees with people walking on the beach all along the snout. Now Halt's great-great-great-granddaddy was supposed to be a famous painter from Germany or Paris or somewhere. They'd forgot his name a long time ago, but Halt said that's where he got his talent from.

Well, he had to boil them bones in a washtub out back, then scrape off any stringy stuff and gristle that was left. After that he had to bleach 'em and then let 'em dry in the sun. Next, he drew him up some little pictures of how he wanted to decorate 'em, and got him some different colors of paint and a bunch of little brushes from Smitty's Hardware and Feed. Once he got everything all set up he started into work. Now, I have to admit, he did a better job than I figured he would and them pictures looked pretty lifelike. But I wouldn't never of bought one.

When he'd finished three, he took them down to the Gator Ranch to show Flavey. Well, that's when he found out if he sold them in the gift shop that Flavey would take half of what he was asking for 'em. When Halt got home that day he was fit to be tied. Couldn't believe Flavey wanted to steal money from him.

So he put up a little lean-to down the road from the Gator Ranch and tried to sell 'em his ownself on the weekends when more folks was around, but turned out didn't nobody hardly notice he was there. Took him three weekends to sell one, and then he up and quit. Like I said before, I wouldn't never have bought one. Couldn't of give me one free.

Since that didn't work he started making jewelry and key chains out of the bones. 'Course, he didn't know no more about making jewelry than a possum knows about playing a fiddle, but that ain't never stopped Halt from doing whatever he wanted. Got him a book on it and before you know it, he's an expert.

He cut the little bones up into slices, polished 'em, and strung 'em together. With the bigger ones he'd paint a mark on them, like a cross or a flower or something, and they didn't look as bad as you'd think. He drilled little holes in the gator teeth and made key chains. After lots of back'en and forth'en, him and Flavey worked out some kind of deal so Flavey sold 'em at the gift shop, but I think both of 'em went around thinking about all the money they was losing doing it that way. Halt used some of the money to fix up his old Model T. Now I have to say that car's his pride and joy. His favorite thing in all the world is riding around town showing it off to everybody.

Early one afternoon in the spring, when the weather was real nice and cool, we're sitting out on the front porch and I'm helping Halt string some necklaces together, when a tall, seedy-looking feller wearing a cowboy hat pulled down low over his face walks up the street and comes to the bottom of the porch steps. "Hello there, Halt," he says.

Halt looks at him over the top of his glasses. "Am I supposed to know you?" he says.

"Yep," the stranger says. "You know me."

"Can't place you," Halt says, looking at the man hard and shaking his head. "What's your name?"

The stranger looks down at his feet and shuffles around a little. "Name's Karl. I'm your brother."

"Karl?" Halt says, dropping the tooth he was working on and standing up. "Karl? Is that you? I'll be damned! You old scalawag! It *is* you!" We both stare at him and my heart jumps up into my throat. Halt puts down his pan of bones, hobbles over to the steps with a great big smile on his face, and puts his hand out.

Karl walks up to him and grabs his hand, then hugs Halt with his other arm.

"My God!! Where you been, you old son of a gun?" Halt says, pulling back. "It's been thirty years!"

"Thirty-one," Karl says.

"Karl," I say, straightening my hair and smoothing down my apron, "come on up on the porch. Let me get you something to drink. Are you hungry?"

Karl smiles and says, "And your name? I know I should re-member it. Sorry."

"Hester," I say. "I'm Hester." Now I know I'm an old married woman, but I start feeling like I did way back in high school, when I first seen Karl. He reaches over and gives me a hug and even though he don't smell all that good, I'm so excited I can't hardly stand it.

"That's right," he says. "Now I remember. You ain't changed a bit in all these years."

"Oh my," I say, touching my hair. "I'm just a mess. How can you say that? I don't look a thing like . . ."

"As pretty as a picture," he says, standing back and pointing at me. "Yeah, look at that smile. I remember you now."

"Aw, go on with you," I say, feeling my face get hot. "Sit down, here in the rocker, sit down. Can I get you some sweet tea?"

"Why, that would be right nice," he says. "I'm a little dry, now that I think about it."

"Me, too," says Halt.

After I put the water on to boil, I comb my hair and wash my face, straighten myself up a little and put on a clean apron. When I go back on the porch they're sitting in the rockers and Halt's saying, "Bubba Stroudamore said he thought he seen you drive by in a car when he was over in Tampa one time, but he wasn't sure."

"Could of been me," Karl says. "I was there 'til about five, six years ago, I reckon. Then I moved over to Orlando."

"What did you do there?" I ask, handing 'em the sweet tea and sitting down on the swing. "Why'd you pick Orlando instead of coming back here?"

"I had a chance to make some money, I thought, anyways." Karl takes a sip from his glass and lights up a cigarette. "Good tea," he says giving me that big smile I fell in love with a hundred years ago. I just about melt, all the while telling myself that I'm almost fifty-two years old and to stop that foolishness and besides, he looks like a raggedy man.

"Met up with a fella in Tampa taught me how to graft citrus trees and I'm pretty good at it."

"What about your wife?" I ask. "Didn't you marry some gal from Mango?"

"Nah," he says, looking at the ground. "Didn't never meet the right girl."

"So," Halt says, giving me one of his under-the-eyebrow looks that always make me stop talking. "Let's get back to Orlando. Ain't nothing there but cows."

"Cows and citrus. That's about it."

"So, keep talking," Halt says.

Karl shifts around in his chair. "Well, I worked for a few years planting and grafting, even saved me up some money. Me and this fella, Henry, got us an old house a few miles outta town near Big Sand Lake. We was thinking about putting in a grove of our own when this feller come along with a deal that was gonna make us rich. That's what he said, anyways."

"Yeah?" Halt leans forward in his rocking chair.

"Didn't you ever get married?" I ask.

"Hester!" Halt shouts out. "Ain't you got something to do in the kitchen?"

That makes me real mad, but I don't answer. Just sit there and watch my hands jump around in my lap.

"So," Halt says to Karl. "What kind of deal was you talking about?"

"We was working for this feller name of Quill—had a big old grove out on the Orange Blossom Trail. Wanted to put in a hotel there."

"But ain't nothing around there," Halt says.

"Ain't nothing in town, neither," Karl says, flipping his cigarette butt into the bushes. "But folks go passing through right often and need a place to stay. That's who we was after. Quill figured to build a place where every single room was a teepee."

Halt just looks at him. "A what?" he says.

"A teepee. Like Injuns live in. A wigwam."

"He's gonna set up teepees for people to rent out?"

"He seen where somebody else done it. Thought it was a good idea."

"He must be some kind of fool," Halt says, starting to laugh. "So what's all this got to do with you?" Halt asks.

"Well, Quill needed some money to get going, so I said I'd help him out."

"Money? You had money?"

"Yeah, for a while I did. No more."

"Where'd you get the wigwams? Get the Injuns to come set 'em up for you?" Halt laughs his big old guffaw.

"Well, no. The Injuns in Florida didn't never live in teepees." Halt just stares at him.

"So the Seminoles wasn't no help. They live in chickees."

"Yeah, yeah. I know all about that," Halt says. "I ain't stupid, you know."

"Well, if Quill had made the teepees out of wood like them folks did up in North Florida, it might of worked. But he didn't have the money, so he just used canvas, the kind that was made for army tents, instead."

"Is that so?"

"Yep. I helped him get the place set up, too; we painted 'em white and then I put red zig-zaggy lines all around the sides. That way they went along with the windows, what was cut all catty-whompus, if you see what I mean. Like a square tipped over on its corner."

"That fella, what's his name? Quill? He's a damn fool," Halt says.

"They looked real good, but what with the moldy smell from the canvas, and the heat, and the skeeters, well, we'll just say things didn't work out. Then Henry got all mad 'cause I'd talked him into putting his money into the teepees, too. He lost a lot, but me, I lost everything. After that, I decided to come back to Toad Springs." Karl turns to me. "You got any more tea, Hester?" he says. "That was mighty good."

"Why sure, Karl," I say, untangling my hands from each other and reaching for his glass. "You want to stay for supper?"

"That's right kind of you," Karl says with a big smile. "I'd be much obliged."

"I can make up the bed in the kids' room for you," I says. "You can stay the night."

"Yeah," Halt says. "You gonna hang around for a while?"

"Why, that's right kind of you to ask. Yep, I figured I might like to stay a few days if it wouldn't be putting you out none."

I bring Karl more tea, with my hand shaking so bad I almost spilled it, then start figuring out what I got that I can fix up for supper. Come up with collards and grits and killed a big old chicken I'd been saving for something special.

Turns out Karl cleans up real good and starts looking like I remembered him. He decides to stay with us for a while and gets a job down to Smitty's, sorting nails and hauling fertilizer. He starts helping Halt with them gator bones and before you know it, he come up with some really good ideas for the jewelry. Since he's got the same great-great-great granddaddy as Halt, I guess that's why he's got the same talent. He starts painting real flowers and fancy designs on the bones and in no time flat, they're selling twice as good as Halt's.

At first I'm so nervous about having Karl around that my hands are going like sixty. I get my words all jumbled up and feel like an idiot. But after a week or so I get more used to having him here.

Karl's always us telling funny stories about Henry and the fixes they'd got theirselves into in Orlando, like the time they was gonna steal a hog outta the police constable's backyard on a dare. It was the middle of the night and the constable's daughter was sneaking out her bedroom window to go meet her boyfriend when she seen 'em. Ended up they made a deal that she wouldn't turn 'em in to her daddy if they wouldn't turn her in.

But they lost the bet about the hog. Another time they got to be heroes when they was huntin' rabbits and found this little boy who'd been lost in the woods for two days. They had theirselves some good times, I'm telling you. But once in a while I think I see a little sadness creeping around the corners of Karl's mouth when he's telling his stories.

He's just so sweet and handsome; I dearly love having him around. He's neat as a pin and don't cause no trouble. He don't yell like Halt does, and he likes to cook. He helps me in the kitchen and sometimes even does the dishes in the evenings. Once or twice I seen Halt giving me a funny look when me and Karl was laughing while we're fixing supper, but he never said nothing, just turned around and walked out.

'Course, once the word gets out there's a single man living with us, all the old maids and widows come by to visit, bringing their best apple pies and squash casseroles, just so they can talk to Karl. He's nice and polite, but he don't never ask nobody to go out or nothing. In the back of my mind, WAY in the back of my mind, I wonder to myself if maybe he loves me the way I loved him in high school, and that's why he's staying here.

When I think things like that I get so bumfuzzled I can't think straight; put the salt in the icebox and pour buttermilk in my coffee. That's when I remind myself that Karl didn't even remember my name, and besides I'm a good Christian woman and I'm married to his brother, so nothing's ever gonna happen even if I wanted it to.

But still, I'd think, what if he ever did . . . When I catch myself thinking like that I get up and go clean the kitchen cabinets or sweep off the porch or something to get my sinful mind back on the right track.

One day Karl asks Halt if he can borrow the car and go over to Tampa 'cause he thinks maybe Henry'd moved over there. He says he'll be extra careful 'cause he knows how Halt dotes on that Model T, and he'll be back the next day. Well, turns out he don't come back the next day, or the day after that, and I'm just worried sick.

When we're at supper the third night he's gone, I'm all in a state but Halt ain't one bit worried. He's mad. "That damn Karl," he says. "If anything happens to my car, he's gonna pay for it. I saved for years to . . ."

"Halt," I say, wringing my hands, "I'm just afraid he might be lying somewhere dead in a ditch."

"If he don't bring that car home in one piece, he's gonna end up dead all right," Halt says. "Deader than a Sarasota mackerel."

Turns out that Halt's down at Smitty's when I hear the Model T pull up out front on the fourth day. "Karl," I yell, running out and waving my arms. "Where you been?"

First thing I see is that the front fender on the passenger side of the car is gone and two of the windows are busted out. *Oh no,* I think. *Halt's gonna kill him.* But I don't say nothing. When he opens the door and I can see he's black and blue, one eye swole almost shut and his shirt's got blood on it. "Karl!" I say. "What happened? Are you all right?"

He stands up and leans on the car. "Guess you might could say it was an accident," he says, pointing to the fender.

"Oh Karl," I say. "What happened to *you?* Oh, good Lord, let's take you inside and fix those cuts."

I put my arm around him and help him into the house. When we get inside he sits on the sofa, then breaks down and starts to cry like a little baby, holding his head in his hands. "I'm sorry," he says.

"There, there," I say. "Let me get some bandages. It's gonna be all right." I want to hug him in the worst way, to make it all better, but I settle for a pat on his shoulder.

He don't say nothing, just wipes the tears away.

"Did you find Henry?" I ask.

He looks at me with the eye he can open up. "Yeah, I found him."

"Did he beat you up?"

"Naw."

"Well, who did?"

"Some fellers I didn't know. It was late last night they come after us on the street. Me and Henry wasn't doing nothing, they just beat us up." He sits there and stares at the floor.

I get a clean cloth and a pot of warm soapy water, and wash off his face. Then I unbutton what's left of his shirt so I can wash his chest and back. I ain't never seen him without a shirt before and he's sure got muscles Halt don't have. Karl don't move or talk, just sits there like his mind is somewheres else. He lets me clean him up but he don't help.

It's like wiping bird doo off that statue of a naked man that's sitting on a rock. I put a Band-Aid on Karl's forehead and one down by his chin, and wrap up a place on his left arm. After I'm done I give him a cheese and tomato sandwich and some milk, and he goes to lie down. I tell him I'll call him for supper.

An hour later Halt stomps in the door, ready to tie Karl up and throw him in the swamp. He yells, "The goddamned fender's gone. *It's gone!* And two of the windows been knocked out. Where the hell is he?"

"Shhhh," I says, wringing my hands. "He's sleeping. He got beat up, Halt. Somebody hurt him bad."

"Beat up, huh. I'll beat him up!"

"You care more about that dang jalopy than you do about your own brother," I say. I knew I shouldn't of said it, but it felt good.

He gets up in my face and gives me one of them squinty-eyed looks. "My brother will heal by hisself. My car won't." His face is real red, and he's spitting when he talks. "He's been gone four days! Where the hell has he been?"

"Tampa, I think. I'm worried about him, Halt. Think he's mixed up with the Mafia or something?"

He looks at me and makes a noise like a hissing cat. "The Mafia? What in God's name you talking about? The Mafia."

"Well, somebody beat him up. They could of killed him."

"Go get him."

"Please, Halt. He couldn't hardly walk. Let him sleep a while."

"You listen to me, woman," he says, shaking a finger in my face. "He's *my* brother and he's living under *my* roof. He's got no right to run off with *my* car for four days and wreck it."

I do what he says, then come back and sit in the overstuffed chair and touch my fingers to my thumb one at a time while he paces up and down. After a few minutes Karl comes hobbling out, hanging his head. He's a pitiful sight. He glances up at Halt and then sits down at the far end of the sofa. "I'm sorry, Halt. I didn't mean to have nothing happen to your car."

"Well, something did happen! Now you're gonna tell me what it was."

Karl looks out the window. "I don't rightly know," he says. "It was parked along the street and when I come out this morning it was like that."

"You saying you wasn't even in the car when it got hit?"

"That's what I'm saying."

"You're lying," Halt says, walking around to stand in front of Karl. "If somebody'd hit the car while it was just parked alongside the road, the other fender would be crunched in."

Karl shakes his head, then looks up from the sofa. "It might look that way, but I swear, Halt, I just parked it on the street and when I come back it looked like that. I'll pay to get it fixed," he says. "It'll take a while but I'll do it."

"You ain't got a pot to piss in or a window to throw it out," Halt says. "How the hell you gonna pay me?"

Karl looks down at the floor. "I know, I know. But I'll come up with something, I promise."

"What did the police say when you told 'em about the car?" Halt says, leaning back.

Karl looks over at me, then down to the floor. "I didn't."

"What? What are you saying, man? You didn't tell nobody?"

Karl looks up at Halt, then down to his shoes. "No, damn it all, I didn't."

"Why in hell not?"

"It wouldn't do no good, that's why not."

"Well, I'm taking it up with Constable Grogan. We'll just see what he has to say about it."

Karl looks worried. "Halt, you don't need to do that. He don't have nothing to do with what goes on in Tampa. They ain't never gonna find out who done it."

By now, Halt looks like he's gonna blow up. "Don't you tell me what to do, you . . . you . . . I'll do whatever I damn well please."

Karl don't answer but gets up real slow, like it hurts him, then heads back into the bedroom and closes the door. I go in the kitchen and don't talk to Halt for a week.

Halt's so mad I'm afraid he's gonna kick Karl out of the house but when Karl starts giving him money for the car, the air clears up a little. If Halt ever called the law, he never said nothing about it. When the car finally gets fixed, Halt swears ain't nobody ever driving it again but him.

Having Karl living with us was a blessing from the Lord, I have to say. He's always telling stories that can get me to laughing even when I'm in a bad mood. And I ain't never seen the likes of the way he can cook. Halt don't even know where I keep the coffee cups, but Karl, my, oh my.

I have to admit that sometimes I stand a little closer to him than I have to, maybe touching elbows while we're both at the kitchen counter fixing supper, or I'll reach over and accidentally touch his hand while we're working on the bone jewelry. I can't believe myself that I got the nerve to do it. But he don't never seem to notice.

Sometimes he's got this far-away look in his eye, like he's wishing he was somewheres else. More than a few times I've asked him, "What you thinking, Karl? A penny for your thoughts," but he just gives me a blank look and gets back to what he's supposed to be doing. A few times I've seen tears in his eyes, and once or twice I thought I heard him crying at night, but I can't ask him about that.

For almost a year nothing much changes; we keep selling the bones at Stroudamore's, Karl keeps working at Smitty's and painting jewelry and he finally pays Halt back all the money. It helps that Smitty give Karl a raise after he painted the whole place and put up a fancy new sign out front.

Finally, Karl gives in and starts going out with some of the ladies. They'll have him over for Sunday dinner after church or take him on picnics down by the lake. They all talk about how handsome and sweet he is and what a good husband he'd make, but I'm glad when he don't take an interest in none of 'em.

One Sunday afternoon when Halt and Karl went off fishing somewheres, this man shows up at the house. He's about my age, I guess, all spiffed up in a suit and tie, neat as a pin with a couple of fancy rings on his fingers. He takes off his hat when I answer the door, and says, "Good afternoon, ma'am. I'm looking for Karl Brisco."

"Oh, he's off fishing for bream with my husband," I say. "They'll be home about in an hour or so, I reckon." He looks nice enough, but I'm thinking, why's a fancy feller like this looking for Karl? He just stands there, staring at me. "You got business with him?" I say.

"Oh no. I'm just an old friend passing through."

"Want to wait for him on the front porch?" I say. "I can fix you some sweet tea."

"Yes, ma'am," he says. "That would be very kind of you."

"You just have a seat and I'll be right back," I say. After fixing the tea I go back to the porch, hand him his glass, and sit down in one of the rockers. "So," I say. "Where you know Karl from?"

"Oh, we go way back," he says. "I met him when we were both working at a restaurant in Tampa twenty-five, maybe thirty years ago."

"That must have been when he first left here."

He looks over at me and grins. "Yes, ma'am. That would be right."

"Don't believe I caught your name," I say. "I'm Hester Brisco. I'm married to Karl's brother, Halt."

"Henry Keith here," he says. "I thought you must be Halt's wife. Heard a lot about him."

"You know Halt?"

"No, ma'am, but Karl talked about him a lot through the years, thinks the world of him. He told me when they were kids he took good care of Halt. When their parents died in that awful accident and all. Raised Halt up himself, just those two kids alone against the world."

I think I'm hearing things. "You must of got mixed up with somebody else. Karl never raised Halt. Their mama and daddy didn't die 'til five or six years ago. And then it was from old age."

The man looks surprised. "Are you sure?" he says.

"Sure, I'm sure. I went to the funerals over in Zolfo Springs, myself. They moved here when the boys was teenagers, and Karl run off when he was fifteen or sixteen. When their mama and daddy went back to Zolfo Springs, Halt stayed here and married me."

Now the feller really looks confused. "Well, that's odd," he said. "At first he told everybody he didn't have a relative in the world. Not a one. Then after I'd known him for ten or twelve years, he said he had a brother, but it took another five years before he told me Halt's name."

Then it dawns on me. "Oh! You must be the Henry that's his best friend."

A big smile shows up on his face. "That's right."

"He's talked about you a lot."

He shakes his head a little and looks out at the yard. "That's right, we were best friends."

I'll never forget the look on Karl's face when him and Halt pulled up out front and he seen Henry talking to me. He jumped out of the car and come running up and they give each other a big old bear hug. They was laughing and carrying on the rest of the night—must have been close to eleven when me and Halt went off to bed and left them two sitting there.

Henry stayed a few days and slept on the sofa. Every afternoon them two would go off fishing or walking in the woods. When he went back to Tampa Karl was real sad and every night he'd have a few drinks of whiskey. Hadn't never done that before. Seemed to me it just made him sadder, but he tried to act like everything was fine.

Still, I could tell he wasn't all right by the way he'd get that funny look in his eye, staring off into space like he done when he first come here. Broke my heart and I tried to cheer him up, bringing him tea when he was listening to the radio after supper, telling him he didn't need to wash the dishes and he could go out on the front porch with Halt. Sometimes he did just that.

Then he started taking long walks every night and sometimes I'd be in bed asleep before he got home. Every once in a while I asked him how he was doing, and he always said he was fine, just tired, that's all. But I knew better.

One night when Halt was over to the church for a deacon's meeting, I went out on the front porch and Karl was sitting on the swing. It was one of them cool, dark evenings and you could smell the jasmine everywhere. When Karl seen me, he wiped his cheeks real quick like he'd been crying.

Instead of sitting in my old rocker, I sat down right beside him. I swear I didn't plan to do it, but without saying one word I reached over and hugged him. He started crying again and I held him tight, like I'd wanted to do since the first time I ever laid eyes on him. "Just go ahead," I said. "Let it all out." And he did. Finally he sat up and blew his nose real good on a handkerchief. "Feel better?" I said.

He don't answer.

"What's the matter?" I ask. "Why are you so sad?"

"I . . . I can't tell you."

"You'll feel better if you talk about it," I say. "Talking's almost as good as crying to let all that sadness out."

He's quiet for a minute, staring straight ahead. Finally he clears his throat and says, "I love somebody I can't be with."

That surprised me now, I have to say. "Love somebody? Who?"

He looks into my eyes and says, "I can't tell you."

"Yes, you can, silly," I say. "'Course you can tell me."

"No. I can't. It's wrong."

"How can loving somebody be wrong?" I say. "Why the Lord tells us to love one another as—"

"It ain't that kind of love."

"What kind of love is it, then?" I say, feeling my hands start to twitch.

"The kind that's wrong." He stands up and faces me. "I ain't gonna tell you who it is, and that's that." His face is all screwed up and tears are coming down his cheeks.

Oh, my dear God in heaven, I think. *He's talking about me.* Then, out of nowhere, I feel real calm. I stand up and hug him again. I can't believe I'm doing this. It's like I'm watching somebody else moving around in my body. He hugs me back and lays his cheek on the top of my head. "You can tell me anything," I say. "I won't think no less of you."

He don't answer. All I hear is crickets chirping.

I lean back and look up at him. "Does this person love you, too?" I ask.

"I'm not sure. I . . . I . . . thought so. But now I don't know."

I pull away and look at him. "Why don't you ask?"

He shakes his head. "I can't. I just can't."

"But if the somebody cares about you, and neither one of you ever says it . . . I mean . . . it would be such a shame . . ."

"I know. I know. But it's wrong. I'm afraid . . ." He takes a step back, then stops.

"Is it one of the church ladies?"

He laughs. "No, most definitely not. I ain't interested in none of the ladies, that's for sure."

Now my heart's beating so fast I feel like I'm gonna faint. "I think I might know who it is," I say, almost in a whisper.

"What?" He sounds nervous. "I don't think so."

I try to talk but can't get any words out.

"I'll get over it," he says.

"Just tell me this now; do they have brown hair?"

"Kind of, I guess."

"And hazel eyes?"

He looks surprised and nods.

"And do they like to cook the way you do?"

"I ain't talking about this no more, Hester. I ain't never gonna tell you. Even if you guessed I wouldn't tell you."

It's like I'm outside myself, watching as I put my hands to his cheeks, pull his face down to mine, and kiss him on the lips.

He jumps back real quick, surprised. "Hester, what are you doing?" he says.

"I'm sorry," I say. "I know it's wrong. But . . . but . . ."

He wipes his mouth and sits down on the swing. He don't say a word.

I am mortified. Worse than when I threw up all over Miss Grimly—way past what I ever thought a person could feel. I think I'm gonna faint. I lose my balance and sit down hard on the swing. I got no idea what to say. "Karl, I'm sorry. I know I shouldn't of . . . It was wrong . . ."

He just sits there. "I'm sorry Hester. I mean . . . I didn't mean . . . I just . . ."

Tears come into my eyes. "It ain't me you was talking about, is it?"

He looks up at me. "Hester . . ."

I stand up and I'm so dizzy I'm seeing stars before I get into the bedroom. I fall on my bed, sobbing my heart out. How could I be so stupid? I'm an ugly fifty-one-year-old woman. 'Course it wasn't me he was talking about.

When I hear Halt pull into the driveway, I make my way to the bathroom and turn on the water so he'll think I'm taking a bath. Soon as I can I get right into bed. How can I ever face Karl again? I made a damn fool of myself. And I'm married to his brother. God'll never forgive me for this. I'm going to hell for sure now.

The next morning at breakfast my hands are shaking and I burn the bacon and knock over a whole pitcher of orange juice. I can't even look at Karl. He eats in about two minutes and says he's gonna walk down to Smitty's. I work up all my nerve and look at him but he just shrugs his shoulders and leaves.

I feel light-headed and can't eat a bite all day. And my hands don't ever stop twitching. Supper that night is even worse. I'm a wreck. My eyes are red from crying, but of course Halt don't notice. Karl gives me a couple of sad looks while we're eating and comes over to give me a hug while I'm washing dishes, but I pull away from him and he leaves the kitchen. I don't ever want to see Karl again as long as I live and I can't believe I've humiliated myself so bad. Besides that, now I'm going to hell for sure.

Then I start wondering who Karl was talking about. Who does he love? If it ain't none of the ladies around here, it must be somebody in Tampa. Maybe somebody him and Henry knew way back and seeing Henry made him remember.

Within the week, Karl moves to Tampa. By that time he'd saved up enough money to rent his own place. He bought a nice new tablecloth and three mixing bowls for me as a thank-you present but I can't use 'em 'cause they just make me think of him. In one way I didn't want him to go, but after that awful night every time I laid eyes on him I wanted to die.

I kept on helping Halt with the jewelry, trying to paint the same pictures on the bones that Karl did, but it always made me start thinking about him so I just started putting little *x*'s on everything. For a long time I wondered about why he told Henry that story about his folks dying young and him having to raise Halt. My best guess is that either he didn't want nobody to be able to find him, or he's ashamed of us. Reckon I'll never know.

Oddest thing is, after all that I don't have to wring my hands so much. Except when Sorrey May's around. It's like the worst thing in the world already happened to me and I ain't got nothing to be nervous about no more.

We still get a Christmas card from Karl every year and it always says he's doing fine and he loves us, but he ain't never come back. I been over to Tampa a few times and I always looked around, but never seen no sign of him.

I just keep hoping that the day will come again when Halt and me'll be sitting on the front porch sorting gator bones and a raggedy stranger will turn up at the bottom of the steps and say, "Hello there, Halt."

Christmas with the Unschooled Masses
by Gladys Heppner

As the second person ever to teach school in Toad Springs—but the first competent teacher—I have learned that trying to help people who don't really want it is an uphill battle. I studied education at Ohio University for over a year, so I knew I was qualified to teach in a small town, even if it wasn't my first choice of a place to live. My husband, Orin, had made an unwise investment and purchased property in the area, which is the only reason we moved here.

One thing I learned at the university is that the illiterate will forever be the unwashed of our world, and I made it my goal in life to raise the standards in this community. I don't believe that the people here had ever even heard that they should be saying "aren't" instead of "ain't" or "children" instead of "young'uns." In all the years I've lived in this town I've done my best to get down to the level of its citizens, but they've never accepted me.

The first teacher here was Carrie June Neal, whose teaching skills were quite limited, but then she only completed the eighth grade. And the fact that her own grammar was appalling didn't help. Even worse, she allowed the children to call her by her Christian name, "Miz Carrie June," if you can imagine. I insisted they call me Mrs. Heppner. Respect is what those hooligans needed to learn. Except for Worthy Perkins, of course. He was my shining star, my only success. Smart young man, Worthy. And I'm proud to say I taught him everything he knew.

But, as I was saying, Carrie June had started teaching in 1914 in a one-room school that we divided in half when I came here in 1918. The wall they put up to separate us didn't keep the sound out, and I was always having to go over to Carrie June's side and tell her to control her children and lower her voice. Not that it did any good.

I prepared my lesson plans every week as I'd been taught in college but it was still quite discouraging. Most of the children were far behind their grade level because they hadn't been taught properly. I had to keep reminding myself that my goal was to change the lives of these poor youngsters and give them a chance to succeed in this world, but at home their parents complained that they were "sounding uppity." There were many times I was ready to give up.

On bad days, when my back was turned the girls would start whispering and the boys would throw spit balls and paper airplanes until I was ready to cry. Sometimes I actually got tears in my eyes and that made everything worse. I usually pretended that I had hay fever and wiped my nose with my hankie, but I don't think I fooled them.

One thing I did right, though. I always graded their papers hard—didn't give them any leeway. Tears and pleading made no difference to me. Right is right and wrong is wrong. By being strict on that account, I knew the ones who passed the tests had actually learned something. Worthy Perkins, the brightest child I ever taught, made a perfect score on almost every test I gave him. Brilliant young man.

I was reared in a very strict home by educated parents and I had no choice but to study hard. When I didn't live up to my father's expectations, he'd stopped talking to me to demonstrate his disappointment in my performance. I believe that to this day, his response is what caused me to become exceedingly upset when I'm unable to complete a task to perfection. Why, when I had to take a test in school, I'd be so terrified I thought I might be having a heart attack. When I took my last final exam in college, I fainted dead away, but not until I'd answered the last question.

I taught school here for over twenty years and had high standards for my students, as my father did for me. In the end, most of them benefited from my rigorous approach.

Orin died a few years after I retired, and I was absolutely lost. I was so distraught that for months I could hardly leave the house. And when I started feeling better I realized that I was absolutely alone. My sons, Russell and Michael, were grown, with families of their own and I seldom saw them. I'd lived in this town for twenty years and knew everyone, but had no real friends to speak of. Of course, that was because I was more selective in choosing my friends than most.

I'd attended church regularly but the few attempts I'd made to participate in group activities were unsuccessful. Without question, I was an outsider. But I knew the time had come for me to force myself to become more active. When I heard they were asking for help decorating the Town Hall for the Christmas party, I decided I'd volunteer, even though I wasn't at all sure they'd want me. I'd seen some pretty little manger scenes once when I was on a shopping trip to Tampa the year before, and in the back of my mind I'd been thinking we could make a few like them and place them around the hall. I'd be doing some good for the town.

The committee met at the Church of Everlasting Liability and those attending were: Ree Perkins and her best friend, Sorrey May Only (who was, unfortunately, my next-door neighbor who carried a vendetta against me), Hester Brisco, and me. When we sat down at the table Sorrey May put herself in charge, of course. "All right, y'all," she said, "this year we're gonna go with the theme of angels."

"Excuse me," I said, speaking in spite of my nervousness, "unless I'm mistaken, the theme last year was angels."

Ree said, "What you got in mind, Gladys?"

"Crèches. You know, manger scenes, with Jesus and Mary and Joseph. We could make up three or four small ones and arrange them in different spots around the Town Hall. I saw some beautiful ones last year when . . ."

Hester Brisco started snapping her pocketbook open and shut like she does when she's nervous, which seems like all the time, and Sorrey May said, "Hester?"

"Well, I, um," Hester said, "if we want to do a manger scene, we shouldn't have but the one. After all, there wasn't but one baby Jesus now, was there."

"Well, of course," I said. "We all know there was just one real Jesus, but if we have different crèches scattered around the hall, then everyone can see the different interpretations."

"I don't know," Ree said. "I mean, the Town Hall ain't got much room since Hank put the library in there. Besides that, making all them little manger scenes would be a lot of work. I guess I could see having one maybe, but I don't think we need . . ."

I felt like I was back in the schoolhouse with disagreeable children again, which was almost more than I could bear. They were going to turn against me like everyone always did. Even as a child I was left out. "I knew I shouldn't have come," I said. "You never listen to me."

"I swan, Gladys," Sorrey May said, rolling her eyes. "Just 'cause we don't agree with you on one little idea . . ."

I pulled out my hankie and started dabbing my eyes. I was embarrassed to be crying but I couldn't help it. "You've never agreed with me on one thing. Why, I saw some manger scenes over in Tampa that were just darling and I'm sure we could make some like them. Improve the quality of the décor. Have something people will really want to look at for a change. Try something different."

"Well, you go right on ahead and do what you want," Sorrey May said. "We ain't stopping you. And maybe we might could use 'em next year."

"If that's too much, maybe we could just have two manger scenes," Hester said, "Maybe one up front and one in the back."

Sorrey May cleared her throat. "Well, I still think the angels are the right way to go. We could make a couple of life-sized ones, maybe out of cardboard, and have 'em standing by the front door to welcome folks when they come in. What you think, Hester?"

"Well, um, I don't rightly know."

"Seems like we ought to be able to decide on this like grown-ups," Sorrey May said. "We shouldn't always have to take a vote on everything."

"Well," Hester said, "I got a idea. How's about we just have a Christmas tree. Just one, and it's outside the building and everybody can bring something from home to hang on it."

I spoke up, louder than before. "Everyone already has a Christmas tree at home with their own ornaments on it. We need something modern, more sophisticated. Something we don't see every day."

"Well, the angels would solve that problem, wouldn't they?" said Sorrey May.

Hester took a deep breath, and touching her fingers to her thumbs one at a time said, "If Gladys don't feel good about the angels, maybe we ought to come up with something we all like."

Sorrey May said, "Gladys ain't *never* gonna like nothing but her own idea. We got to decide what's best for us all and not let one little naysayer tell the rest of us what we're gonna do."

Ree cleared her throat, then said, "Well now, maybe we should all think about it for a week and see what we can come up with."

Sorrey May raised her voice. "Ain't no point in putting it off, is what I'm telling you. Next time we'll just have the same thing all over again. Gladys don't never go along with nothing but her own idea. Never has. Never will."

"Now, now, Sorrey May," I said, trying to contain myself. There's no need to be ugly."

"Ugly? You saying I'm ugly?"

"Frankly, you're being pigheaded," I said.

"I ain't pigheaded, Gladys. If anybody's pigheaded, it's you."

Hester snapped her pocketbook open and closed one last time, then stood up. "Well, um, well . . . um, I got to go."

Ree stood up, too. "Don't leave, Hester. We gonna get this all straightened out. Come on now."

Hester held on tight to her pocketbook. She didn't sit back down but she didn't leave, either. She just stood there.

"Maybe we ought'a take a breather, here," Ree said. "Let things calm down some. Sorrey May, why don't you go fix us all some coffee?"

"That's a good idea, Sorrey May," I said, smiling and folding my hands in my lap.

Sorrey May stared at everybody for a minute. We all know she can't stand being told what to do, but finally she said all right and headed for the door.

"Well," Ree said. "Come on, Hester, and sit back down. Let's talk about Gladys's idea."

I took a piece of paper and sketched out a simple but elegant plan for a large crèche to put by the front door, and they loved it. It took only a few minutes for us to decide that Sorrey May could make one of her cardboard angels to put in the back of the hall.

Then Hester started telling a story about the time she fixed beef tongue for supper one night, which Halt had always said he'd never eat, and how he couldn't tell the difference until he found one little piece of the skin that she hadn't cut off. Then he jerked back from the table so fast that he fell over backward in his chair.

We were all laughing uproariously when Sorrey May came back in. She walked over with a sour look and put a tray with a coffeepot and four cups down on the table between Ree and me. "Ain't got no sugar or cream."

"That's all right," Ree said. "Sit down and let's have some coffee."

Sorrey May kept standing.

Ree said, "While you was gone we done some talking and we're thinking we'll have a big manger scene right up in the front of the Town Hall and one of your big angels in back. Gladys says she'll do the manger scene all by her ownself unless somebody wants to pitch in. And, Sorrey May, I'll help you with the angel if you want."

"Well," Sorrey May said, crossing her arms, "I have to tell you I don't like this one damn bit, all this stuff getting decided while

I'm just being nice enough to go get everybody some coffee. Nobody said you was gonna go on meeting without me."

"Oh my. We're just trying to get things organized, Sorrey May," Ree said. "Didn't mean no disrespect, honey. Come on and sit down."

"Well," Sorrey May said, still standing. "I was planning on making three angels and I was hoping we could all do the angels together, teamwork you know. Working together for Jesus."

"There won't be but one angel," I said. "And it doesn't look as if we'll be working together for anything. In fact, it seems to me that we need to work away from each other. Maybe in different towns." I laughed a little. "Of course that's not really in the Christmas spirit, is it? With love for all and charity for some, or however that goes."

"Well, Gladys," Sorrey May said, "I'm perfectly happy to work with you in the spirit of Christmas. Even though you're the reason I'm a widow today, you and your nasty temper."

"Oh please," I said, rolling my eyes. "Don't start up with that tired old tale of woe. Everybody knows that Lucas had a weak heart. I didn't do anything."

"Then why'd he die over at your house? Just went over there to talk to you real nice about Dirty Sally and you—"

"Ladies, ladies," Ree said, standing up. "That's enough. Sorrey May, please sit down and relax."

Sorrey May raised her voice. "Ree, you can't talk to me like that, even if you are my best friend." Then she turned and looked at me. "It's when you're around, Gladys, that all the trouble starts," she said. "Only when you're around."

I was so angry I was shaking, but I stood up and pointed my finger at her. "That depends entirely on how you look at it," I said. "Actually, it seems to me that you're the one starting it."

"Just settle down, ladies," Ree said. "Let's all sit down and have us some coffee."

I sat down but Sorrey May didn't. Instead she took a deep breath and picked up the coffeepot but her hand was shaking so badly that she almost spilled it. She put the pot down and took another deep breath.

"Here, let me," I said, reaching out. "I'll pour it."

Sorrey May grabbed the handle and jerked the coffeepot toward her. "I don't need no help."

"Be careful, Sorrey May," Ree said. "You don't want to spill it."

Sorrey May squinted her eyes at Ree, took another deep breath, and lifted the pot again. Her hand was still shaking, and as she went to put it back down on the table she tipped it over into my lap. On purpose! Spilled scalding coffee all over me!

I shrieked and jumped up, pulling my skirt away from my legs. I was in agony. I couldn't stop screaming. Ree and Hester came to me immediately, calling to each other about what to do, but the pain was so hideous that I fell back into the chair—and then my skirt stuck to my legs again. "Owwww," I screamed. "My legs!" Hester pulled my skirt up again and that was so excruciating that I thought I'd pass out right on the floor. "I'm scalded! I'm burned!"

In spite of the suffering, I clearly remember that Sorrey May had calmly put the coffeepot down and was just standing there watching when Pastor Blander came running in from his office. "What's going on in here?" he said.

"Don't look! Turn around!" I yelled at him. Pastor couldn't see my legs! That would be indecent! Especially the way they were looking then.

He turned his back and said to nobody in particular, "What happened?"

Hester and Ree were hovering around me and nobody answered him.

"Tell me! What happened?" he called out to the wall.

"It was just a little accident," Sorrey May said. "Just spilled a few drops of coffee, that's all."

When I heard that, I let out another wail.

"Sounds like it's pretty bad," he said. "Sorrey May, come over here and tell me what happened."

"Ain't you never spilled a little coffee on yourself?" she said walking his way. "It's nothing big. Some people just like to make a mountain out of a molehill."

When I heard her say that, it was the last straw. "Look what you did to me, Sorrey May! I'm burned down to the bone! Oh, the pain! You're not even sorry!" I sobbed.

"Can I turn around now?" Pastor Blander called over his shoulder.

"Butter!" Ree said. "We need to put some butter on it. Got any butter around here, Sorrey May?"

"'Course not," she said, sounding like she was bored. "Why would we have butter at the church?"

"Butter's not good enough." I said. "I need to go to Bartow. I have to see the doctor."

"Ladies!" Pastor Blander hollered. "For the love of God! Can I turn around?"

"It's going to get infected!" I said. "We have to clean the wound! But dear Lord, I won't be able to stand the pain."

"Wait 'til I get her dress back down," Hester called over to Pastor Blander as she started lowering my skirt. "There, can you . . ."

"No! No!" I screamed. "That's twice as bad! Take it off! Hold it up!"

"I think it's gonna be all right, honey," Ree said. "Just need to put some butter on it."

"No! Stop!" I yelled. "The pain is unbelievable. I have to see a doctor."

"But, Gladys, don't you think you ought to wait a day and see . . ."

"Ladies!" Pastor Blander yelled.

"You've never been scalded like this," I said to Ree. "I'm going to the doctor."

"Okay, okay, I'll take you," Ree said. "I've got the truck. Let me clear off the seat for you. Be right back."

As she turned to go, Hester called out, "Pastor, I'm standing between you and Gladys's lap, now. You can turn around, but don't come to where you can see anything."

As he moved toward me, I peeked around Hester and saw that he was holding his hand up, blocking his view of my lap.

He said, "What happened?"

I pointed at Sorrey May. "That woman poured scalding coffee on me! On purpose!" I cried. "Just because she didn't like the idea I had for decorating the Town Hall. This was no accident! She did this on purpose!"

He looked at Sorrey May and she said, "Why I did no such thing! How could you even think that? And besides, it was just a few drops."

"Every person in this town knows you hate me," I said. "They've all heard you say a hundred times that I killed Lucas."

"Now, now, ladies," Pastor Blander said, "let's try to stay calm."

"You wouldn't be calm if you were burned all over half your body. The pain is excruciating."

Sorrey May rolled her eyes and said, "Come on now; it wasn't but a few drops."

I leaned around so Pastor Blander could see me and shook my finger at Sorrey May. "So, you just tell me this. If you didn't do it on purpose, why didn't you help me? When I was screaming in agony! You did not lift one finger. Not one little finger."

"I knew you'd turn all this against me, that's why not. Don't matter what I do, you turn it against me. It was an accident, Gladys. A pure-D accident. Just like them raisin muffins was a accident. I'd never hurt nobody on purpose. Not in a million years."

About that time Ree come back in and she and Hester took me outside. I tried not to yell but the pain was too much. As we left, I heard Pastor Blander say, "Sorrey May, I want to talk to you."

The doctor said three spots on my legs were second degree burns and might leave scars, which would have greatly pleased Sorrey May, if it had happened. He gave me some ointment and said I should keep the wound clean at all times. He thought I'd be fine. When I asked him what was the worst thing that could have come of this, he said a bad infection could kill me. Sorrey May would have loved that, I'm sure. This was her way of trying to get me back for something I never did, and I wasn't going to forget it.

For several days some of the church ladies brought me food, but they didn't seem to understand how seriously I was hurt, so after that I had to make do for myself. Russell and Michael came and checked on me, but to tell you the truth, they didn't seem to appreciate what their dear mother had been going through, either.

I was gratified to learn that Pastor Blander fired Sorrey May right after that. She deserved it, certainly, after all the gossiping she's done about everybody in town. Later on Childe Stroudamore hired her over to work in the Gator Ranch Gift Shop, but at least over there she couldn't have her nose in everyone's personal business.

And as much as I hated it, I was still in too much pain to make the crèches so Sorrey May ended up getting her way with having angels for the Christmas party. They were really tacky, I must say. She attached about twenty little tiny gators to the angel wings to advertise the Gator Ranch, which had nothing to do with Christmas at all. I suppose that's the kind of behavior you have to expect from people like her.

And I'm sure our Lord and Savior didn't appreciate it, either.

Sitting Down on the Job
by Polly Thinly

Me, I only had two jobs in my whole life and I had to quit the one I liked best 'cause somebody lied about me for no reason. Why, I was as happy as a clam at high tide when I found out they was gonna let me be the first postmaster for Toad Springs. That's a real important job, working for the United States government, and having the American flag hanging out front proves it.

Used to be, the Post Office was in the back left corner of Smitty's Hardware and Feed Store between the galvanized washtubs and sacks of Purina Horse Chow, and I loved working there. Got to talk to folks who come in to buy everything from bug killer to the pickled eggs Smitty always kept on the counter. And all's I had to do was figure out how much to charge, make change, and put all the mail in alphabetical order—which ain't near so easy as it sounds. Why, some folks have awful handwriting.

When I'd been there a few months, snooty old Gladys Heppner started saying somebody'd opened up her mail before she got it. Said she had some real important private confidential information from her cousin in Ohio that wasn't nobody else's business and she could tell her letters was being steamed open, then glued back shut. Now she's just a plain old schoolteacher and I don't know what big important things she could have going on. I knew what letters she was talking about 'cause they come in these great big envelopes.

But I never tried to open 'em. Why, for crying out loud, I'd never do such a thing. It's against a United States law. I ain't stupid. But Gladys kept carrying on, raising all kinds of sand, saying she's gonna report me to the big Federal Government Office in Tampa. And while she was at it, she must of told every person in town what she thought I was doing and after a while folks start squinting their eyes at me when they come in to get their mail and all of a sudden they don't have time to stop and talk.

Now, I think I know where she got the idea I might do something like that 'cause I'd always read everybody's penny postcards while I was sorting everything. And there ain't nothing illegal about that. When folks come to pick up their mail, I'd say, "I see Aunt Sally's gonna have another operation," or "Looks like Uncle Dave is having fun in New Mexico," or something like that there.

Sometimes they'd look at me funny like I shouldn't be knowing their private business, but I never meant no harm. And it ain't against the law. Why, if something's such a big secret, don't put it on a penny postcard for all the world to see, is what I say.

Before long seemed like everybody in town had their own opinion about me. Finally Gladys and her big mouth made enough people feel like I was doing something illegal that it took every bit of fun out of the job. So I just up and quit. Even though I never done nothing wrong.

One good thing come of working there, though, 'cause that's where Mort started courting me—he worked at Smitty's in the mornings. He could find you anything you wanted in that store, from a post-hole digger to a screw that'll fit an old kerosene lantern from a hundred years ago, but he couldn't never tell you what to do with none of it. He's got his good points but that man couldn't fix a broken promise.

Long time ago I'd decided that if I wasn't married by the time I was twenty-eight I'd marry anybody who'd have me. And I wasn't, so I did. Mort tends toward the heavy side, he's not skinny like me, and he don't have too much energy. His nose is a little bit too long, but he's got a real sweet smile. Now, I knew even back then that he wasn't the smartest feller you'd ever want to meet, and he wasn't never too wild about working a lot—said the kind of job he wanted was one where you could sit down all day and never break a sweat. But I liked that his granddaddy had left him some property with a little house on it, free and clear. And besides that, there wasn't nobody else left to marry.

After me and Mort was settled down we found out we was gonna need more money—I was back to taking in wash by then and Mort was just working part-time like I said. He figured we could grow us some citrus to sell so he took the seeds from some oranges he borrowed from Ollie Trydell's grove down the road, and planted 'em. He said he put fifty-seven seeds in the ground but only eight grew into trees.

Landis Perkins, who had the best groves in the state, told Mort he needed to start 'em out in pots and graft 'em unless he wanted sour oranges but Mort said he figured God knew more about growing trees than Landis Perkins, and he was gonna do it his way. Three or four years later, when we finally got some oranges, they was as sour as the inside of a kumquat and puny to boot.

'Til the trees got big enough to bear fruit, Mort decided to raise chickens—thought all's he'd have to do was toss out some feed and pick up the eggs, and maybe wring a few necks once in a while when somebody wanted a baking chicken.

First thing he buys some little chicks real cheap from old Eustis Trydell up the road. He's Ollie Trydell's big brother. Eustis tells him how to build a fence with chicken wire but Mort figures he can just use scrap wood he can get for free. Turns out he ain't the best fence-builder in the world and all the chickens get out and wander around in the yard 'til the raccoons eat every one. Don't take long, neither.

Then he gets the idea to set him up a whiskey still out in the woods by the cypress swamp; this was back when we still had Prohibition. I'm surprised he can get the thing working, but when he does he's so busy running it he don't care about nothing else.

I'd lie awake nights worrying about him getting caught 'til finally somebody reported him to the law. Mort said when he seen the feller coming through the swamp wearing a badge, he staggered backward, fell down on the ground, and grabbed his chest, like he was having a heart attack. When the guy don't seem to care, Mort jerks around and rolls his eyes up in his head for a while, like he's having a fit but the feller just stands there, watching. When Mort's all done the feller pulls him up and hauls him off to the hoosegow where Holy Rollin' Grogan meets him with a great big smile and a long sermon.

Now, not long before that, Constable Grogan had got born again and for a while there he was trying to save everybody he talked to. So, for hours every day he preached to anybody who was in the jail, most times it was just Mort. After Mort was back home he said he might could of felt bad about what he'd done, but after listening to Holy Rollin' for two whole weeks he decided that was punishment enough, so he don't bother. Anyways, that was the end of his whiskey-making days.

Now, this'll sound funny, but the one thing Mort was really good at was knitting. His mama'd showed him how when he was nine years old and caught the chicken pox and had to stay in bed for a week. He didn't tell me that 'til I found some yarn and knitting needles hid way in the back of the closet. Said he'd been knitting in secret 'cause it calmed his nerves but he didn't want nobody to know.

'Course after I found out, he started knitting right out in the open; why, he made sweater vests and afghans and cute little toy toads, all kinds of stuff that I give for birthdays and weddings and baby showers and such. He'd learned all the different stitches, could do the cable and the basket weave, and even did some sweaters with a big old toad jumping off a lily pad that said Toad Springs underneath. Everybody figured I was the one making everything so I just didn't tell 'em any different. Got myself a good reputation, I did.

Every day, when Mort come home from working at Smitty's, he'd eat lunch, then turn on his radio, get some whiskey—from his stash that the law hadn't found—and go knit on the screened-in porch. That way he can see the lake but at the same time he can see if anybody's coming along so he can toss the yarn down and pretend it's mine. He makes me swear on my mama's head that I'll never, ever tell nobody that he can knit, not that swearing meant anything 'cause my mama was a mean-hearted woman and I hadn't had nothing to do with her in years. Swearing on her head didn't mean diddley-squat.

One Sunday at church Childe Stroudamore said she'd seen one of the vests I'd made and she thought she might could sell some over to the gift shop at the Gator Ranch. Said she'd pay me half of what she sold 'em for. So that's just what I done. Behind Mort's back. Have to say it's the only good thing my mama ever taught me—that a woman needs some money put aside that her husband don't know nothing about, 'cause you can't never tell what's hunkered down, waiting for you just around the corner.

I started asking Mort to knit sweater vests and a few long-sleeved sweaters for my cousins up in Carolina, who he'd never heard of, but he done it without too much fuss. I hid the money in the family Bible, where Mort would for sure never run into it. Had me fourteen dollars in there.

Everything would of worked out just fine if I hadn't dragged Mort over to the Church of Everlasting Liability early one Wednesday evening where they was having a potluck supper to raise money to fix the roof again. Don't seem to matter how many times we pay to get that roof patched up, the damn thing just keeps on leaking.

We had a good turnout, must of been thirty people and there was lots of food. Hank Plenty brought folding tables and chairs so there was plenty of spots for everybody to sit outside. The place smelled like barbequed pork and hot apple pies and everybody was laughing and scratching. Me and Mort was eating Carrie June's fried chicken when Childe Stroudamore come over.

"Hello there, Polly, Mort, how y'all doing?" she says.

Mort keeps on eating, but I look up and give her a nervous smile. "Fine. Just fine."

"That knitting of yours is selling like hotcakes out at the Gator Ranch," Childe says to me. "I'll have the money ready for you on Tuesday and I'm gonna need more of them vests with *Toad Springs* on 'em, soon as you can get 'em done."

Mort looks up from eating, staring straight ahead, a greasy string of chicken skin hanging from the corner of his mouth. Then he looks at Childe. Then he looks at me. I start feeling dizzy.

"Huh?" he says.

"Oh my, the knitting," Childe says. "The good Lord give your wife a real talent for knitting, and she's not hiding her light under a bushel, that's for sure. Matter of fact, I'm gonna get her to come teach a class at the circle meeting so we can all learn to do them fancy stitches."

I feel like a dog caught with the ham for Sunday dinner. "Teach a class? Why . . . Childe . . . I just . . ."

Mort looks at me. "Teach knitting? What the hell you talking about? You . . ."

"I got to get me some more sweet tea," I say, standing up and grabbing my glass. "Childe, why don't you come with me?" When we get off a ways I explain that we need to keep the gift shop business just between us and she says she understands. When I sit back down at the table Mort's frowning and his ears are red. After he wipes his mouth on his sleeve, he says, "What's Childe talking about? What's that about money?"

"Oh, it ain't nothing," I say, while I scoot my three-bean salad around on my plate. "She was just telling me about money from the ladies sewing circle at the church. What them quilts sold for, that's all." And that's the truth. She did tell me that while we was getting the tea.

"How much did they go for?" he says, and stuffs a biscuit in his mouth.

"Sold two so far. Made nineteen dollars."

He has to chew a little more before he can talk. "Damn," he says, spitting out some crumbs, "that's good money." He thinks a minute, then says. "But what was that she said about knitting a quilt? Don't nobody knit quilts."

"Hold on just a minute," I say. "Never Riley just come in with one of her custard pies. Let me get you some before it's all gone." I come back with two pieces of pie and give 'em both to him. He digs right in and I go off and visit with as many of the ladies from church as I can find.

When I finally go back to the table he squints his eyes at me. "Well, I'm done eatin'," he says, "and you've talked to everybody here, so it's time to go." On the way home I tell him all the gossip I heard, hoping he'll forget to ask me about what Childe said, but when we get in the house, he sits down in his chair in the living room and starts in. "All right, Polly. Now you gonna tell me what's going on."

I sit down on the sofa—I still didn't have no idea what to say. "Well, er . . . Childe seen a couple of your sweaters and she thought they was real nice."

"But she said your knitting was selling like hotcakes. And you can't knit."

Now, Mort's never raised a hand to me, and you don't see it often, but he's got a temper that can get ugly. My heart's beating so fast I think I might faint. I take a deep breath. "Well, since Childe liked them sweaters so much I showed her one of the Toad Springs vests. Then she wanted me to leave it there at the gift shop. Just to see if somebody'd buy it. So I did. That's all."

He gives me one of them squinty sideways looks. "And?"

I know I'm caught now. But I ain't telling him about the money I got in the Bible. "Well, it's . . . I mean . . . I just found out Childe sold that vest. I didn't say nothing to you 'cause . . . 'cause I didn't know what you'd think. I was afraid you'd be mad. You always said you didn't want nobody to know you can knit."

"So, what'd it bring?"

"She's gonna give me four dollars."

"Four dollars! For one vest? Damn! That's a lot!"

"Well, yeah," I say, hoping he's so happy about the money he'll forget to be mad.

"So, when you getting it?"

"Um . . . Tuesday."

"What you thinking of doing with it?"

"Saving it, of course. For emergencies."

"Oh." He wrinkles his brow and stares at me for a minute like he's trying to figure out what I said.

I keep talking so he can't keep thinking about it too hard. I say, "I bet Childe could sell some of them little toad toys you come up with. Why, you can keep making everything and we'll just let her think I'm doing it."

He's sitting there, shaking his head. "Four dollars!"

After a while, Mort decides that I *have* to learn to knit. Otherwise it's bound to come out that he's doing it and he'll be the laughingstock of Toad Springs. "And besides," he says, "if we're both making stuff we can bring in more money."

Now, I hate to knit. Back when I was ten or eleven years old Mama decided she was gonna teach me, and I despised every single minute of it. All that fiddling around with a piece of string that won't go where you want it to. And you make one little mistake and you have to unravel the whole damn thing. Last thing in the world I wanted to do was get into the knitting business, but I'm so glad that Mort paid more attention to getting the money than he did to me selling his knitting behind his back, I go along with him. At least I act like I go along with him.

I'm left-handed, so I tell him he has to figure out how to knit left-handed hisself before he can teach me. He tries, but good as he is at knitting he says he can't do it backward and gives up. But before I can even feel happy that I don't have to knit nothing, he says we'll just do it right-handed. He's dead set I'm gonna learn, and he calls me stupid when I can't do it. I can't stand him hanging over my shoulder giving me orders to do it this way and that way, and it don't take long 'til I'm ready to strangle him. The real truth is, when I don't want to learn something, I ain't gonna learn it and finally he gives up.

I keep taking the stuff he makes down to Stroudamore's every Tuesday, but of course after that Mort gets the money—uses it mostly on buying drink for his jug since his homemade moonshine's run out. Says he needs to have it so he can concentrate. But that's all right. I still got my fourteen dollars.

Childe's always nagging me to hurry it up, that she needs more to sell. Says she don't have no idea how I get it all done since I'm still washing clothes for folks and I just tell her I ain't getting much sleep lately. Mort even gets to where he cut down his hours working at Smitty's and had them needles going from dawn to dark. He was always complaining that it wasn't no fun no more when everybody and their aunt Tillie wanted something outta him but I just remind him that at least he ain't out working in the fields all day.

It's early one Saturday afternoon in October when Hester Brisco come by unexpected. I'm out hanging clothes on the washline in the side yard and Mort's up on the screened porch in his rocker. Later on he tells me he's concentrating real hard on a sweater, one of the ones that has "Toad Springs" on it, trying to get the toad's feet to look just right. There he sits, in the middle of balls of yarn with them needles clacking away when he hears a little noise and looks up. Hester's standing there on the porch, staring at him with her mouth hanging open, 'til as a statue, like Lot's wife. She don't say a word.

"Hester!" Mort says. "What in hell you doing here?" He throws down the knitting, stands up, and tries to take a step, but he trips on the rocker and goes crashing to the floor. Then he looks up at her and says, "I just been trying to fix Polly's knitting needles."

"You all right?" she says while he's getting up.

"Dammit, woman. Ain't right to come sneaking up on folks."

"Didn't mean to, Mort. Sorry. I wasn't really sneaking, just come by. Um . . . What's wrong with the needles? Ain't never heard of fixing broken knitting needles."

"Ain't nothing wrong with 'em now. Got 'em done," he says, holding up his elbow, looking at where he scraped it. "Polly's out in the side yard."

"I didn't know you could knit."

"Told you! I wasn't knitting. Just fiddling with Polly's needles, like I said."

"Oh . . ." She gives him a funny look. "Sorry. Heard you cut your hours at the hardware."

"That's right. Just took some time off to fix things up around here. There's lots of upkeep to a house, you know."

"Yeah, I noticed that third step there's kind of wobbly."

"Yep, I know that. I'll go get Polly for you."

"No need," she says, turning back toward the door. "I'll go around to the washline. You just sit back down there."

Well, now that Hester caught him, everybody's gonna be knowing about it. After she leaves, Mort's beside himself, figuring there wasn't no way he's gonna be able to hold his head up in Toad Springs. Best he figured he could do was just stay home and don't never go where folks'll ever see him and make fun of him.

The next Tuesday I take some stuff to Childe to sell, and a bunch of the ladies are there, wanting to talk about Mort and his knitting. They ask me if we're both doing it together and who come up with the idea. I figure the cat's out of the bag and so I go on and tell 'em he does it all, so then everybody wants to talk to him about this stitch or that one and how did he come up with the pattern for the toad on the lily pad. When I get home I tell him about it. All he wants to know is what the men had to say.

"Well, there wasn't no men there," I tell him. "But the ladies are all excited about you."

"I ain't going into town 'til I hear what the men are saying."

I go to church by myself for two weeks, and once I seen Hank Plenty wearing one of Mort's sweaters. Not the kind with the toad on it, though. Don't none of the men say a word about Mort.

After about three weeks he was going crazy just staying at the house, so that Tuesday he took the sweaters in to Childe instead of me doing it. He said the ladies he run into told him how smart he was and they want him to teach a class. That made him feel better and the week after that he got up the nerve to go to church with me. We come in just as it was starting so we wouldn't have to talk to nobody. I see folks pointing at us and whispering while Preacher Blander's talking, and afterward a bunch of the ladies come over to see Mort. He answers their questions and tells 'em he'll think about teaching 'em some of the tricks he knows. He's feeling real good.

When we walked out the door, Preacher Blander shook his hand but didn't say nothing about the knitting. Mort was smiling real big when we walked down the front steps, 'til one of the fellers who was working out at Hank Plenty's ranch hollered, "Hey Mort! You wear a granny shawl while you're knitting?" He laughed and elbowed his friend.

Then the other feller yelled out, "How you like them soap operas on the radio? The ones all the ladies listen to?" Then the two of 'em walked away laughing.

I could see him tense up some, then, maybe 'cause Preacher'd just talked to us about love and tolerance, Mort give 'em a little smile, waved his hand at 'em, and kept on going. As time went by he got some pretty good teasing and he wasn't always smiling about it, but the ladies all loved him, said he was smarter than most, 'cause it was a helluva lot easier to sit on the screened-in porch knitting in a rocking chair, looking out at the lake with a jug by your side, than it was to pick strawberries or mow orange groves. After a while, some of the men even come around and started ordering sweaters that had turkeys and dead deer and the like on 'em and that made Mort real happy.

Some days while I'm rolling the yarn into balls for him, I think back to all the jobs Mort's had, like starting the orange grove and trying to raise chickens and running that whiskey still. But in the end, Mort got what he wanted all along. A job he could do sitting down.

Who Says You Can't Cheat at Bingo?
by Wilton Mayfield

Now, my pop was a traveling preacher man. He preached at the Fiery Freedom Holiness Baptized Church in Toad Springs one week, then traveled around to other towns the next. He didn't much like working with his hands, and since he was gone so much, us kids had done most of the labor on the truck farm. I think that's why he decided to be a preacher, so he didn't have to work so hard. Strange, ain't it, he's the one turned me against the church. If God's rules hadn't of changed every time Pop didn't agree with 'em, maybe some of it would of stuck.

So, the whole scandal come to light when Aunt Never was visiting her cousin Ruby over in Kissimmee. Ruby went to church every Sunday and she wanted Aunt Never to meet this preacher she liked, name of Burtis McAffee, and his sweet wife, Lilly. That's when Aunt Never recognized that Burtis McAffee was really my pop, Harold Mayfield. After the church meeting was over, she went right up to him and she told us later that he acted like he never seen her before in his life.

He said he had a long-lost twin brother that looked so much like him even their mama couldn't tell 'em apart, and for some reason, nobody knew why, his brother run off one day and wasn't never seen again. Said maybe that other fella in Toad Springs would turn out to be his brother. Even pretended to be all excited about finding him, but Aunt Never knew he was outright lying 'cause Pop had this burn scar on his left hand—run from the outside of his little finger down to the wrist.

Mama told us when he was a kid somebody dared him to stick his hand in the fire. He done it, thinking God would keep him from getting burnt. But I reckon God must have been looking the other way that day. Anyhow, every time Pop put his hands together to pray you could see the scar—wasn't no way to hide it.

The evening that Aunt Never got back home she come by our house for a neighborly visit. "Ida," she says to Ma, "you ever heard of a feller name of Burtis McAffee?"

"Don't believe I know that name," Ma says.

"Well, does Harold have a brother that's tall and skinny and looks just like him?"

"A brother? No. He don't have no brother."

Ma said Aunt Never give her this funny look before she said, "Well, there's a preacher over in Kissimmee with that name. Only that Burtis McAfee is really Harold Mayfield. And he's got a wife name of Lilly."

"What are you talking about, Never? You ain't making no sense."

Well, Aunt Never went on and on about what she'd seen over at Ruby's but at first Ma didn't believe her. Aunt Never was just that kind of person. You couldn't trust that anything she said was true. But when Pop come home that night Ma told him what Aunt Never'd said.

At first he'd just look shocked. After a minute, he said, "Darlin', when I met you I knew right on the spot that you was the one and only for me. You the only gal I ever loved in my whole life."

"I ain't asking do you love me, Harold," she says, putting her hands on her hips and squinting her eyes at him. "I'm asking you about Lilly McAffee."

Took a while, but he finally told Ma that he met Lilly when he was first getting into preaching in Kissimmee. She'd just got married a month before and her new husband run off and left her after three days. Pop wanted to help her out and so he practiced his preacherly consoling on her and somehow, he didn't know how it ever happened, things got to where she said if he didn't marry her she'd kill herself. So what could he do? Even if he didn't love her, he couldn't be a party to somebody killing theirselves. Anyway, not long after they got married he started taking his preaching out on the road, and that's where he met Ma and truly fell in love.

Ma asked him where he got the name Burtis McAffee and Pop told her that his real name was Austin McAffee, and Burtis was his uncle who'd got killed up in North Carolina while he was trying to get a big old buck he'd shot back to the house. Freak accident. That deer was slung over the back of a mule, and when the mule got spooked by a rabbit it reared up and threw that deer right on top of Uncle Burtis. Smashed him flat as a noodle. Like I said, freak accident. He'd just made up the name Harold Mayfield.

A few days after hearing all this Ma decided she'd take her own trip to Kissimmee and see just what she could find out. Got Halt Brisco, who was always ready to take folks around in that old rusty rattletrap of a Model T he loved so much—if they'd buy the gas—and off they went. Turned out Ma and Lilly had a nice long talk and when Ma told her the whole story, Lilly didn't seem all that upset; said she was tired of Pop's lazy ways and was thinking about going up to live with her family in Ohio.

After them two talked a while, they come to find out that they each had three girls and one boy, they both hated to quilt, and their favorite dessert was grapefruit pudding. They even looked alike, wore their long brown hair braided into a bun in the back. Ma said her and Lilly could have been good friends if things would of been different.

Well, by the time Ma got back home and kicked Pop out of the house, Aunt Never'd told the whole town what was going on, being she was the telephone operator and didn't mind passing any news she heard along to anybody who'd take the time to listen. 'Course they put him right out of the church. Everybody was so mad at him that nobody'd take him in, so he slept in the shed out behind Smitty Mallet's Hardware and Feed for a while. But before long, lo and behold, he was working in our fields out back every single day. Couldn't believe he was doing that, especially since he was still sleeping in the shed.

Just to teach him a lesson, for a while there Ma took us all to the Church of Everlasting Liability every Sunday, the one that Pop said was his mortal enemy 'cause they was always trying to steal his parishioners while he was on the road. He didn't go with us, of course, but he told us that the whole time we was there, he was having his own private church meeting by hisself, all dressed up, preaching and praying and singing all by his lonesome.

Pop kept begging Ma to let him move back in, but she said she had to think long and hard about it, emphasizing the "long." She was waiting for a real good answer about why he'd married her when he already had him a wife. The best he could come up with was that that Ma was the love of his heart and he couldn't live without her, but at the same time, back then he couldn't leave Lilly 'cause she'd kill herself. And once he got into the mess, he couldn't see no way out. But God as his witness, Ma was the only one he'd ever wanted. Loved her so much he'd took the risk of going to hell to have her.

"And just what did God say about marrying me when you was already married to somebody else?" Ma asked him.

"You know I don't do nothing without checking with the man upstairs," he said, holding up his right hand, "and he said it was all fine. God as my witness."

Me, I couldn't never understand why he'd go on praying to the Lord who'd tell him it was all right to marry two gals at the same time and lie to them both. But then my pop seemed to be able to get the Lord to tell him that what he wanted to do was all right, even when Spivey's old hound dog could of told you it was wrong.

Sometimes I think you just got to shut your eyes and throw all common sense out the window if you're gonna be good church-going folks. Like I said, it ain't never made no sense to me, and when Pop quit going to church, I did, too. I hadn't never liked sitting on them hard benches for hours every Sunday morning and

Wednesday night, twiddling my thumbs while he stood up there preaching the wrath of God.

But after all this hoopla I give some serious thought to how Pop and Pastor Blander from the Church of Everlasting Liability look down their nose at everybody and tell us how we're supposed to live our lives when mostly they ain't got no idea about how to live their own. I say, if you can't even trust your own preacher to follow God's rules, how in the hell are the rest of us supposed to be able to do it?

And it really got me when they decided to hang that big old picture up in the front of the church—like the Catholics have— of poor old Jesus, hanging up there on the cross with all them thorns sticking in his head so blood can dribble into his eyes, and blood coming down his side and some people calling that picture beautiful. Hah! Beautiful? What it is, is some poor guy getting tortured to death. Ain't nothing pretty about that. Talk about not seeing what's right under your nose.

Naw, something just ain't right. Makes me wonder if God's even up there at all. And if he is, why ain't he doing a better job of things down here. Unless maybe he's doing the best he can. And if that's the case, he ain't doing no better than the rest of us.

A couple of years after Ma let Pop move back into the house and we was finally selling enough vegetables to make ends meet, I was out back digging weeds with him one day. I must have been about fifteen and I most generally done my best to be over on the other side of the field when we was out there at the same time, you know, I'd be pulling hornworms off the tomatoes on the north side while he was digging carrots on the west side, but this day we was both hoeing weeds around the squash plants. Like he's always doing, he asks me, says, "Wilton," he says, "what are you doing to save your soul?"

I don't say nothing. Just keep working.

"Don't want no child of mine going to hell," he says.

Here we go again, I think to myself. "I ain't going to hell," I say, and chop weeds faster, moving down the row away from him.

I hear him suck air through his teeth and I can just see the snarl he gets on his face when he does that, even though I'm looking the other way. He spits and says, "So, what makes you think God's gonna let you into heaven?"

I don't say nothing.

"You answer me, boy."

I clench my jaw and keep looking at the ground. "Didn't say I was going to heaven."

"Well, you got to head one way or the other."

I look over at him. "I don't aim to head any ways at all. When I'm dead and gone, that's just where I'll be. Dead and gone."

"Well, that's just stupid, boy. You can read. It's all right there in the Bible." Pop shakes his head. "You got to go to church, boy. You got to believe in Jesus."

I take a deep breath. "*You* don't go to church," I say.

"That's different. Me and the good Lord, we got an agreement."

"And what's that?"

He leans on his hoe. "Well now, I'd say that's between me and him, boy. Ain't none of your damn business."

"In that case, maybe what's between me and the Lord ain't none of *your* business." When them words come outta my mouth I know I gone too far.

He throws his hoe down into the squash plants, gets all puffed up and red-faced, and says, "You getting way too big for your britches, Wilton Mayfield. You may have got taller than me but I'm still your pop, and the Ten Commandments say you got to honor thy father and thy mother."

"Well, I don't believe in the Ten Commandments. So I don't have . . ."

He sticks his chest out like a big old Tom turkey, squints up his eyes and takes a few steps my way. I back off. He stops, then picks up his hoe.

Don't know why, but I said, "Just what you think I done that's so bad it would send me to hell?"

He gives me the turtle eye and snorts. "You don't pray to the Lord and praise his holy name. You don't strive to live a perfect life."

"But can't nobody live a perfect life. You say that yourself. If you gotta be perfect to get into heaven, ain't nobody gonna be there."

"Only those that *strive*, boy. *Strive* to be perfect. *Strive* to walk God's path."

"Ain't nobody going to heaven or hell, anyway. There ain't no such place."

"You are blaspheming the Lord, talking like that, Wilton Mayfield." He's yelling and shaking his fist at me now, those stringy cords in his neck sticking out. "He's gonna smite you dead if you don't change your ways. You'll burn in the fiery furnace . . ."

Don't know what took hold of me that day but I look right at him and say, "What about you? Where you goin' when you die?"

He stops and raises his hands up to the sky, still holding his hoe, looking around for Jesus, I reckon. "I done made my peace with God and the Lord forgives anybody who comes to him with a humble heart and begs for forgiveness."

"So, even after what you done to Ma, you still think you're goin' to heaven."

He drops that preacher look and squints his eyes at me. "You got a smart mouth on you, boy. I done told you I made my peace with the Lord and with your ma, too. It ain't none of your damned business. That's private. Between me and your ma and God."

I lean on my hoe and look at him. "All right, Pop. Here's how I see it. If you strive to be perfect, God promises you flutter trees and lakes of honey and streets of gold. But if you die a sinner," I say, holding up my finger at him, "and you said a hundred times that everybody dies with sins on their soul 'cause ain't nobody perfect, then you get to go to hell and burn in a fiery furnace for eternity. Now that just don't make no sense."

"Wilton, the Lord works in mysterious . . ."

I know I'm just asking for trouble walking away from him, but I throw my hoe down and head over to the water bucket we got sitting under an orange tree.

He comes along side me, hollerin', "We ain't never gonna understand the Lord. You just *gotta* believe! You *gotta* have faith!! *Be-lieve!*" He's dragging his hoe with one hand and raising his fist with the other. "You can't talk about God's laws that way. Not in front of me. I won't have none of that."

I take a deep drink of that nice cool water while he's carrying on, then hold out the tin cup to him. He snatches it out of my hand and I head back to the field, surprised he ain't tried to hit me. He keeps on yelling while I go back to hoeing squash, then after a while sits down in the shade. He hollers out a couple of Bible verses, prays at me real loud for a while, then gets quiet. When I look his way, he's walking off down the road, headed for home.

On that day I decide I ain't never gonna talk to him about God again. If he starts going off at me, I ain't gonna answer. I'll just walk away from him and his crazy ideas. And that's just what I done, too.

Me and Arvella got married when I was eighteen and she was seventeen. Her and her family'd moved to Toad Springs when she was thirteen and they started going to Pop's church. 'Course that was after he'd got kicked out but I'm sure they heard about him. Might be why her folks wasn't too crazy about her marrying me.

Anyway, she pretty much left me alone about going to meetings until we had Junior. After that, she decided I should start going with her and her folks. Now, I'd told her from the start I didn't believe none of that hogwash. Maybe I didn't call it hogwash when we was courtin' but I'd made damn sure she knew I wasn't gonna be going to no church.

Anyhow, was the oddest thing, every time Arvella had a new baby, she'd start up on me again. She was at the church every spare minute she had, which wasn't much, but after all the young'uns was in school she started going to circle meetings where, you ask me, her and her best friend, Sweetie, spent all their time there complaining about their husbands.

I thought I was being real good, never fussed about her and all the kids being gone every Sunday morning and only getting soup for supper every Wednesday 'cause she had to go over to the prayer meetings. And, like I promised her, I never tried to talk the young'uns out of believing whatever she told 'em, even though I didn't always feel good about that.

I remember this one time Junior come to me when he was six or seven years old. He'd been crying and looked real worried. I was sitting on the front porch in my rocking chair and he climbed up on my lap. "Daddy," he said, "ain't you scared of going to hell?"

I give him a hug. "Why you asking me that, Junior?"

"Preacher and Grandpop say you're going to hell 'cause you won't go to church."

For a minute I couldn't think of nothing to say. Then I sat him up and turned him around so we're face-to-face. "What's your ma say?" I asked him.

He looked kinda trapped, like he's in trouble. "She says you might could, lessen you change your ways."

I think for a minute. Then it comes to me. "Well, Junior," I say, "I know that's probably what they think, but it just ain't true. I got me a little secret here that Preacher and Grandpop don't know about. Your ma don't know it, either. Now, if I tell you, you promise you won't tell nobody?"

He looks real eager to hear. "Yes, sir. I promise."

"'Cause this is a secret between me and God. And he don't want you to tell nobody, neither."

"Okay, Daddy. I won't."

I sit back and take a deep breath. "Well, son, the secret is that I'm going straight to heaven. And God told me you are, too."

He grins and puts his hands over his mouth.

"But you can't tell nobody now. Remember."

"What about Mama?"

"Mama's going to heaven, too. We're all going straight to heaven."

"But why don't God want us to tell?"

"Well, Junior, I don't know. He didn't tell me why. But like your grandpop says, the Lord works in mysterious ways."

Junior gives me a big hug, then runs to the front door.

"Remember now, it's a secret," I call after him. Then I lean back in the rocker and think how smart I am. 'Til it comes to me.

I done just what my pop done. I twisted things around make 'em turn out the way I wanted.

As time went by, Junior took to looking more and more like his grandpop. Everybody said so. Sometimes when I'd catch his profile, I'd get a shiver up my spine—it would make me cringe. I caught myself watching him to make sure he didn't start acting like Pop. Didn't know what I'd do if he wanted to be a preacher.

As it turned out, he was just about the luckiest young'un in the state of Florida. Ma said he was like that old King Midas. Everything he touched turned to gold. He'd win the Easter egg hunt every year, come in first at the church cakewalk, and you couldn't hardly beat him at cards. That's the one thing Arvella let us do that was against the church. Play cards. She just couldn't see the harm in it long as nobody was betting money. Said it was a good way to keep the kids outta her hair.

After Pop left the Fiery Freedom Holiness Baptized Church they got this feller name of Murphy Goins to be pastor there. He had his own ideas on how things should run and along with making everybody sit in the same place every Sunday and getting the church to buy him a shiny red robe and a big red velvet chair for him to lie back in with his eyes closed while everybody else was singing hymns, he figured out how to bring in more money.

What he come up with was Bingo games. Ma and all the ladies at the church was in a tizzy when he started 'em up, and Pop near about had a conniption fit even though he never went there. A lot of the men understood that they had to do something, 'cause the Church of Everlasting Liability was outshining 'em; had more members and even had a new coat of paint on their church building. The men was determined to get more money coming in, but the women said it was gambling and gambling was a tool of the devil.

Anyways, that money from the devil got 'em some nice new pews that had a back on 'em so folks could relax a little during the preaching, maybe even take a little nap if Preacher wasn't coming on too loud. Arvella said they even got a couple of new members, come over from the other church so they could play Bingo without feeling guilty. Now, you didn't have to be a member to play so some folks just sneaked over for the Bingo whether they felt guilty or not.

Junior had been going to that church with his mama twice a week since he was little and Preacher Goins had took a liking to him. He'd take Junior along on fishing trips with his boys and was always talking about how smart he was; quick as a minute and sly as a fox, he said.

The Bingo games kept getting bigger and bigger, and Junior must of been about twelve when there was so many people coming every week, they had to move the pews around to make room for everybody. Junior was a big strapping kid by then and he got picked to set the place up every Saturday night. Then, Preacher said if it was okay with me and Arvella, he could play two Bingo games for free.

It was fine with me but Junior and the preacher had to do some fast talking to get Arvella to agree. When she finally did, she said he could play for one month. But that's all 'cause she didn't believe in gambling. Now, when Junior started winning, the first thing he done was buy her a pretty little vase with roses on it.

That's when she decided that Bingo just might be a gift from the Lord. Wasn't too awful long before Arvella was going to Bingo night herself once a month or so. Wouldn't never play more than two games, though. Said she didn't want to push her luck too far,

and she was always looking for a sign from God that she should
stop. Never got one, though.

Well, I started to hear that them *good churchgoing people*, like
they called theirselves, was saying that Junior won at the Bingo
games so often that he must be cheating. First of all, it really
burned my grits to think anybody'd accuse my boy of cheating
when everybody knew how lucky he'd always been. And second
of all, there ain't no way to cheat at Bingo. Them godly folks was
supposed to be honest and charitable and I was supposed to be a
lying sinner, but looked to me like things was backward.

Evenings, after supper, him and me would sit on the porch
while Arvella and the two girls cleaned up the kitchen. Most
nights he'd get around to asking me to come to the church and
play Bingo, but for a long time I figured it was just a trick to
get me into the building and I said no. Them folks thought if
I walked into that place, God could just snatch up my soul and
make me a believer. Hah.

One night Junior said that if I come, maybe I'd win money
like him. Truth be told, I'd thought about that myself; since I was
Junior's papa, maybe I'd have same kind of luck that he had. After
all, everybody always said he favored me. So it was one Saturday
night in the spring when I decided to go play a game or two of
Bingo and just see how it went. We had all the crops planted and
the weeds hadn't had a chance to start taking 'em over yet, so I had
a little extra time.

I hadn't been inside a church in ten or fifteen years and I
have to say I was surprised at how good the place looked. New
paint inside and out, them new pews all had cushions on 'em—
'course they wasn't near as good as the red velvet the preacher
had on his chair, but at least they was softer than wood. They'd
moved the pews around so we could set the long skinny benches
along in front of them, like little tables where folks could set their
Bingo cards.

People started coming in about six o'clock and the ones from
Toad Springs was saying things to me like, "Glad to see you finally come to your senses, Wilton," and "Coming home to the Lord

at last," and "Arvella's been waiting for this since Hector was a pup." Hearing stuff like that made me want to run right out the door and I told 'em I was only there for the Bingo, wouldn't be going to no church meetings. But they just give me this look like they knew the Lord was sneaking up on me and I'd be right there with 'em pretty soon.

Halt Brisco shook my hand. "Just trying to get hold of some of that luck of Junior's, are you, Wilton? It's a little odd, you ask me," he said. "Ain't never in my life seen a young feller win at something so many times."

Then Aunt Never come along. "God's sure favoring your boy," she said. "I hear he's always around here with Preacher Goins." She points her finger at me and says, "That boy was sent here to save your soul, Wilton Mayfield. Maybe he'll be a preacher hisself one day."

That's all I need, I thought to myself. *Junior, a preacher.* I rolled my eyes but didn't say nothing back, just walked off. Ain't no use talking to that woman. Don't matter what you say, when she passes it on to somebody, it ain't nothing like what you told her.

Well, when it come time to start the game, Preacher give a five-minute prayer about how they needed money for the church and may God bless everybody, even the sinners. I didn't bow my head or close my eyes, just looked around at the top of everybody else's head and thought real hard about what fertilizer I'd be buying for the tomato plants so I wouldn't have to hear everything Preacher was saying.

When he was finally done, Hester Brisco give everybody as many Bingo cards as they wanted along with a little bag of beans so they could put a bean on the Bingo numbers when they got called. She took in the money, and said after a few games, folks could get more.

Junior went up and got him a bunch of cards, then took a seat on one of the back pews over in the corner and laid 'em out on the bench in front of him. I decided for the first game I'd just stand in the back and watch. There must of been twenty people there and when it started up and Preacher called out them numbers so fast I couldn't tell you how Junior kept up with him, having to look at every one of them cards.

Junior won the first game, and when I moseyed over to where Hester was to get me a card and some beans, she was counting the money. I watched real close and seen they'd got six dollars and fifteen cents so far. Then I said, "Hester I'm surprised to see you here. I thought you was a member of the Church of Everlasting Liability."

"Umm . . ." she says, wringing her hands in her lap and looking all around her, "well . . . um, fact is you'd be right about that. But . . . um I used to play Bingo when I was little and it never seemed to do me no harm. I figured it wouldn't hurt none if I was just to help out, you know."

"Oh. Well, you're probably right there," I say, handing her my dime. "Don't seem to me that Bingo is what you'd call a real dangerous game."

"Well, thank you, Wilton. Here you go." She hands me a card and I go find a seat near Junior.

When I started playing I noticed Halt Brisco had moved over and was standing off to the side with his thumbs hooked over his belt, rocking back and forth, watching every move Junior made. I turned toward Halt and right away he looked up to the front at Preacher Goins who was calling out the numbers. When I looked back down at my Bingo card I could see outta the corner of my eye that Halt went back to watching my boy.

"Bingo!" Junior yelled and the other folks groaned.

"Call out your numbers," Preacher said.

Junior did, and with a big smile on his face, Preacher said, "Come on up here, son. You won again."

That's when I went over and said, "Halt. Why you been looking at Junior?"

"I'm just watching the game," he said, rocking back on his heels.

"You got a problem with the way my boy's playing?"

"Well," Halt said. "Like I told you, strikes me a little odd he wins so much."

"He's lucky. He's always been lucky."

"You askin' me, this here's more than luck."

"What's that you're saying?" I'm getting fired up now and I try to keep my voice down but people start looking at us.

"You heard me," he growled back.

"You saying my boy's cheating?"

Junior comes hurrying our way with a worried look, putting his winnings in his pants pocket. "What's the matter Dad?"

"This man thinks you're cheating, Junior. When somebody accuses my son of cheating I ain't gonna let it slide."

"Aw, Dad, it don't matter what he says."

Halt pipes up, "I ain't said he was cheatin'. You said that, Wilton. I ain't never said that."

"Then why you watching him so close?"

Now everybody's staring at us. Preacher's looking worried and he comes over and puts a hand on my shoulder but I shrug him off.

"Gentlemen, gentlemen," he says. "We're in the house of the Lord. We can't have no voices raised up in here unless they're raised in joy. What's the problem?"

I stare at him. "You got a man in your own church building who's lying through his teeth. He's saying my boy's cheating. You telling me I shouldn't do nothing about that?"

Preacher takes a step back and says, "Cheating? No, no. I'm in charge here and I'd never allow something like that. Calm down now, the both of you." He takes out a handkerchief and rubs his forehead. "Ain't nobody here cheating, Halt."

Then he turns to me. "And Wilton, we welcomed you in here even though we all know you're a heathen. If you're gonna start raising sand, you got to leave."

"Ain't here to start no trouble. I'm here to look out for my boy, who's in this place every time the doors open up. And somebody's accusing him of being a cheater."

Preacher's all red in the face and his hand is twitching. "You gonna have to leave, Wilton. Now. We don't want no trouble."

"I'll leave," I say, "but you ain't heard the last of this." I give that damned preacher and Halt the squinty eye, turn, and start walking right out of that place.

Junior's following behind me. "Dad! Dad! What you gonna do?"

I stop and he comes to stand in front of me. "Halt Brisco was saying you're winning too much. Saying you ain't being honest. Now, I know my own flesh and blood. And I know you don't never lie. Besides, can't nobody cheat at Bingo, anyway."

Junior looks away from me and we start walking toward home.

"That's right, ain't it?" I say. "Can't nobody cheat at Bingo."

He looks off at the setting sun. "Well, sometimes what looks to be cheating ain't really."

I grab him by the shoulder and turn him around to face me. "Looks to be cheating? Either it is or it ain't."

He looks like a cornered rabbit. "Well . . . It ain't really cheating if you . . . if you . . . if you gonna use the money for something good."

"What are you talking about?"

"Well, Preacher Goins says God needs money for his church, so if there's a way we can help the Lord get what he needs, we have to help him. If it's God's will . . ."

I can't hardly believe what my boy's telling me. "So, let's see here. If the church needs something, say"—I hold up one fin-ger—"like that fancy new window they just put up, or"—I hold up a second finger—"another velvet chair for the preacher or"—I hold up a third finger—"a new stove for the preacher's house, say, things like that, then it's all right to cheat? And lie?"

"Well, you putting it that way don't sound too good. But you see what I'm telling you. You won't go to hell if you're just doing the will of the Lord, Daddy. That's what Preacher says."

I stop and turn him to face me. "And what do you think? You think it's all right to do that?"

"Well, yes, sir," he says. "Sometimes. I mean . . . That's what Preacher said."

"I'm askin' what *you* think, boy."

"Well, ummm . . ."

"So, taking money from folks and lying to 'em about it is all right. That's what you're learning at church?"

"Well, Preacher says at least they're in the house of the Lord, and they're enjoying theirselves."

"I can't believe my own son . . ." I shake my head, can't hardly even look at him. "So how y'all been doing this? How in hell can you cheat at Bingo?"

He looks down at his shuffling feet. "I ain't supposed to tell."

"I'm your daddy and you're telling me."

"Um . . . um . . . I don't want to get him in trouble."

Now I'm hollerin'. "You tell me, dammit! Now!"

He steps back from me, looking scared. "Well . . . well . . . I always get six cards. And Preacher fixed it so I get the same ones every time and he knows what's on 'em." He stops talking, stands on one foot, then the other.

I don't say nothing.

"An . . . um . . . since he's the one calling everything out, sometimes he calls out one of my numbers instead of what he pulls out of the bag. Don't nobody ever check."

"How'd you think you was gonna get away with this? Didn't you worry about getting caught?"

"Well, sometimes . . . But he . . ."

"Ain't this the same man who tells you that you could go to hell for lying?"

"Well . . . yes, sir. But you already told me ain't no way I'll ever go to hell. So I didn't never worry about that part."

I can't believe what he just said to me. I turn and head back toward the church.

"No," Junior calls out and runs to get in front of me. "Daddy! No! Please stop! Please, please don't go back. Not in front of everybody . . ."

I stop.

"Not now. Please."

"Just how'd he talk you into this?"

"Well . . . he lets me play for free. And I get to keep part of what I win. Most of it goes to him but I keep some. It ain't much."

"So, how much you win last week?"

"Thirty-three cent. Like I said, it ain't much."

"May not look like much to you, but thirty-three cents'll buy a chicken, boy. How much did Preacher get?"

"I don't know. Maybe four or five dollars."

"Now, who else knows about this?"

"Nobody."

"Well, son, you just won your last Bingo game. You ain't never going back to that place long as Goins is there. You hear?"

"Yes, sir," he says, crying now. "But . . . I never meant to do nothing wrong. I try to be honest. Preacher said . . ."

"You ain't going back there. That man taught you it's all right to lie to get your way. I'm a heathen, like he said, but I know what's right and what's wrong. You can go to the Church of Everlasting Liability if you want, but you're done with this one. I swear, Goins ain't getting away with this."

I sent Junior on home, crying, and I went back to the church. Preacher's up front calling numbers and I march right up the aisle and stand in front of him. "Goins," I say, "you're a liar! Ain't nothing but a cheat. You been lying to everybody who comes to these games."

He turns pale as a flounder's blind side.

"I want you to tell everybody here in this room what you been doing to my boy. Or I'll tell 'em. Right now."

"Wilton Mayfield," he says, not moving from his spot, "you . . . you're in a holy place. You can't talk like that in here."

"We'll see about that," I say. I turn around and everybody's sitting on the pews, leaning over their Bingo cards with their mouths hanging open, holding their beans in their hands. Halt's standing in the back with his thumbs in his belt loops, smiling.

"This man took my young'un and taught him to cheat and lie. That's what your holy man here's been doing. Taking an innocent child . . ."

"Wilton Mayfield," he yells, coming down from his perch, "you're the one lying and God ain't gonna forgive you for what you're doing."

"You want me to come back in here with Junior? You want him to tell all these folks what you done?"

"I ain't done nothing wrong," he said, holding his hands together like he's praying and looking around at everybody. "I been doing my best to keep this church going since your daddy left. Now that man's a liar!"

"I ain't my daddy. And I don't hold with what he done. But this here's about you, Goins. This ain't about my daddy."

By this time folks have stood up and they're watching close.

"He set my boy to steal money from you all," I said. "Every week he calls out the numbers on Junior's cards so he'll win and then he takes most of Junior's money back and keeps it for hisself."

"I knew there was something fishy going on," somebody says.

"Oh yeah. Can't nobody be that lucky."

"I been wondering about the same thing . . ."

"That's not true," Goins says, turning to everybody. "I'd never do nothing like that."

The crowd starts talking among theirselves. "I believe you, Wilton," Halt hollers from the back. "Ain't never trusted Goins. Glad there's at least one man here willing to say what we been thinking."

A couple of people go up to stand beside Preacher, but most start walking toward the door and I go with them.

"Wait . . . wait . . ." Goins calls out everybody.

I don't stop to talk to nobody, just head down the road.

On my way home, I felt good that I'd stood up for what was right. But I felt bad I had to talk about Junior like that. But there wasn't no other way.

And, since Aunt Never was there everybody in Toad Springs knew about it an hour later.

Wasn't two weeks after that, Preacher Goins left the Fiery Freedom Baptized Holiness Church—said God had called him to a bigger one over in Frostproof. That was after he'd cried out loud to his flock, tears and all, and said he meant well, that he'd just been trying to help folks, but he'd got misled by the devil hisself. Said he'd repented of his sins and God had forgiven him. But the folks in the church didn't.

Now, this is when my pop come back into the picture. Him and Ma was still living in the old house and he'd settled down some by the time he hit sixty. Why, I'd even talk to him once in a while when I didn't have to. He'd always wanted to preach again and I reckon this must of looked like his last chance.

Right away he volunteered to take over for Goins, and since there wasn't nobody else around to do it, the members voted to bring him on just 'til they could find somebody else for permanent. Ended up, though, he was there for years.

First things he done was to outlaw Bingo and get rid of that velvet chair. He give the shiny red robe Preacher Goins left behind to some of the ladies for them to cut up and use on a quilt, and just wore his regular Sunday go-to-meetin' suit, the same one he'd worn to those church meetings he'd held all by himself every week in his own living room.

Some folks still didn't like him and moved over to the other church, but the ones who stayed said his preaching was different; still some stuff about hell and damnation, but a lot of the fire'd gone out of him and everybody liked him better than before. Don't know what got into me, but I decided I'd try to be more open-minded and give him the benefit of the doubt, so I went once to listen, but he still didn't make sense to me. I didn't never go back after that.

Me and Junior learned a hard lesson that night about how folks can twist things around in their own heads to make 'em look good when they really ain't. I had to tell to Junior that I'd just made up that story about God telling me we was all going straight to heaven. But I told him that I believed there wasn't no hell or heaven to go to anyways. Feller's gotta think for hisself, not let some fast-talking fancy man's words take hold of him. It's something we all got to watch out for.

Ended up that Junior didn't like the way his grandpop preach-ed either, and before long he was staying home with me on Sunday mornings. Didn't make Arvella too happy, but that time I broke my promise to stay out of the Sunday-go-to-meeting situation at our house and stood up for Junior. While Arvella and the girls went to church, Junior and me would sit on the front porch and drink coffee and talk about God and Jesus and what we thought was right and wrong while everybody else was getting told what they ought to think.

I wouldn't give nothing for them Sunday mornings. My Junior's smart as a whip and he sure enough thinks for hisself. Now, he might look like my pop but I thank the heavens I don't believe in that he ain't nothing like the old man. Ain't no way he'll ever be a preacher. That's for sure.

Epilogue
By DeLoyd Stroudamore

There's been lots of changes in the last thirty to forty years; one of the big ones was World War II, when most of the men went off overseas, but didn't all of 'em come home. And them that did come back didn't seem like the same fellers who'd left.

Anyways, after the war there was lots of building going on and we got our new Interstate Highway 4 and Florida State Road 60. Turned out to be bad news for Toad Springs 'cause the travelers started bypassing our little town. The Reptile Ranch went out of business in 1958; now it's a strip mall with a grocery store, a drugstore, and a coffee shop.

There's still orange groves and strawberry farms around, and now there's a fancy new subdivision out at Grasshopper Lake, what they call a "gated community"—so they can keep out the riffraff—that would be us. Them folks drive into Tampa for work every day.

The Green Gator Hotel burned down in 1952, and the Blue Eyed Gator Restaurant got closed down by state inspectors a year or so later after some trouble with food poisoning.

There's still a few of us descendants of the founding families around but most of the young folks moved off to the big cities for a more exciting life.

Acknowledgements

The interest and assistance of the following people have made this book possible.

The descendants of the Riley family of the tiny town of Mango, Florida, who handed down stories from days gone by, and whose voices I still hear in my head.

My writing groups: POP (Publish or Perish) including Abe Spevack, Ann O'Farrell, Barbara Schrefer, Lee Summerall, and Maureen Cain, for their detailed critiques, good common sense, and generous encouragement through the years; John O'Farrell for editing the entire manuscript not once but twice; and the Pinellas Authors and Writers Organization, whose influence made me realize that writers are "my people."

And last, but certainly not least, my publisher, Jason Aydelotte and the wonderful Grey Gecko staff, who have been patient, encouraging, and understanding, without fail.

About the Author

Susan's family came to Florida in the late 1800s and has been there for five generations. She borrowed from, as she says, "memories of our old cracker family stories" while working on *Seashells, Gator Bones, and the Church of Everlasting Liability*. The book was a pleasure to write, she says. Most of the characters just sort of magically appeared on the page.

For Susan, there's nothing more interesting than family relationships. For over thirty-five years, her extended family has gathered every single July 4th and Thanksgiving to catch up. She's always thought it fascinating that they are so very different from each other – if she weren't related to most of them, she probably wouldn't even know them. But she loves them dearly.

Susan currently resides in Dunedin, Florida and is active with several writing groups.

Connect with Susan

Email:	susan@susanadger.com
Facebook:	facebook.com/AuthorSusanAdger
Web:	www.susanadger.com

Grey Gecko Press

Thank you for purchasing this book from Grey Gecko Press, an independent publishing company that focuses on new and emerging authors, bringing readers the best in fiction and non-fiction at reasonable prices in all formats.

With books in nearly every genre of fiction and non-fiction, there's something for everyone, and you can be sure that buying books from us leads directly to the support of independent authors like Susan Adger. Grey Gecko pays our authors some of the highest royalty rates in the business and strives to produce only high-quality books.

Visit our website to purchase our titles, pre-order upcoming books at a discount, sign up for our free monthly newsletter, and find out about two great ways to get free books, the Slushpile Reader Program and the Advance Reader Program.

And don't forget: all our print editions come with the ebook absolutely free!

Authors First!

www.greygeckopress.com

store.greygeckopress.com

www.ingramcontent.com/pod-product-compliance
Lightning Source LLC
Chambersburg PA
CBHW031231210726

48287CB00003B/741